ANCHORED TO THE SHARKMAN

JADE WALTZ

Published by: Jade Waltz

Release Edition v3: January 7th, 2024

E-Book ISBN: 978-1-952420-37-5

Paperback Print ISBN: 978-1-952420-55-9

PreMade Book Covers by Atlantis Book Design:

http://https://www.atlantisbookdesign.com/

CONTENT / TRIGGER WARNING:

This book contains references involving:

- Biting / Blood Drinking (Hero)
- (Near) Drowning (Heroine)
- Gun Violence (Heroine)
- Kidnapping (Not Done By Hero)
- Murder
- Torture (Not Done By Hero)

And others who needed a helping hand when circumstances were dark and grim.

No matter how dark things seem, there is always someone who loves and cares for you.

Your life matters—always.

ONE

ISLA

A steady rumble of thunder was punctuated by blinding cracks of lightning and an onslaught of rain, each brilliant flash cutting through the darkness and echoing a terrifyingly sharp clap that made my heart skip a beat. The ocean swelled with energy, rolling mounds of pitch-black fury that surged forward with untamed force, each one crashing against the sturdy hull of the boat with a resonating slap, rocking it every which way.

The sea sprayed its cold, salty mist into the air—mingling with the rain—leaving every surface glistening with droplets, soaking everything it touched—including me.

Ropes cut into my flesh, a sharp counterpoint to the numbing cold as I lay on the stern of the boat, bound and helpless. My legs were bound together, my arms secured behind my back, my freedom stolen away by the two people I'd once trusted most in the world.

Sam—the man I'd once loved—loomed over me, his eyes cold and merciless beneath the glimmering rain. Beside him stood Rose—my ex-best friend—her face a mask of twisted satisfaction. Their figures were silhouetted against the storm, looming over me with sadistic glee.

"What's the matter, Isla?" Sam called out over the howl of the wind. "Didn't expect you would end up like this?"

"Shut up, Sam," I spat back, my teeth chattering from the cold. The rainwater mixed with my tears, but I refused to let him see me falter, to grant them some sick pleasure from my pain.

Rose laughed, a harsh sound that cut through the surrounding tempest. "She's always been a dumb one, hasn't she?"

My heart raced in my chest, dread mingled with wrath at the circumstance I was in. I knew my odds of survival were minimal, especially given my current vulnerable state, but I refused to give up and let them get away with this.

"What is it that you really want, Sam?" I growled, angry at myself for trusting them once again.

The roar of the storm echoed around us as he considered his answer.

"I want you out of my life." Sam's voice was brutally firm, cutting clear through the storm. "Forever."

A harsh, humorless laugh bubbled from my throat.

"Out of your life?" I shot back, the storm's chaos reflected in the turmoil in my voice. "I've been out of both of your lives, Sam. I moved, blocked you everywhere, and even changed my number. You're the one who sailed into the middle of the Atlantic after tricking me to meet you both and knocking me out. If you didn't want me in your life, you would never have figured out how to contact me and reached out to meet up and apologize—"

"Isla, you're always the fool. Too kind for your own good. Too trusting. Did you really think we were going to apologize to you?" Rose's voice carried a bitter chill that surpassed the relentless ocean winds.

Fury bubbled within me. "I didn't think it was a flaw to hope the good I once saw in you both had returned. But clearly, I was mistaken." My voice was raw, echoing the tumult of emotions inside me.

Sam's laugh echoed into the tempestuous night—a harsh, ugly sound that mirrored the ugliness of his soul. "Good in us? You've always been good for one thing, and it was never about you. It was your family's company and grandfather's money that I wanted, but you had to go and ruin that. Did you really believe that I wanted to be with you?"

A frigid wave of realization crashed over me. "What do you mean?" I stammered, my voice barely audible over the roar of the storm. "Why kidnap me? Why bring me out here?"

He knelt as a burst of lightning highlighted his menacing grin, a glint of malice in the darkness. "Because, *darling*, if I couldn't get your family's money through marriage and your timely demise, then kidnapping and holding you hostage was the next best thing."

Tears blurred my vision as I turned toward Rose. "You... You were in on this? Was our friendship ever real to you?"

Her laughter was an icy dagger to my heart. "Oh, Isla. Did you honestly believe I was going to save you?" she taunted. "I'm everything you're not, and I do it so much better."

I watched in numb disbelief as she flashed a large, diamond-encrusted ring on her finger, a garish spectacle I hadn't noticed before. The gem glinted spitefully, reflecting the sparse deck light as it cast a cruel luminescence over her victorious grin.

"Oops," she said, feigning innocence, her voice oozing

with glee. "Didn't you hear? We got married. I can give him everything you couldn't…and more."

Before I could utter a word, Sam's hand shot out, ensnaring Rose's waist, pulling her close. Their lips met with a ferocity that mirrored the surrounding storm, a grotesque display of their twisted unity.

A wrenching sensation tore through me, as if the daggers they'd plunged into my back twisted and dug deeper. I was powerless, forced to watch their spectacle, each kiss an echo of betrayal reverberating through me.

The shrill ring of a smartphone interrupted their obscene display. They broke apart, Sam smirking at me as he answered the call, wiping his mouth with the back of his hand.

Sam's laughter rang out over the line as he answered, his voice saturated with mockery. "Finally decided to give in to my demands, huh?"

"Demands? What demands?" I yelled, my voice raw, echoing my confusion and fear.

Rose's eye roll was a clear, disdainful answer. "You really haven't figured it out yet, have you, Isla? Your life is nothing more than collateral in a deal. It's either your grandfather coughs up the money or…well, it's your life."

"You can't do this!" I cried out, the fury in my voice slicing through the storm's howling winds. "You'll be tried for murder!"

Rose's laugh was harsh, mocking. "We've thought about that. And with the government all tied up about aliens and that missing crew on the *Stardancer*…you know, the one that was attacked and exploded? They have bigger things to worry about than some spoiled rich bitch."

Her words hit me like a punch to the gut. My world felt as chaotic as the stormy ocean that surrounded us. It was a vile

ANCHORED TO THE SHARKMAN

plan, one I'd never imagined someone I'd called a best friend capable of conceiving. But the worst part was the realization that in their eyes, my life, our past, our memories meant nothing.

Every word from their lips, every derisive laugh, was another layer of betrayal, another wound to my already bleeding heart.

"Pay up now, old man," Sam barked into the phone, his demand reverberating around the storm-ravaged deck. "If I don't get a notification from my digital wallet in the next five minutes, then your darling granddaughter will be swimming with the sharks you love so much."

"No!" I screamed as my heart pounded in my chest. "Don't do it, Grandfather!"

"Shut up, bitch!" Rose snarled, bending over to grab the front of my shirt. Her fingers were like icy claws against my skin as she hoisted me up by my collar. She drew back her other hand and struck me hard across the face. The sudden force sent me sprawling back onto the deck with a painful thud.

Pain blossomed across my face, a raw, burning agony that blurred my vision and filled my head with a disorienting hum. My world spun as I lay there, the faces of Sam and Rose wavering above me. The salty tang of blood on my lips was a bitter reminder of Rose's brutal assault, while their mocking laughter echoed cruelly around me.

"Do you want proof?" Sam roared into the phone, a cruel glint in his eyes. "Fine, I'll give you proof."

He strode over to me, his boots thudding heavily against the deck. Gripping my hair, he yanked me up. Pain exploded at the back of my skull, a sharp, wrenching sensation that had me gasping. His spit struck my face, instantly washed away by the relentless rain.

"Look at your pathetic bitch of a granddaughter," he growled into the phone, thrusting it in front of my face. "If you don't meet my demands, this will be the last time you see her."

On the screen, I saw my grandfather, gray-haired and stern in his black suit. His icy blue eyes bore into me, filled with a steely determination that belied the fear lurking within them.

"Be strong, my Isla," he said, his voice firm despite the strain in his eyes. "Help is on the way."

"No, don't," I pleaded. "Don't give him the money."

He shook his head, a look of resolve hardening his features. "Your life has no price tag. You're the last living reminder of your grandmother and your mother. I won't lose you, too."

Sam let me drop back onto the drenched, frigid metal deck, snatching the phone from my hand and scowling at the waterlogged screen. "You're too cocky," he spat, his voice filled with venom. "I think we need to up the stakes."

"You won't get away with this," my grandfather shot back, his voice as icy as his blue eyes. "I will dismantle your family's business. I'll make sure both you and Rose pay for what you're doing."

As I lay on the cold, unforgiving deck, I clung to my grandfather's words. Help was on the way. I just needed to stall to give him more time. I trusted my grandfather. He always kept his word. All I had to do was stay strong and calm until his help arrived.

"You can keep talking, old man," Sam sneered, an ugly grin stretched across his face. "But the fact is, Isla's here with me, in the middle of the Atlantic, and you're not here to protect her. Your words mean nothing to me."

Tossing the phone to Rose, he laughed as she made

mocking kissing faces at the screen. I could hear my grandfather's frantic voice, but the words were lost in the cacophony of the storm.

Sam sauntered over, his boots clunking on the wet deck, and grabbed me by my armpits. He hoisted me up, dragging me toward the boat's edge.

I kicked and screamed, struggling to escape his grasp. The ship rocked wildly beneath us, the towering waves threatening to tip us over. But my attempts were in vain. He was stronger, crueler, and he didn't flinch as I fought.

"You can find her body in the depths of the ocean." His face twisted into a sinister smile as he yelled at the phone that was pointing at us, putting on a show. "Maybe, if you're lucky, you'll find Atlantis while you're at it, since you love collecting exotic pieces for your private museum."

With a malicious, triumphant laugh, Sam flung me over the railing. The world spun in a disorienting whirl as I was thrown into the tempestuous night.

His malicious grin, distorted by the onslaught of rain, was the last human detail I registered before the ocean swallowed me whole. The crashing sounds of the storm were muffled by the consuming depth, replaced by a hollow, haunting silence that seemed to echo the very heartbeat of the sea itself.

Icy tendrils of current coiled around me, pulling me deeper into the inky blackness. They pierced my skin, seeping into my bones and sapping the warmth from me.

It was a biting, merciless cold, cruel proof that I was dying alone in the ocean deep.

TWO

KY'RN

Who would travel this far from land amid a massive storm?

Only someone insane would risk being this far out from land when their vessel is incapable of handling the rising waves or the treacherous storms.

Unfortunately for them, if they venture any closer to *Atlantis* and run into trouble, I wouldn't be able to summon assistance to save them.

Humans must not discover our secret underwater base. Not when relations were strained as a result of the recent incident involving the human space vessel, *Stardancer*, crossing into Yzefrxyl territory and failing to heed their warning shots. The IPA was now working with the human government, attempting to alleviate the chaotic situation by assisting refugees lost in space and compensating the relatives of those who died.

We were here in stealth to study the Earth's oceans and learn more about modern human society. The leaders of the IPA hoped to utilize our newfound knowledge to try to negotiate a peace treaty with the human government in exchange for their species joining the ranks and allowing aquatic species to settle within Earth's oceans.

But unfortunately, those peace talks haven't been successful.

Humans hadn't united under one government, but instead under hundreds. Each had their own opinion on the situation, and whether they should trust us aliens.

My mission was to lead my soldiers in defending our base borders, ensuring that humans did not approach the protective force field, preventing us from being detected by their inadequate technology.

"There's a vessel too close for comfort," I pathed to my scouts on duty with me. *"I'll let you know if I need assistance. I hope by banging on their hull and messing with their electronics, I can spook them enough to leave this area."*

"Do you require assistance?" Scout Daixa responded, the tone of her mental voice revealing her eagerness. *"Everything appears to be in order here. The large commercial vessel has turned away from us, and there are no other vessels on my side of the base."*

"No, I think I'll be fine." I came to a halt right behind the ship's stern and scowled, my eyes narrowing as I pondered why they'd come to a standstill. *"It should be another quick job, and hopefully, they'll be on their way."*

"They shouldn't be out here, Commander," Scout Ephi pathed sharply. "Especially not during a storm. *Are they crazy?"*

"Or they are on a death wish," Daixa remarked. *"I'm not sure why humans enjoy taking unwarranted risks. It's almost as if they like putting the Fates to the test."*

"Or them being here was written in the Stars." I circled the small vessel far below the water's surface, assessing its equipment, shocked by the lack of military protection. It appeared to be a pleasure vessel, one that wealthy people used to enjoy themselves at sea. The storm raging above was hurricane-like, creating currents that were a challenge even for my strong tail and muscular arms. I had to exert considerable effort to remain stationary. *"Whatever their reasoning, I want them gone before they're swallowed by the swelling waves."*

I was just about to bang on the boat to make my presence known when a loud splash pierced through the cacophony of the storm. Something, or rather someone, had been thrown into the water just behind me.

Turning swiftly, my eyes fell upon a bound form—a female human, bloodied and bruised. Her scent, rich with blood, filled my nostrils, igniting a primal focus within me. The coppery tang tantalized me, stirring an urge deep inside. I needed to know how it tasted, yet my instincts screamed another command.

This trapped female needed rescuing, needed to be saved from drowning. Her long hair, a vibrant array of colors like the coral reefs of my home, flowed around her in the water, a stark contrast to her pale, injured skin. Her clothes, a pair of torn pants and a shredded shirt, clung to her slender form.

Her eyes captivated me, calling out to me, begging me to save her.

As I reached out to her, my fingers gently grazing her arm, the vessel's engines suddenly roared to life, the ship jolting and beginning to move away from us.

Without a moment's hesitation, I scooped her close to my chest, ensuring her safety from the dangerous propellers.

Her mesmerizing sapphires, locked onto mine, piercing

through my predatory nature, awakening a fierce protective instinct within me. I knew then, with an unshakable certainty resonating in my chest, that I had to save her, to shield her from the unknown horrors she had faced on that vessel.

With powerful strokes of my tail, I propelled us toward the water's surface, feeling her body go limp in my arms.

As we broke the surface, the storm raged around us, and the ship made its turn, heading back toward land and away from Atlantis. I instinctively turned my back to it. My broad shoulders acted as a shield, protecting the injured, bound woman from the crashing waves.

Holding her close, I felt her coughing against my skin, as her eyes fluttered closed. Her head lolled to the side, revealing a face marred by an angry, reddening mark—a stark reminder of her recent ordeal.

I brushed her hair back gently, away from her face, feeling the soft yet clammy texture of her skin under my fingertips. My concern grew as I realized how cold she felt— far too cold for a human. Water splattered from her lips with each weak cough, amplifying my worry.

With a gentle grip on her chin, I transmitted my thoughts to her mind. It was an ability inherent to my kind, to communicate through touch with those who were not of our species. "*Let me breathe for you, and give you back your life.*"

Leaning in, I pressed my lips against hers, closing my eyes to concentrate. I channeled all my body's energy into this act, breathing for the both of us. I filled her lungs with rich, life-giving air, drawing the foreign water from her airway.

She coughed against my lips, a sign that life was returning to her. When I felt her breathing stabilize, I pulled away, my hearts pounding with a mixture of relief and satisfaction.

Scanning the stormy waters around us, I noted the

absence of any human vessel. Summoning help from Atlantis was out of the question; I couldn't risk revealing its presence, and she couldn't know of the IPA's presence in Earth's waters.

Thinking quickly, I used her bound hands to my advantage. Lifting her arms, I placed them around my neck and maneuvered her onto my back, securing her with the ends of her bindings, tying them around my waist.

Her life was now in my hands, and I was determined to see her safe.

Knowing fully well that humans were not built to endure the ocean's harsh conditions, especially not in these stormy ones, I made a decision.

To rescue her, my only option was to swim to shore with her on my back. This would allow her to breathe and enable me to swim as fast as possible through the surface waters.

With every fiber of my being straining, I battled against the swelling waves, my powerful strokes guided by instincts honed from a lifetime in the ocean. The rain and wind were relentless, pummeling down on us, but my resolve was unyielding.

I refused to let this human—this female—perish on my watch.

Her mind was a quiet enigma, her consciousness veiled in darkness, yet her steady breathing and the rhythmic beating of her heart reassured me.

She was alive, albeit unconscious. Faint impressions of fear, pain, and betrayal seeped through her mental shields, igniting a surge of protectiveness within me.

Whoever had beaten, bound, and cast her into the sea to drown had committed an unforgivable act. If not for my intervention, I would have been a witness to her murder.

As her skin grew colder against my own, my concern intensified.

However, the first glimpse of land on the horizon, a glimmer of hope surged within me. The sight fueled my determination, igniting a renewed urgency in my strokes.

I swam faster, every muscle in my body straining toward that distant salvation. She needed warmth, safety, and care —and I was her only hope.

As the storm clouds began to recede, the first hints of dawn started to paint the sky, signaling the arrival of a new day. My hearts raced as a surge of worry and urgency coursed through me. Being discovered in these tense times, especially while carrying a bound and injured human female, could lead to catastrophic consequences. The tensions between Earth and the IPA were a delicate matter, and this situation could easily spark unwanted conflict.

With careful movements, I navigated past jagged rocks toward a secluded beach, a hidden haven away from prying eyes. The sight of dwellings perched upon a distant hill gave me a flicker of hope. It was crucial that she be discovered by the locals, or at least have a chance to find help once she regained consciousness.

Dragging my body across the sandy shore, I moved us away from the lapping waves. It was essential to place her far enough from the tides that would inevitably rise later.

Laying her gently on the soft sand, I took a moment to observe her. Her chest rose and fell with a steady rhythm, a reassuring sign amidst the uncertainty of her condition. And yet, I couldn't help but feel a pang of concern.

My instincts screamed to stay, to protect her, but I knew the risks were too high. She was vulnerable, alone, yet I had faith they would find her, care for her—but I must prevent them from finding me with her.

In the dim light of dawn, her features appeared peaceful, belying the ordeal she had just endured.

Using my sharp talons with careful precision, I sliced through the bindings at her wrists, legs, and feet. I cast the remnants aside, ensuring they were far enough from her so as not to entangle her in her vulnerable, unconscious state. Observing the blueness of her lips and the clamminess of her skin heightened my concern. It was clear she needed more help than just freeing her from her physical restraints.

Faced with her vulnerable state, I knew I had to take a risk. My only hope to ensure her recovery and give her a fighting chance at life was to share some of my life's essence with her. This act of transferring vitality was a revered practice among my kind, often used to restore a fallen comrade or warrior.

However, she was human, and the effects of my blood on her were uncertain, but it was a risk I had to take, especially with the looming threat of being discovered.

Propping myself up on one arm, I bit into my thumb, drawing forth a small pool of my blood. Carefully, I placed my bleeding thumb against her lips, introducing my life essence to her.

As my blood seeped into her mouth, a faint sigh escaped her lips—a sign that she was reacting to my essence. Encouraged, I pressed my thumb further, ensuring my blood dripped directly onto her tongue.

Almost immediately, her breathing became more pronounced, and her hands clawed at the sand, signs that it was beginning to work.

Feeling confident that she had received enough, I withdrew my thumb and licked the wound to seal it.

Cupping her cheek tenderly, I leaned down and pressed a

soft kiss onto her forehead. Closing my eyes, I reached out to her mind with a simple, heartfelt message.

"Live, my little fish."

With one last lingering look, ensuring she was as safe as I could make her, I turned back toward the ocean. As I retreated into the sea, the first rays of dawn cast a golden glow over the beach, and my hearts were heavy, knowing that I would have to report to the prince for what I'd done.

THREE

ISLA

I jerked my head out of the water, gasping for air as I shattered the still surface of the bathtub. My hair, heavy and slick with moisture, clung to my face and neck. My heart pounded as if it were trying to break free from my chest, each drumming beat echoing the terror of my recurring nightmare.

My body convulsed with violent shivers. The once-comforting bath water had gone lukewarm, and it was now a reminder of my ordeal—the almost-drowning, the betrayal. I clung to the edge of the tub, knuckles white, as I struggled to contain the flood of memories.

Those terrible, damning memories were the reason why I was trapped here, away from the life I used to know.

My hand groped blindly for the drain button, pressing it down with a shaky determination. The water, once inviting, now held the ghost of my fears, and I was eager to banish it.

"Enough," I muttered, my voice echoing in the steam-filled bathroom.

As the water drained away, I uncurled from my defensive huddle, forcing my stiff muscles to obey. I reached for the oversized fluffy towel, pulling it around my shivering form like a protective cocoon.

I stepped onto the cool marble floor, letting the familiar luxury of my surroundings serve as a soothing balm against the turmoil of my thoughts.

The soft fabric enveloped me, offering a simple comfort that I clung to. "It's okay, Isla," I murmured to myself, making my way to the sink. I reached for a smaller towel, gently pressing it against my hair to soak up the excess water. "You're okay."

I had to keep moving forward. The past was just that. Past.

I had a new life now, a life that was carved for me.

A shimmer of movement caught my eye in the foggy mirror. A pair of amber eyes—so warm, so familiar—were staring back at me. The sharkman's eyes. They always seemed to find a way into my thoughts—into my dreams—especially during the darkest of times.

A startled gasp tore from my lips, my heart slamming in my chest as the memory of those intelligent eyes gripped me, thrusting me back into the past.

Those were the eyes that had saved me that dreadful night, the eyes that brought hope when despair was my only companion.

I flinched back, squeezing my eyes shut as if that could shield me from the past. The soft fabric of the towel was still in my hand, and without thought, I used it to frantically wipe the mirror, erasing any remains of the phantom eyes.

When I dared to look again, it was my own face that stared back at me, my eyes red-rimmed and haunted. But I managed a weak smile, an affirmation of my own strength.

A small victory over the fears of my past.

I took a deep, steadying breath, gripping the edges of the

sink until my knuckles turned white. Each exhale was a release, each inhale was a promise to myself. I was not the same person they had thrown into the ocean anymore.

I was safe.

Reaching for the towel again, I began to dab gently at my hair, using the small action as a way to ground myself in the present. Each pat of the soft fabric was a reminder that I was here, in the safety of my grandfather's private research facility.

Each breath was a reassurance that I was alive, that I had survived.

Each day, I stepped further away from the wounds of the past and closer toward my future. A future that wouldn't be marred by Sam and Rose's unforgivable betrayal. They thought they could snuff me out, but they were wrong.

I was no longer the naive girl who had believed in their pretense of friendship, who had accepted Sam's proposal with starry-eyed dreams of love. I was Isla, the survivor. The girl they thought they'd discarded but who had risen from the depths.

With my grandfather's unyielding support and protection, I was safe and had been granted a second chance.

But the same could not be said for Sam and Rose.

For the last year, my grandfather had hunted them relentlessly, his vengeance as deep and unstoppable as the ocean's currents. It had stirred a current of vengeance within my family, a tide that would surge and swell until justice washed ashore.

They'd made a grave mistake by crossing my family, by attempting to exploit our past ties and my innate goodness for their greedy machinations. I'd walked away from our engagement with grace, cutting them out of my life after discovering

Rose in Sam's bed. I had sought to move forward, to live free of their toxicity.

But they hadn't allowed that, had they? Their greed had led them to this, to a life of constant pursuit and impending retribution.

And the money…it was mine by right.

They had sought to use me, to manipulate my grandfather through me for their personal gain. But they would not succeed. I would ensure that.

As I stepped into my RoBo Changing Room, I studied my reflection, tracing a finger down the mirror's surface.

I called out to Navi, the ever-cheerful AI that controlled the building's network system. "Navi, get me my lab uniform and put my hair up in a high ponytail, please."

Navi's cheerful voice replied, her tone never wavering from its programmed positivity. "Right away, Isla. Will you be requiring makeup today?"

I shook my head. "Not today, Navi."

Instantly, robotic arms whirred into action, unfolding from the ceiling and walls. They were quick and efficient, helping me into my uniform and deftly pulling my hair into my desired neat style. When they retreated, Navi's voice returned, softer now. "Do you find it to your liking?"

I turned in the 270-degree mirror, taking in my reflection. The red-rimmed eyes were less noticeable, the pallor of my skin less ghostly beneath the professional attire.

"Yes, Navi. Thank you." I managed a nod, appreciating the care Navi had taken. "Tell Dr. Violet I'm on my way to the lab," I ordered as I stepped out of the RoBo Changing Room.

"Of course, Isla. Should I also arrange for your breakfast to be delivered there?"

"Yes, thank you, Navi." I motioned to my apartment door,

and the control panel flickered to life. A simple wave of my hand, and the door unlocked with a soft *beep*.

"The green apple cinnamon oatmeal and a hot vacuum flask of vanilla chai, correct?" Navi confirmed.

"That sounds perfect. Thank you." I offered her a smile. Although Navi was just an AI, she had become a constant presence in my life, providing comfort and support in her own way.

"It is my pleasure, Isla." Her response was immediate, filling the room with warmth. "Dr. Violet has been notified of your arrival, and your breakfast will be prepared as per your request. Have a wonderful day."

"Thanks, Navi. You, too," I said, smiling despite the tight knot in my chest. Her programmed cheerfulness was a welcome distraction, a balm for my frayed nerves.

I stepped out of my apartment, giving one last look at the sanctuary I had made for myself as I swiped my hand over the door's control panel; the satisfying *click* of the lock echoed in the pristine white hallway.

As I walked toward the lift, I felt the weight of the world falling away. Here, in the heart of my grandfather's empire, I was protected from those outside… only to be tormented by my thoughts and memories.

No matter how hard I tried, I couldn't forget that night and those glowing amber eyes that haunted me every time I closed my eyes.

The lift took me downward, deeper into the heart of the facility. The glass tube enclosing it gave me a view of the encroaching darkness as we descended below the waterline.

Each passing moment, each level descended, was like a vise tightening around my chest. The water surrounded me on all sides, a tangible reminder of that night, of my betrayal and subsequent plunge into the chilling depths.

My heart pounded as the water got darker, the memories it invoked threatening to overwhelm me. My palms ached as I clenched my fists, the nails digging into my skin. I had to force myself to take slow, measured breaths.

"Everything's okay, Isla. You're safe," I murmured to myself, drawing on every ounce of my courage to keep the panic at bay. "Control, Isla. Take control."

I took slow, deep breaths, in…out…in…out…

"It's okay. I'm safe."

I kept repeating those words to myself until they formed a mantra, a soothing rhythm that helped slow my racing heart.

Every time I took this lift, no matter how many times I hoped I could be free of the anxiety it caused, I was disappointed in myself for my weakness.

Finally, the lift came to a stop, the double doors sliding open with a soft hiss. I nearly ran out.

"Morning, gentlemen," I greeted the two guards posted by the lift, forcing a smile on my face. They nodded at me, their expressions stoic but their eyes sympathetic.

They knew my story, my struggles.

Everyone in the facility did. All had been handpicked by my grandfather, all sworn to protect me, to keep me confined within the safety of these walls.

But confinement or not, this was my haven.

This was where I found solace, in the very heart of the ocean that had nearly claimed me.

The world couldn't hurt me in here.

The sight of my grandfather conversing with Dr. Violet was the first thing that greeted me as I entered the lab. It brought a smile to my face to see him active in his condition.

Dr. Violet, my boss and mentor, was both a unique individual and a force to be reckoned with, with her gray hair spiked in an unconventional style that mirrored her personality. The oversized lab coat and lavender pants were her trademark, along with a purple mug always filled with hot cocoa and marshmallows.

My grandfather was a striking figure as well, the power of his presence unmistakable despite his age. His sharp eyes seemed to hold a million secrets, the weight of countless scientific breakthroughs etched into his weathered face.

"Morning, Isla!" Dr. Violet greeted me first, her eyes sparkling with excitement.

My grandfather turned around and beamed at me, wrapping an arm around my shoulders in a warm hug, the familiar scent of his expensive cologne enveloping me like a weighted blanket.

"We have something exciting to show you," he said, a matching sparkle in his eyes.

"Is it another piece for your exotic private museum?" I teased. My grandfather had an insatiable curiosity for the bizarre and extraordinary, and his personal collection was filled with treasures that would make any explorer green with envy.

He chuckled, a deep, booming sound that filled the lab. "Something better," he promised, shooting a glance at Dr. Violet.

My heart skipped a beat at his words, a flurry of possibilities racing through my mind. "Did we finally get revenge?"

The thought of Sam and Rose finally facing the consequences of their betrayal sent a shiver of satisfaction down my spine.

My grandfather's eyes turned steely, the light-heartedness vanishing in an instant. "Not yet," he said, his voice a low growl. "But we're close. Their families have abandoned them, so their resources are running low. They won't be able to hide much longer."

His words rang with a promise, a vow of retribution that filled me with a sense of impending closure. The nightmare was almost over. Once they were taken care of, I would finally be able to leave these walls without fear.

That chapter of my life would finally come to an end, and I'd be able to move on to the next knowing they couldn't hurt me anymore.

The air in the lab seemed to shift as my grandfather led me toward the test aquarium room. Each step echoed in the stark, sterile corridor, the world holding its breath in anticipation. Dr. Violet matched my pace, her face an unreadable mask of intrigue.

"I know I've been nagging you about how you were saved," my grandfather confessed as we walked. His voice was soft, remorseful, an unfamiliar tone that left me feeling uneasy.

I chewed on my lower lip, anxiety knotting in my stomach, the memories of that harrowing time threatening to surface. The chill of the ocean water, the fear, the hopelessness—it all came rushing back like a tidal wave. The sight of that creature—part man, part shark—had been burned into my mind.

It was a topic we'd rehashed countless times, each conversation leaving me feeling rawer and more exposed. My miraculous survival, the tale of my unlikely savior, was not easily accepted by those around me. They'd said I was hallucinating, seeing things under the influence of the cocktail of drugs they'd pumped into me.

Nonetheless, given the recent revelation that aliens were real, I'd hoped that someone other than my grandfather and Dr. Violet would believe me.

Sighing, I looked up at my grandfather, searching his familiar face for a hint of understanding. "I've been telling the truth. It…it was like a merman, but with a shark tail. It cut me loose. It saved me."

We came to a halt before a door marked *Top Secret*, the ominous label sending a chill down my spine. My grandfather's hands gripped my shoulders, his intense gaze meeting mine. "I know," he said, his voice a murmur barely louder than the hum of the underwater facility. "I believed you then, especially after the recent *Stardancer* incident. I've known you were telling the truth this whole time."

A shock ran through me, my heart pounding in my chest. "What are you saying?" I asked, my voice trembling.

Dr. Violet moved past us and keyed in the access code, placing her hand on a scanner. The door beeped in response, sliding open to reveal a sight that made my heart stop and my breath hitch in my throat.

The light in the room beyond was soft and ethereal, reflecting off the water in a gigantic top-of-the-line tank that occupied most of the space.

There, in the expansive display aquarium, swimming amidst the artificial currents, was a figure that had haunted my thoughts for months.

I wasn't crazy. It was real. And it was here.

The merman with a shark's tail.

The very creature from my memories that had saved me.

The one I had started to believe was a figment of my drugged imagination was right in front of me.

FOUR

ISLA

For a moment, I could only stand there, my heart pounding in my chest as I stared. A dull buzz began in my ears, growing in volume until the background noise of the facility faded away. The weight of memories, of what had once been and had now returned, bore down on me with an intensity that threatened to break my resolve.

My thoughts scrambled back to that fateful night when the raging sea threatened to swallow me whole. Desperation had clouded my senses, yet I vividly remembered a mysterious savior, one with glowing amber eyes.

Was this really him?

The same creature that had vanished into the depths of the ocean after saving me?

My past and my present collided.

Wobbly-legged, I managed to take a hesitant step, my fingers trembling as they extended toward the tank. Every part of me was drawn to him, like a moth to a flame. Yet, despite the familiarity, an eerie undertone of tension settled in the pit of my stomach.

How had he ended up here, confined and on display?

The merman seemed to feel the pull, too. He gravitated toward me, his graceful hand coming up to mirror mine on the opposite side of the thick barrier. The glass, a stark reminder of the chasm between our worlds of land and sea, felt ice-cold against my skin.

His amber eyes were mournful, but they still held an unspoken connection—a tether that had inexplicably bound us during our brief encounter.

Turning slightly, the merman tilted his head, a gesture so profoundly human that it sent shivers down my spine. His gaze never wavered, capturing mine with an intensity that spoke of recognition—and of silent pleas.

The intense glow of his gaze followed my every move, tracking me with an intelligence that could not be ignored.

Blinking hard, I shook my head as I pulled my eyes away from him, turning my head to look at my grandfather. "How…how did you find him?" I asked, my voice barely a whisper.

He cleared his throat, unable to conceal his mischievous grin. "Our offshore cameras captured footage of him. I managed to erase it before it caused a panic, but I kept a copy to study," he explained smugly. "He was caught off the coast of Miami, almost halfway to Bermuda. On the border of the Bermuda Triangle, of all places."

He leaned in closer, his voice just above a whisper. "With the recent tension over the *Stardancer* incident, people are demanding answers. I used my influence, pulled a few strings, and managed to purchase him through the black market before the discovery was publicized."

The implications of his words hung heavy in the air. They had captured my savior, held him captive for their own curiosities. And my grandfather, the man I trusted above all others, was part of it.

I turned back to the glass, my heart pounding in my chest. "What are your plans for him?"

My grandfather, the renowned marine biologist, looked at me with a mixture of fondness and seriousness in his eyes. He adjusted his spectacles and sighed. "Isla, my dear," he said, his voice low and measured. "This creature is unlike anything we've ever encountered. I paid a hefty price for him. He may have saved you, but he is also a scientific marvel—a living bridge between our world and the depths of the ocean."

I blinked, trying to comprehend the weight of his words. "But shouldn't we be thanking him for rescuing me?" I asked, my voice barely a whisper. "He risked his life to save mine."

A shadow passed over my grandfather's face, his features tightening. "I understand how you feel. But this creature is a rare specimen. His existence holds immeasurable scientific value. We have the opportunity to study him, to learn from him, and perhaps even find a way to protect other species on the brink of extinction."

My heart sank, my hand still against the cool glass, feeling the vibrations of the water from the other side. His words hit me like a tidal wave crashing down around me. I couldn't deny the importance of scientific discovery and preservation, but it felt like a betrayal to keep my savior imprisoned.

The man standing before me had raised me, taught me to respect and cherish life in all its forms. Now he was willingly keeping a sentient being captive, rationalizing that he was acting for the greater good.

It felt like I didn't know him anymore.

I forced myself to swallow down the anger that was rising within me. "So you're just going to keep him locked up? Use him for your research?"

His eyes softened slightly. "It's not that simple, dear."

"He's not another piece for your collection, Grandpa," I snapped, struggling to keep my voice steady. "He's a sentient being. Since he decided to save me, he must be capable of thoughts, feelings…empathy."

He gave me a pointed look, his gaze drifting to where my hand still rested on the glass, against the hand of the sharkman inside. "I'm aware of that. And that's why I need you. You've already established some sort of connection with him. You could be the key to communicating with him."

"But what about his rights? His life?" I countered, my voice rising in anger. "This is wrong. It goes against everything you've taught me."

"He's a *creature*, Isla. Either from an experiment, hyperevolution, or even from that alien government that has shown interest in our world since the *Stardancer* disaster." His response sent a chill through me, wrapping around my heart with an icy grip. "He has no rights here on Earth. Not until our government has reached an agreement with the Interstellar Protections Agency. Only then can we ascertain if he was sent by them or not, and how he came to be."

That wasn't what I wanted to hear. "And until then? What's your plan for him?" I pressed on, my eyes scanning the sharkman's form behind the glass. The way he was watching us, his gaze unwavering, sent shivers down my spine.

Could he understand what we were saying?

My grandfather's gaze flickered to Dr. Violet before landing back on me. A sly smile formed on his lips as he answered, "We'll care for him. Treat him well." His gaze fell on my hand, still resting against the glass. "Nurture your connection with him."

"Like a pet?" I swallowed the lump in my throat, attempting to fight back the tears welling in my eyes.

My grandfather nodded. "His life, for now, is here." His expression softened slightly, but his voice was firm. "We're the only ones who can ensure his survival. Outside, there are people who would exploit him, harm him…even kill him for what he represents."

I could hardly believe what I was hearing. This was not protection. This was imprisonment. The creature who had saved my life was now being used as leverage, a bargaining chip in an interstellar game of politics.

A lump formed in my throat. "But he's not a pet. He's not an object to be studied. He's a sentient being, just like us." The words poured from me, a desperate plea. "He saved me. He has every right to be free."

My grandfather turned his gaze to me. "I understand your feelings, but he's an alien. Like I said, until we settle things with IPA, he has no rights here on Earth."

As I looked back at the creature behind the glass, his amber eyes met mine, and I saw understanding there, a shared determination. I made a silent vow then and there. I would find a way to free him, no matter what it took.

"Well, I don't agree with that," I stated, my voice firm, meeting my grandfather's gaze head-on. "I won't be party to keeping him prisoner."

The older man raised his hand, forestalling my protest. "Isla," he began, his tone conciliatory. "You don't get a say in this. And if you cause any issues, I will revoke your access to the lab. You'll have to spend your time above the surface."

I glanced back at the sharkman, his amber eyes burning with an intensity that completely overwhelmed me. His unwavering gaze seemed to pierce through to my very soul, silently begging me to aid him.

If I were barred from the lab, there would be no one to defend him. I wouldn't be able to live with myself if anything happened to him in this lab. I'd once thought my grandfather would never resort to immoral research practices, but now, I couldn't be sure. It was evident that my grandfather was no longer the noble man I had known. Perhaps it was his age or the fact that he had almost lost me—the last member of his bloodline—but something changed him.

For now, I had to go along with his demands so that I could keep access to the lab, even if I wasn't even sure where to start in communicating with the sharkman.

I swallowed hard, pushing down the wave of anxiety that rose in my throat.

"Dr. Violet, Grandfather." I took a deep breath, my pulse racing in my chest, and mustered the confidence to do whatever I needed to ensure the sharkman's comfort during his stay with us. "What have you tried so far to communicate with him?"

Dr. Violet sipped her steaming hot cocoa, her gaze distant for a moment as she gathered her thoughts, her hands gently cradling her mug. She sighed softly before meeting my eyes, her expression tense with disappointment. "Isla, we've tried various methods to communicate with him," the renowned ichthyologist explained, her voice carrying a hint of frustration. "We brought a waterproof touch screen to the ledge, hoping that it would intrigue him, but he ignored it completely. It seems he's not responsive to our technological approaches."

Dr. Violet looked to my grandfather for his guidance. His weathered face held a thoughtful expression as he gazed at the tank. With a measured sigh, he slowly pivoted toward me, piercing gaze locking onto mine.

"He is my gift to you," my grandfather began, his voice steady and calm. "You obviously have a bond with the creature. If you think he might trust you enough to communicate with him, then try it. If you're successful, we might be able to contact his people and work out some deal."

"I…I don't know…" I began, my voice shaky. "Shouldn't we let the government deal with the IPA to determine whether he's one of theirs? Why don't you use your connections to get a direct line to them?"

He cut me off with a firm wave of his hand. "We both know how useless our leadership has been regarding the whole alien situation. I'd rather not have others learn what we have and try to seize the exotic items I've amassed over the years."

Unethically…

I turned back to the glass, staring at the creature beyond. I felt a pang of sympathy for him. He must feel so isolated, trapped within the confines of the tank. He hadn't moved since I placed my palm on the glass, his amber gaze was still fixed on me.

"This is a lot to process," I said softly, more to myself than to them. "You want me to befriend the creature who saved me...to communicate with him, despite his lack of interest so far..."

"Yes, and I believe you can do it," my grandfather said, his voice sharp and commanding. His words were firm, leaving no room for doubt or hesitation. "I'm confident you'll figure it out, Isla. And I believe he has faith in you as well."

As I looked into the amber eyes of the creature, the shark-man, I found a flicker of something else: hope.

I was not sure if I was capable, but I nodded. "All right. I'll try."

I felt a spark of defiance ignite within me. I would not be a part of this. I would not betray the trust of the creature who had saved my life. Whatever my grandfather's plans were, I vowed to do everything in my power to set him free.

To repay the debt I owed him for saving me.

No matter the cost.

"You don't have a choice," my grandfather said, his voice cold and hard, leaving no room for argument. "You're the only one who can do it. And you will."

FIVE

ISLA

The doors slid shut behind us, enclosing Dr. Violet and I in the quiet solitude of the aquarium lab. The weight of the recent revelation pressed heavily upon me. I felt betrayed by someone I'd trusted—once again.

I dropped my hand from the glass, instantly regretting the loss of connection with the being who'd saved my life.

Spinning toward Dr. Violet, my boss and mentor, I couldn't contain the turmoil boiling within me any longer. "Why didn't you warn me?" I demanded, my voice tinged with anger and hurt. "You could've informed me my grandfather knew who'd saved me all along. Knowing him, he most likely hired someone to find and capture him, and yet you never mentioned a word to me."

She turned to face me, her expression guarded, then walked away with purpose, heading toward the wall of screens displaying various graphs and information.

Her avoidance only heightened my frustration. It was clear she had her own reasons for keeping me in the dark.

Rolling her eyes, Dr. Violet sighed heavily. "Isla, as much as I respect you, it's not as if warning you would've made a difference," she said, her voice laced with exasperation. "When your grandfather sets his mind on something, he will do whatever it takes to make it happen. And you, my dear, are living proof of that."

Her words struck me like a blow to the chest. The truth of them hung heavily in the air. Yes, I had always known my grandfather to be relentless in his pursuits, but to hear it spoken aloud, to have my own existence be used as an example, stung deeply.

My survival, my sheltered life here, was a testament to the overwhelming force of my grandfather's will. It felt suffocating, as if I had no control over my own destiny, not trapped within this research facility until he finally hunted down those who had tried to end me.

Anger and frustration swirled within me, intertwining with a desperate longing for freedom and independence. "I am more than just a pawn in my grandfather's plans," I retorted, my voice quivering with the rage boiling within me. "I deserve to know the truth, so I can be prepared for what lies ahead."

Dr. Violet's gaze softened, and for a moment, I caught a glimpse of understanding in her eyes. "I apologize if I seemed dismissive. I understand your concerns, your need for transparency. But sometimes, even the best intentions can complicate matters further. I'll do my best to be open with you moving forward, but at the end of the day, it's your grandfather I must report to. He has the final say over what we do, not just here, but in our entire lives. I can't betray him, or he'll make finding a new job impossible."

"I know exactly what you're talking about," I said, my voice tinged with a mix of bitterness and resignation. "Living under my grandfather's influence has been my reality for as long as I can remember, especially after what happened to my parents. He blames himself for introducing me to Sam and Rose, given their families' previous dealings with him. But that's all in the past now. I just hope he finds them and deals with them accordingly."

Dr. Violet's expression softened, understanding flickering in her eyes. She asked the question that lingered in both our minds, "Do you think your grandfather will do to them what they did to you?"

I shrugged and strolled over to the small dining table, reaching for my breakfast. The comforting aroma of vanilla chai tea and apple cinnamon oatmeal filled the air, momentarily distracting me from the weight of the situation. I picked up a knife and stabbed one of the apples, relishing the satisfying crunch.

"They will get what they deserve," I replied, my voice firm and resolute. There was no ounce of regret in my words. I was done being controlled by others, done being a victim of their manipulations.

I wanted this chapter of my life to end.

Dr. Violet chuckled, a glimmer of amusement in her eyes. "Feeling feisty today?"

I nodded, setting the knife down and turning to face her. "I'm sick and tired of others dictating my life," I said, as a determined fire ignited within me. "I want all of this," I paused, waving my hand around the room, "to end. I want to take back control."

"Hopefully, they'll be taken care of soon," she remarked, nodding. "Their families have abandoned them, and your grandfather has made it known that anyone supporting them will feel his wrath as well."

"Hopefully," I echoed. I knew that justice needed to be served, that Sam and Rose needed to face the consequences of their actions. But deep down, a part of me longed for closure, for a sense of healing that extended beyond their punishment.

As I twirled the knife in my hand, my attention was irresistibly drawn back to the tank.

I studied the sharkman's features, taking in the unique blend of human and aquatic traits that defined him. He was undeniably handsome for a shark merman. His upper body exuded strength and power, with well-defined muscles sculpted like those of a seasoned swimmer. His teal skin, adorned with dark-blue patches and a mesmerizing turquoise speckled pattern, seemed to shimmer in the ambient light of the lab.

His hands, webbed and adorned with black talons, held a strange allure, simultaneously powerful and graceful. Those same traits were reflected in his lower half, resembling that of a shark in all its dark-blue glory. The combination of colors and patterns, overlaid with the glowing turquoise swirl, created an aura of mystery and danger.

Short, spiky, dark-blue hair topped his head, accentuating those burning amber eyes that seemed to hold wisdom and experience. I found myself contemplating the intricacies of his biology, wondering about the number and appearance of his teeth.

Despite his mesmerizing beauty, he was ultimately a predator.

But I wasn't afraid.

In fact, this predator was the reason I stood here today, alive and filled with a newfound sense of purpose. This creature had risked everything to save me, proving that beneath his primal nature, there existed a capacity for empathy and compassion.

A surge of gratitude welled up within me as I locked eyes with him once again. An unspoken promise lingered between us, an unbreakable bond forged in the depths of that fateful encounter.

He had given me a second chance at life, and in return, I would give him the same.

Tentatively, I approached the glass, the knife still in my hand. My heart pounded in my chest, adrenaline rushing through my veins at the prospect of touching him once more. Not wanting to acknowledge his existence, not because he was another reminder of that night and he wasn't a fabrication of my imagination, but because I was the one who blamed him for being here.

I'd never had the chance to thank him for saving me. If there was anything positive about this scenario, it was that I might be able to return the favor.

He moved in sync with me, his amber eyes never leaving mine. When I was close enough, I lifted my hand slowly and placed it on the glass. As he mirrored my movements, laying his hand on the glass against mine, there was a subtle shift in his gaze, something close to recognition and interest.

He leaned in closer, his movement generating ripples on the surface of the water, until our faces were close enough that we could almost kiss, if it weren't for the glass barrier between us.

"I won't hurt you," I whispered, feeling absurd speaking to a creature who probably didn't understand a word I was saying. Yet, I couldn't shake the feeling that he could sense my intentions, understand what I was trying to communicate.

I slid the knife onto the palm of my other hand and pressed it against the glass, pointing the handle toward him. I hoped my message was clear—this was an offering, a peace gesture.

He looked at the knife, then back at me. His gaze softened, and I could swear there was a hint of understanding in his eyes. He copied my gesture, pressing his other palm against the glass over the handle, as if accepting my offering.

I let the knife fall onto the ledge, my gaze never leaving his. "I promise you," I said, my voice barely above a whisper. He leaned closer, his gaze focused on my lips as I spoke. "We're going to get through this. Together."

SIX

KY'RN

How had it come to this?

As I stared at the human female I'd saved, I wondered what she was thinking. As she sat there eating her meal, I saw her long hair was like a curtain of multicolored seaweed—shifting from purple to blue to green, rather than the dark brown it was when I last saw her—as it fell about her shoulders. She kept observing me with concern behind her wall of hair, as if she was attempting to hide her interest in me.

I, too, was facing the consequences of my own curiosity.

The Interstellar Protections Agency had classified humans as an adolescent species, still learning to explore their own sol system. But their first foray into interstellar travel had led them straight into the territory of another race.

The results had been devastating.

Humans now knew they weren't alone in the universe, and not all were accepting of this revelation.

I had been caught in the midst of it all, my insatiable curiosity leading me to investigate the presence of a vessel within the vicinity of the IPA's secret base during a hurricane. It was there that I'd found the helpless human female, on the verge of her doom. I couldn't stand by and watch her perish, so I had rescued her, unaware of the chain of events that would follow.

And, in a moment of weakness, I—a high-ranking IPA commander—swam dangerously close to a hydrothermal vent —and got burned.

I trembled at the thought of the experiments my former captors had performed on me. The pain and the indignity still lingered, a constant reminder of the cruelty I had endured.

And now, somehow, by the Stars' Will, I found myself in the hands of the very human female I had saved.

And in her eyes, I saw a mix of confusion, compassion, and concern that distinguished her apart from the rest. Refreshingly, she lacked the cruel apathy of the other humans I had encountered.

She was different.

She had seen the fear and desperation in my eyes, and instead of exploiting it, she had offered me salvation.

At least, that's what I hoped from her earlier display with her weapon.

A strange sense of irritation coursed through me as I swam laps around my glass prison, unable to divert my attention from the female who strode back and forth across the laboratory, her delicate fingers tracing the edge of the knife that she had presented to me moments before.

My eyes tracked her every feature, taking in the tense line of her shoulders, the furrow between her brows, the way her lips moved as she muttered words I could not hear.

I wished I could reach out to her, to bridge the gap between us.

But without the touch of her skin, I couldn't communicate with her…

A plan began to form in my mind. It was risky, and I had no guarantee that she would understand. But it was the only option I had. I swam closer to the glass, my hearts pounding in my chest.

I pressed my hand against the cool surface, then dragged it downward, tracing a simple pattern over and over again—a series of dots and lines, an ancient symbol of my people.

A plea for help.

I glanced up, catching her attention. She looked at me, then at the symbol I had traced on the glass. Her brow furrowed in confusion, and she approached slowly, as if fearing that any sudden move would scare me away.

If it wasn't for my bleak circumstances, I would've found comedy in her reaction, but instead, a tiny flame of hope surged within me.

She reached up, her delicate hand retracing my symbol on the glass wall. I watched her intently, my gaze locked on her every movement, as she spoke softly to her companion behind her. There was an undeniable energy between them, an excitement that radiated through the room.

Her companion tore her attention away from the multitude of projection screens before her, her eyes flickering between the long-haired female and me. They exchanged words, their voices brimming with excitement. I tried to catch fragments of their discussion, hoping to comprehend what they were saying, but the sounds echoing within the water drowned them out.

And then, without warning, the female from my past broke into a run. She dashed along the glass wall of the aquarium, her steps echoing in the chamber.

Curiosity sparked within me as I watched her run up the stairs, her long colorful hair trailing behind her. I pushed myself off the glass wall, propelling toward the surface.

As I burst through, I noticed her above me, peering down from the ledge wrapped around the tank. Her eyes sparkled with exhilaration and anticipation, like a youngling about to embark on their first hunt, reflecting the brilliance of the illumination within the chamber.

What was she up to?

I remained still, allowing her to take the lead, to guide our interaction. The last thing I wanted was to scare off the only ally I might have in this facility.

She reached for the tablet on the table, her movements deliberate yet filled with an eagerness I couldn't ignore. She positioned herself beside the ledge, the soft glow of the room casting gentle shadows on her features, accentuating the deep concentration in her eyes.

I watched in awe as she attempted to recreate the symbol I had just traced on the glass. To my surprise, her depiction was accurate, each line and curve reflecting the essence of the symbol.

Peace.

I had written the word *peace*, a concept that held significance for my kind, and she had presented it back to me. I knew she couldn't fully grasp the weight of what she had written. Still, the fact that she had made the effort, that she had attempted to communicate with me in a way that bridged our worlds, touched something deep within me.

She offered me the tablet, holding it out for me to take.

At that moment, I realized she was striving to overcome the gap between us, to communicate on a level deeper than just observation. She sought to have a conversation with me, face to face, as equals.

A surge of hope coursed through me.

Could it be possible? Could this human female truly see me for who I was, rather than what I could do for her? Was there a chance for acceptance and understanding in a world that had shown me nothing but cruelty and confinement?

My hand reached out in a moment of raw vulnerability, fueled by a deep-seated need. It wasn't a deliberate motion, but rather an instinctive reaction to the pull of her presence.

The warmth of her skin met the coolness of my fingers as they wrapped around her wrist tenderly, holding back the full force of my strength. It wasn't a show of dominance, but rather one of silent desperation—a wordless plea urging her to stay, to not sever the burgeoning bond that had started to form between us.

Our eyes met, and in the vast pool of emotions reflected in her gaze, I discerned a truth. She possessed a deep reservoir of compassion and understanding that seemed to course through her very being. This essence beckoned to me, much like the allure of sunlight to someone submerged in the shadowy depths of the ocean, promising warmth and clarity.

A soft intake of breath escaped her lips as she registered my touch. Her eyelids fluttered, revealing wide, surprised eyes that searched mine for understanding, for intent. Yet, instead of recoiling or expressing discomfort, she remained still, allowing the connection to deepen.

Her partner's voice grew louder as she shouted from down below, her concern echoing through the chamber.

Ignoring the commotion, I focused on the connection between us, establishing a telepathic link. I reached out to her mind, my thoughts intertwining with hers, and reassured her that I meant no harm.

"I only want to talk," I pushed the words into her consciousness.

"How is this possible?" Her brow furrowed. *"How can I hear your thoughts and understand you?"*

With a mental sigh, I responded, *"It is a natural ability*

43

that many species within the IPA possess, especially between mates. Those who bind themselves together develop the capacity to communicate on a deeper level without having to touch. It is a gift bestowed upon us by the universe."

"But how are you speaking directly to me?" She pressed further, her curiosity unyielding. *"Is it because of our encounter, the bond we formed? Did something happen between us when you rescued me?"*

I shook my head, my gaze steady as I replied. *"I did not bond with you intentionally. When I found you, you were bound and helpless. I freed you from your restraints and carried you along the surface, bringing you to the nearest human settlement."*

Her brow furrowed again, her confusion evident. *"But why would you save me?"* she asked, her mental voice tinged with a hint of vulnerability. *"Do you regret it?"*

"I regret getting caught," I confessed, my mental voice tinged with bitterness. *"But I don't regret saving you. You deserved a second chance at life. It was the right thing to do."*

Her companion had managed to make it up to the ledge. I tensed, but she raised her hands in surrender as she approached us, and the tension in the air seemed to ease slightly. She turned her attention briefly to her companion, exchanging words before refocusing on me.

"Tell her that I mean no harm to you," I requested, my telepathic message clear and resolute. *"Let her know that I come in peace and only wish to engage in conversation."*

I watched as the female in the white coat kneeled beside her, her gaze shifting between my face and the spot where my hand grasped her companion's wrist.

"This is my mentor, Dr. Violet," she explained, both vocally and telepathically introducing her to me. *"She works*

for my grandfather, who purchased you. We've been tasked with attempting to communicate with you and obtaining answers to any questions my grandfather may have for you."

Dr. Violet nodded and offered me her hand in a gesture of goodwill.

However, something within me hesitated. Dr. Violet had not abused me, and yet, she didn't possess the same peaceful aura as the human I had saved. My instincts were directed by a complex blend of experience and caution, and right now, they solely trusted the one I had saved.

I declined her offer and kept my distance for the time being. My attention returned to Dr. Violet's student, the one I was touching.

"What is your name?" I had a genuine desire to learn more about the female who had ignited a flame of hope within me.

Her eyes met mine, a hint of a smile tugging at the corners of her lips. *"Isla,"* she replied, both her vocal and mental voice soft yet brimming with a quiet strength. *"It means 'island.'"*

The name held poetic beauty. Isla, like an island, generated visions of tranquility amidst turbulent waves. It seemed appropriate for this woman who had become my beacon of hope, my refuge in a world of uncertainty.

"Isla," I said aloud, relishing the sound of her name as it rolled off my tongue. A smile tugged at the corners of my lips as I repeated her name. It held a certain melody, an assurance that resonated deep within me.

"Thank you, Isla," I replied, my mental voice soft, tinged with appreciation. *"Your name fits you."*

A small smile played on her lips, and my hearts swelled with warmth.

Though there was an undeniable connection between us—

a shared longing—a mutual desire to learn more about each other—it was also tinged with uncertainty and fear.

The promise of trust and acceptance hung heavy in the air, tempting and terrifying at the same time. Was it worth getting to know her for a chance at solace?

Or was this why was there a hesitation hidden in the depths of her eyes?

"What's your name?"

"I am Ky'rn, a Makezu commander." My chest swelled with a sense of accomplishment and responsibility as I spoke, my mental voice betraying hints of both pride and obligation. *"My unit was tasked with a mission to study Earth and its vast waters, to see what the IPA can do to assist with its poor conditions, and to ascertain whether there was a chance for aquatic species to settle in your waters."*

"Ky'rn." Her eyes shone with genuine concern, and she leaned in slightly, her tongue briefly darting out to moisten her lips. *"You can trust me."*

Her words reverberated deep within me, igniting the spark of hope that had long been smoldering within my heart. The flicker of hope that had been barely alive suddenly roared to life, threatening to consume me entirely. After a year of captivity and torture, her declaration was a lifeline for my shattered soul. In her eyes, I saw a glimmer of light amidst the darkness that had engulfed me for so long.

"I owe you a life debt, Ky'rn," she declared, her mental voice steady as her expression softened. *"And I intend to repay it. But you must trust me and give me the answers that I need."*

"I will answer whatever I am able to." I understood the weight of her promise, the magnitude of the debt she sought to repay. *"Your trust in me is not misplaced."*

SEVEN

ISLA

D r. Violet's inquisitive gaze met mine. "What is he
saying?"

I hesitated for a moment, unsure of how much
to disclose. The weight of keeping secrets from my mentor
tugged at my conscience, but the knowledge that she was still
tied to my grandfather's employ lingered in the back of my
mind.

Nevertheless, I owed it to her to provide some information. Hopefully, all she would tell my grandfather was that I
was communicating with the sharkman as he'd asked me to.

"He introduced himself as Ky'rn," I said, trying to keep
my voice professional. I didn't want her to know how thrilled
I was to be able to communicate with the creature who had
saved me. "He was sent here by the IPA to study Earth's
waters."

"Why would the IPA want to study our waters?" she
asked skeptically, side-eying Ky'rn, her mistrust visible in her
narrowed gaze. "Have they been monitoring Earth this whole
time?"

I shrugged, grappling with the complexities of the situation. "Water is a precious resource, and Earth possesses an exceptional abundance of it compared to other planets we've studied. Considering Ky'rn is an aquatic species, it's likely they've been looking for other water-rich planets, and that their interest lies in the unique properties of our oceans' ecosystems."

Dr. Violet nodded, but her expression quickly shifted to one of deep suspicion. "What if they're the reason behind some of the mysterious ship disappearances?" she questioned with a hint of accusation. "Throughout history, we've had countless vessels sink or vanish on clear nights…Could they be responsible?"

"You don't believe in ghost ships, do you?" I teased lightly, attempting to ease the tension in the air. "Vessels haven't gone missing for years!"

"Who knows how long aliens have been studying us?" Dr. Violet's expression hardened as she leaned away from the tank.

"It doesn't really matter anymore, does it?" An unrestrained chuckle escaped my lips as I bared a wide, toothy grin, finding amusement in the current state of humanity. "Sadly, our arrogance blinded us, thinking we were invincible, only to be harshly reminded of our place when we dared to fly too close to the sun," I said, anger lacing my words. "We were humbled, painfully so, realizing our so-called advanced technology was nothing but child's play compared to the aliens within the IPA. We're just infants, naively taking our first steps in a universe where they reign supreme."

"Which is why this is too good an opportunity to not take advantage of." Dr. Violet's gaze shifted between me and the tablet, her hand reaching out toward me. "Let's take this chance to get Ky'rn to answer some questions while he's still willing to communicate with you."

With a wary eye, I gingerly handed over the tablet to her, my movements deliberate and slow, conscious of not startling or offending Ky'rn. I was intent on preserving the delicate bond we had just begun to establish, hoping to gradually build his trust.

However, as Dr. Violet grabbed the tablet from me, her hands swiftly navigating its interface, I couldn't shake off a nagging feeling of distrust. Her swift, precise movements seemed overly calculated, as if she was concealing something or had an ulterior motive. This heightened my sense of caution, prompting me to scrutinize her behavior and the possible consequences.

The last thing I wanted was for her to sever the fragile bond I'd created with Ky'rn before I had a chance to nurture it.

Ky'rn's voice echoed in my mind, cutting through my thoughts. *"What is happening?"*

"My mentor, Dr. Violet, is going to ask you a few questions, if you're willing to answer." I hoped he would be open to sharing more about himself, as it could help us understand him better.

I'd love to learn more about the creature who rescued me in the hopes of gaining his trust.

Ky'rn's response came swiftly, his voice holding a hint of caution. *"As long as the questions are not too invasive."* Given how vulnerable he must feel after being held captive for so long, it was a legitimate caveat.

Dr. Violet wasted no time diving into the conversation. "Ky'rn," she began, her voice steady and professional, "we have some questions for you, if you're willing to answer."

Dr. Violet listed her first few questions to me, and I relayed them to Ky'rn, mentally noting how clinical they were thus far. *"My mentor wants to know if the condition of the tank is to your liking,"* I pathed. *"Is there anything we can change or improve?"*

"It's good enough," he conveyed with calm assurance, confidently tilting his head. *"My species is capable of surviving in a wide range of water conditions, including Earth's salt or freshwater, and even brackish water."*

As his words sank in, I felt a wave of relief rush over me , like a tide retreating after a storm. The current setting appeared to provide him with the required conditions for survival. Knowing he wasn't in immediate danger eased the knot of worry that had been tightening in my chest since my gaze landed on him. His safety, which had been a constant source of concern, now felt somewhat assured, allowing me to breathe a little easier.

But I knew I couldn't become complacent, for as long as Ky'rn was within my grandfather's possession, his life would always be hanging in the balance, subject to the whims and decisions of a man whose motives I could no longer trust.

With a nervous glance over my shoulder, I hesitantly shared the information with my mentor. I couldn't shake the doubt in my mind, wondering if I was making the right decision by trusting her with everything he'd told me so far.

"Thank you for sharing that with us, Ky'rn." She nodded appreciatively. "It's fascinating to learn about the adaptability of your species."

She quickly jotted down notes on the tablet, her focus unwavering as she documented our interaction. She had shifted into a purely scientific mindset, seeking to understand the needs and adaptations of this fascinating aquatic alien before us.

My heart swelled with empathy as I gazed into Ky'rn's warm, amber eyes. I could see the faint lines of worry etched into his forehead, and I felt a strong desire to ease his anxieties and to allay any doubts or concerns he had. Without hesitation, I reached out and placed my hand on his shoulder, offering a reassuring squeeze.

"How can we make you more comfortable here?"

His gaze shifted momentarily toward Dr. Violet, as if seeking reassurance. *"I'd like to know that no one will conduct any more experiments on me,"* he responded, his voice soft and vulnerable, his gaze returning to mine.

As I thought about Ky'rn's past, tears welled up in my eyes. He had been through unimaginable pain and suffering at the hands of those who favored luxury and exotic collections over life. A lump formed in my throat as I thought about all he had endured. Anger boiled within me, directed towards the heartless individuals who had caused him so much harm. My emotions were in conflict, torn between wanting to comfort him and seeking justice for him.

As an alien species in a world that had only recently discovered the existence of intelligent life beyond our own, he faced the stigma of being an invader. The fear and animosity that some held toward his kind was unavoidable.

But to me, he was more than an alien interloper.

"Ky'rn," I said, my voice filled with unwavering conviction. *"You are a hero in my eyes. It doesn't matter where you come from. You deserve to be treated with respect and have your rights acknowledged. I will do everything in my power to protect you until I can get you out of here."*

A moment of silence passed between us, as the tension between us seemed to grow thicker with each passing second.

Was he debating whether he should believe me?

He smiled and gently squeezed my hand. *"Thank you."* I could feel the sincerity in his words, and it brought a warmth to my heart that spread through my entire body.

Dr. Violet leaned in, her curiosity piqued as she instructed me to ask Ky'rn about his dietary preferences. She wanted to ensure that he was receiving proper nutrition and asked if he enjoyed the frozen fish that his previous owner had provided him with.

I relayed the question to Ky'rn, whose amber eyes intensified, their thoughtful focus seeming to dissect each word, weighing the question with a hint of suspicion.

"Frozen fish is acceptable," he responded, his mouth pinched. *"But I prefer live fish. The larger, the better. I enjoy the thrill of the hunt."*

I wondered how he managed to fulfill his hunger within the limits of the tank, knowing that his previous owners would not have allowed him such luxury. The image of him devouring a fish larger than himself sparked a sense of awe within me.

"Are the Makezu similar to our earthly sharks?" I asked, eager to learn more about his species. *"And, forgive me for asking, but would you ever eat a human? Despite what most people think, our sharks dislike the taste of humans and won't attack one unless provoked. I blame our media for perpetuating that myth, which has caused many people to be afraid to swim in the ocean."*

There was a glint of laughter in his eyes as he shook his head, a broad smile exposing his pointed fangs. *"Yes, we share similarities with your Earth sharks, but we are not driven by the same instincts. While I am capable of hunting and consuming fish, I have no desire to harm humans. Our diets are distinct, and I seek sustenance from non-sentient sources."*

The knot of tension in my stomach released, as I absorbed his words. I could see the sincerity in Ky'rn's eyes, and it was reassuring to know that he didn't view humans as mere prey to be hunted.

At the very least, that was one less thing I had to be concerned about.

"If you trust me enough not to flinch away when I grab your wrist," he continued, his mental voice soft like a whisper in my head, *"are you afraid to share the same tank with me?"*

His teasing made my heart flutter, and I found myself drawn to his mischievous charm. If Ky'rn had intended to harm me, he would have had ample opportunity to do so, but instead he had rescued me. His actions spoke of bravery and compassion, not of a predator seeking to consume its prey. The strength and power he possessed were undeniable, and yet, he had chosen to protect me instead.

So, I grinned at his lighthearted comment. I had trusted him enough to let him touch me and communicate with me telepathically, and perhaps I should consider swimming with him.

But that would have to wait for another time.

I turned my attention to Dr. Violet. "Is there a way we can provide live fish for Ky'rn to hunt in his tank?"

She peered at Ky'rn and sighed. "Unfortunately, it would be challenging to maintain a steady supply of live fish. However, I can discuss the possibility with your grandfather and see what he thinks."

The mention of my grandfather stirred conflicting emotions within me. While I yearned to protect Ky'rn from my family, I also had to be practical. Dr. Violet's willingness to consider the idea showed her commitment to ensuring Ky'rn's well-being, but I knew I couldn't fully trust her.

I relayed the information to Ky'rn, and he nodded. A sudden alarm on my smartwatch sent him into a state of alertness, his gaze sharpening as he focused on the source of the sound.

"It's okay!" I reassured him, gripping his wrist to keep him from jerking away. *"It's a reminder for me to prepare for my dinner party with my grandfather."*

Glancing at my watch, I realized with surprise how time had flown by.

The conversation with Ky'rn had occupied my thoughts so completely that I had unknowingly skipped lunch. My focus had been fully taken by the connection we were forming, and my heart had been captured by it.

I could see the disappointment in Ky'rn's eyes as I uttered my apologies. *"I am sorry, but I must leave now,"* I said, my heart aching with an unexplainable longing. *"Could we perhaps continue our conversation tomorrow?"*

"I would look forward to that." His gaze shifted toward Dr. Violet. *"Should I be worried about her?"*

I sighed heavily. *"Dr. Violet's heart is in the right place,"* I admitted, *"but my grandfather holds her loyalty. I'm the only one you can fully trust."*

Understanding washed over Ky'rn's features as he nodded in acknowledgement. *"I will be vigilant,"* he assured me. *"Thank you for treating me like an equal, with respect."*

His words of gratitude touched my heart. *"It's the least I can do."*

"Farewell, my Isla." His voice held a depth of emotion that sent shivers down my spine. The way he said my name, with a mixture of familiarity and affection, ignited a flame within me.

As he released my wrist, his gaze locked with mine, and time seemed to stand still. I held his gaze for a lingering moment, lost in the depths of his amber eyes. They were like beacons of light in the midst of the darkness, a reminder of what I had clung to in despair that fateful night.

A thousand unspoken words passed between us, a silent

promise that we shared. But as much as I longed to stay, duty called. I reluctantly tore my gaze away from his captivating presence.

An unsettling sensation nestled itself at the back of my mind—the unmistakable feeling of being observed, of unseen eyes tracking every movement. Taking a deep, steadying breath, I rose from my kneeling position by the tank, feeling the moisture from the ground seeping into my pants. With one last lingering look, I raised my hand in a gesture of parting, silently vowing that our paths would cross again.

With a heavy heart, I turned away under the ever-watchful eyes of Dr. Violet. Sensing something in her gaze, I shot her a soft smile. "It's time for me to prepare for the dinner party. Are you okay with me leaving?"

She clasped my shoulder, her eyes scanning my face as if searching for something. There was concern etched on her features. "Of course," she replied gently. "Go and enjoy yourself. We will continue our work tomorrow."

"Have a nice night."

"You too, dear." She released me and turned her attention to her tablet, resuming her work.

Slowly, I turned to leave, glancing back once more to see him watching me leave, his amber eyes gleaming softly in the dim light of the tank. It was an image that would haunt me, tugging at my heartstrings and reminding me of the commitment I had made.

I would find a way to free Ky'rn. It was the only thing I could do for him now.

EIGHT

KY'RN

As Isla disappeared through the doors, leaving me alone with her mentor, a sense of unease settled over me. She was my only chance for freedom, my connection to the outside world, and now she was gone.

The tank felt cold once again, void of her vibrant presence.

I admired Isla's radiance. Her essence shone like the sun's rays dancing on the surface of the ocean. There was a purity to her mind, a lightness that contrasted with the darkness lurking in the depths of her thoughts. I couldn't shake the feeling that there was more to her story, a hidden pain that resided in the shadows.

My attention shifted to her mentor, who offered me a soft smile and extended her hand toward me again. I dismissed her gesture this time, too, uninterested in engaging with anyone except my Isla.

If Isla didn't fully trust her mentor, then neither would I. I couldn't afford to make any mistakes, to ignore the warning signs that surrounded me.

Resigned, I lowered my head beneath the surface of the

water, watching as Isla's mentor cast a disappointed gaze upon me. She retreated down the stairway, returning to her workstation and leaving me alone in the quiet tank.

I began to swim around the perimeter, my thoughts consumed by Isla. There was an undeniable pull, a magnetic force that drew me to her.

It was as if our destinies were intertwined, our paths colliding once again.

As soon as my fingers had contacted her pale, delicate wrist, I was ensnared once again by her enchanting presence. A rush of sensations had flooded my mind, overwhelming me with an intoxicating mix of desire and admiration. Every nerve in my body seemed to pulse with electricity as I struggled to comprehend what was happening to me...

Her touch had been like a drug, addicting and impossible to resist. In that moment, I had felt completely under her spell, helpless but content in her captivating grasp.

Not that I wanted to.

I couldn't explain the intense attraction I felt toward her. Maybe it was just a chemical reaction, or perhaps it was something deeper and more primal.

An inexplicable pull emanated from her, drawing me in and igniting a primal desire to possess her. Every nerve in my body screamed for me to take her, to claim her as my own, to fiercely protect her from anyone else's grasp. The intensity of this instinct was overwhelming and consumed me completely.

As I rubbed my fingers together, I could still feel the searing electricity coursing through me, the lingering sensation from where our skin met. Every touch from her was like a jolt of reality, confirming that the intense connection we shared on that fateful night was no figment of my imagination. It was an undeniable force pulling us together, leaving me desperate for more.

Each time our bodies had touched, a strange sensation coursed through me. Her skin was like nothing I had ever felt before, soft and smooth yet unfamiliar.

Was there something about her that made my body react this way? Was it some chemical or pheromone she emitted that caused this intense reaction?

Either way, I couldn't deny the intense reaction my body had to her skin. It left me feeling conflicted and unsure of what to do next.

I had always prided myself on my ability to lead my people and keep them safe, even in the face of defeat. But I've never experienced this reaction with other humans or females that I've encountered.

Why was my entire being responding to Isla in this way? My body, mind, heart and soul were all affected by her presence.

She seemed to be designed specifically for me, drawing me toward her and igniting all of my senses as if I were tracking prey.

I frowned as a pang of regret tugged at my heart. If only our meeting had occurred under different circumstances, in a world where our connection could flourish without the weight of secrecy and uncertainty. It seemed unfair that fate had brought us together in this complex web of intergalactic politics and human intrigue.

Yet, even in the midst of it all, Isla had shown me a glimmer of hope. She had treated me as an equal, a being worthy of respect and understanding. Her genuine care and consideration had touched my soul, leaving a lasting imprint.

She saw beyond the confines of my appearance, embracing the essence of who I was.

In her eyes, I wasn't a mere prize to be studied or a test subject to be prodded and examined. She recognized my worth—me, for who I was, without actually knowing my fortune or caring about *who* I was amongst the IPA.

In a universe where humans were still finding their place among the registered species of the IPA, Isla had become a beacon of possibility. She had shattered the preconceived notions that weighed me down, reminding me that there was goodness and compassion to be found within humans.

The stagnant water flowed over my skin as I contemplated the enigma that was Isla. Her existence sparked a longing within me, a desire to learn more about her, to unravel the intricacies of her mind and heart.

It baffled me, the depth of my fascination with her. She wasn't of my kind. She wasn't even aquatic. And yet, there was an undeniable pull, a magnetic force that drew me toward her. No matter how hard I tried, I couldn't get the image of her face out of my mind. Her eyes, filled with compassion and understanding, seemed to pierce through the depths of my being. The memory of her gentle touch, how she had reached out to me with genuine care, sent ripples of warmth down my spine.

I pondered the reasons behind this inexplicable attachment. Had my isolation and solitude over the past year driven me to seek connection with any being who showed me kindness and understanding? Was I simply grasping at the first lifeline thrown my way?

But there was something more to it, something deeper that defied rational explanation. Isla had awakened emotions within me that I had long thought dormant. Her presence brought a sense of vitality and purpose to my life, filling the void that had plagued me for so long, even for the brief moment we'd conversed.

Was I becoming too attached, too wrapped up in her existence? Was I projecting my desires and yearnings onto her, seeking solace in her presence? Or was there something more profound at play? Something that surpassed the boundaries of mere companionship and hinted at a deeper connection between our souls?

I looked up when the older male re-entered the lab space, turning to speak with Dr. Violet. I watched their interaction, unease stirring within me. I couldn't comprehend the details of their conversation, lacking a universal translator to understand their words, but the tone of their exchange spoke volumes.

Dr. Violet, who had initially stood at attention, seemed to deflate as he addressed her. There was a flicker of tension in the air, a subtle shift in the atmosphere that hinted at an underlying power dynamic. I no longer wondered about the nature of their relationship and the extent of his influence over her.

Isla was right. Her mentor would never go against her grandfather's wishes—she feared him far too much to consider it.

I watched as Dr. Violet showed Isla's grandfather the tablet, pointing to me in the tank and then gesturing toward the ledge above. His response was a smirk, a hint of amusement playing at the corners of his lips. He patted her back before pointing her toward her workstation, leaving the room without another word.

The moment the doors closed, Dr. Violet released a heavy sigh, her gaze fixed on the tablet in her hands. Her face bore the weight of remorse and concern.

Something about it didn't sit right with me.

The dynamics between Isla, Dr. Violet, and her grandfather seemed complex, tangled in a web of power, control, and conflicting interests. It made me reflect on what Isla had shared with me—her fear of her grandfather's influence.

Was that the source of the shadow that lurked in the recesses of her mind?

The unease that gripped my hearts deepened, and I vowed to myself that I would protect Isla from any harm that might befall her...

NINE

ISLA

T tugged at the hem of my snug purple dress, hoping it wouldn't ride up any further. I couldn't fathom why my grandfather had insisted on my presence at this business dinner when all I wanted was to learn more about the enigmatic aquatic alien he had "gifted" me residing in the depths of our research facility.

But as always, my grandfather kept his own counsel. It was better not to question him and just do what he asked.

He adjusted his tailored suit jacket, his eyes gleaming with pride as he looked at me. "You look amazing, dear," he remarked, a wide grin stretching across his face. "The spitting image of your late grandmother and mother."

"Thank you." Blushing at the compliment, I glanced away. I wasn't one to enjoy getting dolled up, and this formal attire only emphasized my unease, but being compared to mother and grandmother's beauty made me feel more like I was actually a part of the family. "I feel like a fish out of water."

"My dear, I know you're not quite accustomed to this scene," my grandfather acknowledged. "But it's necessary to remind others who you are," he added with a gentle smile, extending his arm for me to hold.

I hesitated for a moment, the desire to bolt conflicting with the obligations that bound me this evening. Ultimately, I determined it wasn't worth arguing with him and accepted his arm, intertwining mine with his.

It was only one night, and tomorrow morning, I could return to the research lab to learn more about Ky'rn.

Even after a year living in this facility, I was continually astounded by its grandeur. The black marble floor gleamed under the warm light, reflecting the sparkle of the gilded detailing on the high ceiling. Sapphire stones were inlaid in intricate patterns along the walls, lending a soothing aquatic hue that contrasted beautifully with the opulent gold accents.

A crystal chandelier hung in the middle of the hallway, its brilliant light casting a myriad of colors on the reflective surfaces.

The walls bore the occasional piece of expensive artwork, each a masterful depiction of underwater scenes, honoring our family's maritime legacy and fascination.

My heels clicked against the polished floor as we walked, the sound echoing through the vast corridor. The air was perfumed with a blend of sea salt and cedar, the signature fragrance of our estate. The sound of distant laughter and clinking glassware indicated we were nearing the dining hall.

Despite the elegance around me, I felt an overwhelming sense of dread. I was dressed in silk and lace and surrounded by grandeur, but all I wanted to do was exchange my high heels for a pair of safety boots and my dress for my well-worn lab coat.

My fingers tightened around my grandfather's arm. He patted my hand reassuringly, but his attention was elsewhere. As we neared the entrance to the dining hall, I took a deep breath and cast a wistful glance over my shoulder, longing to dash to the elevator and return to the depths of the ocean, to the lab where Ky'rn was.

As the doors swung open, revealing the grand ballroom, I felt a surge of anxiety bubble in my stomach. But I refused to disappoint Grandfather. I straightened my back, raised my chin, and forced a smile onto my face.

I would endure this for Ky'rn, for the hope of a future where we could both be free from our confines.

The ballroom was a dazzling sight, filled with important figures from the government and business world mingling and socializing. Their conversations and laughter created a symphony of voices that echoed throughout the expansive space.

All eyes turned toward us as my grandfather, the esteemed host of this lavish dinner, made his grand entrance. He held his head high, radiating authority and confidence. I followed closely beside him, trying my best to exude the grace and poise expected of the heir to his fortune.

"Ladies and gentlemen, distinguished guests, I stand before you tonight with great pride and joy." My grandfather's voice boomed through the ballroom, commanding attention. "I am honored to introduce to you my beloved granddaughter, Isla. She is not only the heir to my wealth and empire, but also a shining beacon of the future of Boze Marine Co."

A wave of applause and appreciative murmurs rippled through the room as all eyes turned toward me. My cheeks flushed, nervousness coursing through my veins. I forced a smile, my gaze shifting from face to face, trying to take in the sea of expectant faces.

"My dear Isla has grown into a remarkable young woman, embodying the values and spirit of our family," my grandfather continued, his tone filled with pride. "With her intelligence, grace, and unwavering dedication, I have no doubt that she will carry forward our legacy with utmost brilliance."

The applause swelled once again, washing over me like a tidal wave. I lowered my gaze, my hands clasped tightly together in front of me, feeling the weight of the responsibilities that awaited me.

I was the heir to my family's wealth, fortune, and business, but I hated the pressures that came along with it.

"In this rapidly changing world," he continued, his tone becoming more impassioned, "we must come together, bridge the gaps that divide us, and embrace the potential that lies in collaboration. Tonight, we celebrate the power of connections, the power to break barriers, and the power to shape a future that knows no boundaries."

The guests seemed to lean forward, captivated by his words. My grandfather's ability to capture an audience was unmatched, which made him a threat to our rivals.

A wave of excitement swept through the room, and my pulse fluttered. This was the moment my grandfather had been preparing for, a chance to showcase not just his wealth, but his vision for progress and prosperity for future generations.

My grandfather guided me toward the VIP section, positioned on a raised ledge overlooking the rest of the ballroom. Five individuals, clearly related by their shared features, occupied the seats, dressed to impress in their finest clothes. Their matching bright blue eyes followed our every move, expressions a mix of curiosity and boredom.

The older gentleman at the table leaned in and whispered something to the youngest man, who appeared to be around my age. Without hesitation, he stood up and descended the steps toward me. His confident stride and the warmth in his eyes told me that he was here to offer his support.

His manners were impeccable, and his charm flowed effortlessly as he extended his arm to me, his smile almost dazzling. "Good evening, Miss Isla," he said, his voice as smooth as silk. I recognized him as Roman, the son of one of my grandfather's closest business partners.

"Good evening, Roman," I returned his greeting, tugging my arm from my grandfather to accept Roman's. Despite his charming exterior, I couldn't shake the unsettling feeling that I was merely a pawn in the midst of another of my grandfather's grand plans.

My instincts told me that introducing me hadn't been his primary reason for hosting this dinner party, and I was terrified to find out what was.

As Roman led me up the half flight of stairs, I stole a glance over my shoulder, taking in the sea of faces that watched us ascend. I was used to scrutiny from the scientific community. Many of my peers had spread rumors that I'd only gotten into my prestigious marine biology program through my family's influence. But this was an entirely different kind of attention. I was being treated as if I was royalty—a princess being led to the throne in her own castle.

At the top of the stairs, a private dining area overlooking the grand hall greeted us. An intricately carved wooden table, laden with food and surrounded by plush oversized chairs, dominated the space.

Roman pulled out a chair for me next to a woman who bore a striking resemblance to him—presumably his mother, whom I hadn't met yet.

As my grandfather introduced Roman's family, I couldn't help but feel a pang of discomfort under their stares. It was as if they were scrutinizing a new item at a charity auction.

Roman's grandparents, with their air of authority and the weight of their family empire, had an imposing presence. Both radiated the same old money arrogance as my grandfather—anyone beneath them held no value.

"Isla, it's good to see you out and about. Ever since the… incident, it's been a trying time for you, I'm sure." Roman's grandmother's words cut through the air but were tinged with sympathy.

I nodded, my smile faltering for a moment. The mention of the incident reminded me of the darkness that had enveloped my life, the trauma I had experienced. It was a wound that hadn't completely healed, a scar that still caused pain, and encountering Ky'rn had ripped it open again.

It had been difficult to move on from what had happened, but I couldn't let it define my entire existence.

"Thank you." I nodded. "It has been a challenging year, but I'm trying my best to move forward."

Roman's grandmother reached out, her hand resting gently on mine, her touch both reassuring and stifling as she squeezed my hand. "You're a strong young woman, Isla. I'm confident that you can overcome anything."

Her eyes held genuine warmth as she nodded, seemingly understanding the weight of my words. I wondered if she, too, had faced her share of struggles in life, being a leader in the powerful Aurora Cosmetics Empire.

Her words were meant to offer encouragement, but they only served as a reminder of the expectations placed upon me. I felt like a puppet in a carefully choreographed performance, with everyone else dictating my moves and decisions.

Roman's mother, a poised woman with an air of sophistication, offered a supportive smile. "It takes strength to endure, my dear. Remember, you have the support of our family as well."

I appreciated the sentiment, though I wasn't entirely sure if the support was genuine or just a social nicety. After all, they were here to discuss a potential partnership between our families, which made it difficult to discern the true motives behind their kindness.

Our plates arrived, showcasing beautifully prepared fish. A waiter gracefully placed our meals before us, and I picked up my fork, trying to focus on the food in front of me instead of letting my thoughts drift to my savior, trapped in the lab below.

As the fragrant aroma of the dishes wafted through the air, I tried to maneuver my knife and fork to slice the filet, but the delicate fish seemed to resist my efforts. Each attempt to cut through left me more flustered than the last, and I felt a flush of embarrassment creeping up my cheeks. The tender flesh either slipped away or was mercilessly squashed beneath my inexpert hands.

I bet Ky'rn could tear through a fish the size of himself effortlessly, but here I was, struggling to cut a filet.

"Need a hand with that?" Roman's smooth voice broke my concentration. I looked up to find his eyes twinkling with mirth. He glanced at my plate, the subtle arch of his brow betraying his amusement.

"I've got it, thanks," I replied hastily, my pride slightly wounded. The polite smile I forced didn't quite reach my eyes.

He leaned in, bouncing an eyebrow playfully. "Are you sure? I've been told I wield a knife quite proficiently. But if you change your mind, let me know."

I chuckled, the tension dissipating. "Thank you, Roman, but I think I can manage." I paused, glancing down at the mangled piece of fish. "Do you always offer to cut a lady's fish for her?"

His face reddened slightly. "Only when I'm trying to impress," he admitted sheepishly, a playful glint in his eye.

Throughout dinner, everyone engaged in hushed conversations about trivial matters. Their voices washed over me like a distant tide while guilt gnawed at me with each bite I took. Here I was, dining on exquisite fresh fish, while Ky'rn subsisted on a diet of frozen, lifeless prey.

It brought the disparities between our worlds into stark relief.

As the evening wore on, I tried my best to engage in the conversation, taking occasional sips from my wine glass to mask my discomfort. I couldn't shake the feeling that I didn't fit into this world of societal expectations and family legacies.

Suddenly, Roman turned to my grandfather with an eager expression. "Sir, I've heard so much about your collection. Would it be possible for me to see it?"

My grandfather's eyes sparkled with pride. "Of course, Roman." He lifted his wine glass toward me, his probing gaze locked onto mine. "Isla, why don't you give him a tour of the garden on our way to the museum?"

A lump formed in my throat at the suggestion.

My grandfather was eager to marry me off, and this walk in the rooftop garden was clearly his way of pushing me to consider Roman as a potential spouse.

Forcing a polite smile, I agreed, rising from my chair. "Of course, Grandfather."

Roman seemed to catch on and stood too, his eyes never leaving mine. "After you," he murmured, offering his arm.

Tentatively, I took it, leading him through the grand ballroom and into the hallway adorned with sparkling chandeliers and priceless artworks. As we approached the door leading to the garden, my pace quickened, eager for the fresh air.

The music from the grand ballroom was muted as we stepped out into the moonlit garden. The cool night air was refreshing, brushing against my skin and rustling the leaves of the meticulously maintained plants.

I stood still for a moment, taking a few deep breaths to calm my heart and allow the heat to drain from my body after being trapped inside the ballroom with all those bodies and lights shining down on us.

I hated the expectations and burdens that came with our family names. Amidst the grandeur and politics, was there room for genuine emotion? For personal desires and dreams? A connection built on shared dreams and aspirations, rather than duty?

The thought of commitment, especially under external pressure, made me wary.

I yearned for the freedom to forge my own path, in love and in life. The fact that Sam and Rose were still at large, lurking in the shadows, hidden from both my grandfather and law authorities, made me feel confined more than the facility's walls and island location did.

"You have a beautiful garden here," Roman commented, glancing at the exotic flora that surrounded us. Each plant had been handpicked by my grandfather from various parts of the world.

"Thank you." I nodded, forcing a polite smile. "My grandfather takes great pride in it."

"Your grandfather seems to take pride in many things. Especially his collection." His curious eyes searched mine.

I exhaled a sigh and led him down the stone pathway. "He does. He's always had a strong interest in collecting unique and exotic stuff—it gives him something to do—but since my parents died, he's become more preoccupied with his collection."

We stopped in front of a magnificent fountain, the water cascading in rhythmic patterns, shimmering under the moonlight.

"I've heard rumors," Roman said, his gaze fixated on flashing lights dancing on the water. "About his most recent acquisition."

I felt a lump in my throat. Was he referring to Ky'rn? I played coy. "Oh? And what have you heard?"

He looked up at me, eyes sharp and assessing. "Just that it's something…otherworldly."

Swallowing hard, I managed a small laugh and nudged his shoulder. "You know how rumors are. They're often bigger than the truth."

Roman nodded, though I could see he wasn't entirely convinced. "True, but my connections have never been wrong."

Curiosity gnawed at me as Roman's words hung in the air.

What was he getting at? I didn't have much time for pleasantries and social niceties, not when my mind was constantly preoccupied with thoughts slipping away from here to the urge to check on Ky'rn.

I leaned closer to Roman, dropping the act. "Could you please cut to the chase?" I hissed. "What's so important that we have to sneak away like this?"

His gaze flicked over our shoulders, to where the guards stood stoically along the wall, ever watchful. He leaned in closer, his breath warm against my ear. "Act like we're together," he whispered urgently, "like we want to run off for a private moment."

I followed his gaze and nodded, trying to maintain a composed facade. Inside, confusion and fear threatened to overwhelm me, my heart racing and palms sweating, but I forced myself to keep still and outwardly calm.

His brown eyes were dead serious. I'd have to play along if I wanted answers.

My mind raced as I forced a fake giggle, as if we had just shared a private joke. I took his hand and led him toward the private balcony, wondering what on Earth could be so important that it required this level of secrecy.

The stone balcony defied gravity, extending fearlessly over the roaring sea below, surrounded by a white marble archway and dense shrubbery. Perfect for what Roman had requested, outside the confines of my private suite.

The moon, high above, covered the world in an ethereal, silvery cloak. The brilliance of the moonlight was rivaled only by the artful garden lights that dotted the garden, each one strategically placed, guiding us while adding to the evening's enchantment. The soft night breeze murmured through the trees, teasing the strands of my hair and tickling my nose with salt as it ruffled the hem of my dress.

The gentle crash of waves below was accompanied by a mesmerizing sight. Just beyond the frothy whitecaps, deep beneath the water's surface, the underwater lab emanated a soft glow, like a beacon in the heart of an abyss. Its luminescence created a dance of lights upon the water, hinting at groundbreaking discoveries and untold marvels.

Surrounding the lab, immense walls rose from the ocean floor. These structures, formidable and awe-inspiring, served not just as fortifications against the elements but as barriers against prying eyes. They ensured that the research work within the lab remained shielded from prying eyes and the outside world's relentless curiosity.

Only a select few were permitted on this garden floor. The

fact that my grandfather had suggested I bring Roman here gave me cause for concern.

Roman gently withdrew his arm from my grasp and leaned on the balcony railing, gazing out at the waves.

"I know what lingers below the waters," he began, his voice low as he jerked his head toward the underwater lab. "That's why I'm here."

I frowned in response to his cryptic statement. I didn't want to jump to conclusions and make my fears come true, but my growing unease was hard to ignore.

"I don't understand," I replied cautiously. "What are you talking about?"

"You already know, but I'll play your game." He chuckled as he gripped the railing and leaned backward. "You don't know the reason for tonight's dinner, do you?" he asked, his gaze piercing.

I shook my head, feeling a sense of dread settling in. "What do you mean?"

With a sigh, he stepped closer, taking my hand gently and pressing a soft kiss to the back. The gesture was both comforting and unsettling. "My family bid for your hand in marriage, Isla," he confessed, his words hanging heavily in the air. "Tonight was a test, to see how we fit."

The world around me seemed to blur as I struggled to comprehend the enormity of what he was saying. It couldn't be true. It couldn't be.

"No," I whispered, shaking my head in denial.

Roman's grip on my hand tightened and he pulled me closer, wrapping his arms around me in a protective embrace. His voice was a hushed murmur in my ear as he revealed the painful truth. "Your grandfather has been searching for a rich and powerful heir to be your husband, in order to protect you and continue your family's legacy. Tonight's dinner was to showcase to families with eligible sons that you're ready for an arranged marriage."

The pieces fell into place, and I couldn't deny the truth any longer. His murmured words sent a chill through me, and it all began to make horrible sense.

Why else would my grandfather have gifted me Ky'rn, if not to use him as a bargaining chip to secure my compliance.

My hands clenched into fists, nails digging into my palms as frustration bubbled up in my chest. How dare they try to continue to control my life, especially in such a cold and calculated way?

"I won't accept an arranged marriage," I declared, through clenched teeth, narrowing my gaze, daring him to contradict me. "Not to you, not to anyone. I'm sick and tired of others dictating my life and keeping me in this gilded cage. It's just a glorified prison, no matter how lovely it is."

He pulled away slightly, his eyes widening in surprise as they scoured mine, a hint of a smirk playing at the corners of his mouth. Then, he gestured toward the lab beneath the water's surface, where Ky'rn was held, and posed a question that stopped me in my tracks.

"But what if agreeing to marry me is the only way to save the Makezu commander you care about?"

TEN

ISLA

"How do you know about Ky'rn?" I asked, my voice trembling with disbelief.

Roman pursed his lips and shook his head. "I can't disclose that yet," he replied cryptically, "not until you agree to my terms."

Frustration welled up inside me, and I pushed away from him, crossing my arms and rubbing them as if I could physically ward off his words. Once again, I felt trapped, cornered by forces beyond my control, and every fiber of my being yearned for an escape.

"You're not much different from my grandfather," I accused him bitterly.

"That's not true." Roman's gaze never wavered. "Unlike your grandfather, I can help you get away from here, if you want. You could have the freedom you've always desired without needing to worry about being betrayed again."

My eyes narrowed and I shifted my weight as I studied him, unsure whether to trust him or not, my heart hammering with indecision. He stood there, tall and imposing, with the same smooth smile on his face that my grandfather always wore when manipulating someone. My fingers twitched, caught between my desire for independence and the rising anxiety that I was bartering with someone as cunning as my grandfather.

"How can I blindly believe what you're saying?" I questioned, my brow raised. "Why would you want to help me, then? What's in it for you?"

"You can't." He sighed as he brushed back his long brown hair. "All I can give you now is my word. You'll have proof of my good intentions in due time."

I scoffed, shaking my head. "Your word? That's supposed to be enough? After what I've been through, the betrayals, the lies…"

He stepped closer, his eyes intense. "Isla, I know it's hard to trust. And frankly, you shouldn't trust anyone blindly, not even me. But I've been watching, listening…and I've seen what you've endured. It's not right. No one should be treated like a pawn, especially not by family."

My defenses wavered for a split second. "And why do you care? Why help me?"

"You're the only person who can help me in return." Roman's words hung heavy in the air.

I furrowed my brows. "How can an arranged marriage between us help me free the alien?"

"How about we establish a few things first?" Roman crossed his arms, still watching me closely. "What do you think about him?"

I felt the weight of his gaze, his judgment pressing down on me.

"He's…extraordinary," I began slowly, thinking of Ky'rn's amber eyes and the intensity they held. "He's more than an animal, some specimen to be collected and studied. He has thoughts, feelings, a soul. When I look into his eyes, I see intelligence, sadness. He's begging me to let him go. He's gone through so much, and the notion of him being confined, of being used…it breaks my heart."

Roman seemed to soften a bit at my words. "I understand your feelings. But what do you intend to do about it alone?"

"I don't know yet," I admitted, my voice barely above a whisper. "But I can't just stand by and let my grandfather use him for his own gain. He deserves freedom, just like any of us."

Roman nodded, his demeanor contemplative. "You care for him deeply, don't you?"

"I can't deny the odd connection we have." My cheeks flushed at the recollection of the intimate way we'd communicated. "He saved me when he had no reason to. And I owe it to him to try and do the same."

Roman's demeanor softened, a glimmer of understanding in his eyes. "Connection?"

"It's complicated." My voice trembled with the weight of my words as I swallowed hard. My stomach churned as I weighed the difficult decision ahead of me. An arranged marriage? Considering it made my skin crawl, but the prospect of assisting Ky'rn in escaping the clutches of my family's research facility fueled a fire within me. As I stared down at my quivering hands, I knew I couldn't back out now, no matter how afraid I was or how unsure I was about Roman's genuine intentions, particularly with regard to Ky'rn. "Do you think I wanted this? Do you think I had a choice?"

He continued to watch me, waiting for more.

I took a shaky breath, memories flooding back. "He saved me once, long before all of this. I owe him my life. So when my grandfather handed him over as some…gift, as an exotic pet, I felt so guilty, and so angry. It was almost as if he was mocking me, giving me Ky'rn like he was some object, some expensive possession that others in our high society own to brag about, like he was some fancy limited-edition car or the only copy of some painting from a famous artist. It was then that I'd noticed he'd changed. He's no longer the person I used to inspire to be. He's gone too far for reasons I don't understand, but I can't stand by and watch him keep Ky'rn imprisoned."

He sighed and nodded. "So this is personal for you, too."

I hesitated, my gaze darting back to the ballroom doors, then back to Roman's waiting eyes. "Very." I nodded, meeting his gaze head-on. "So tell me, Roman, why should I trust you with this? What's your real interest in all of this?"

Roman's gaze shifted to the guards stationed outside the ballroom doors, his hand nervously stroking through his hair. He sighed deeply, his gaze intense, choosing his words carefully. "It's not just about Ky'rn. It's about what he represents. The IPA knows your grandfather is holding a decorated commander, but they can't tell the public because they might reject an alliance if they knew aliens have been visiting and studying Earth for millennia without human awareness.

"It's critical that we free him without your grandfather's knowledge, to prevent a potential conflict that might end in the IPA invading and taking control of Earth. If your grandfather knew who he's actually captured, I'm afraid he would have tortured him for information rather than given him to you as a pet."

Roman leaned in closer, his warm breath teasing strands of my hair. "What do you see when you look into my eyes?"

As I locked eyes with him, a flicker of vulnerability passed over his face before he composed himself. "I see layers, Roman. I see ambition, but also…empathy," I said, leaning in closer. "But why should I trust you? How do I know you won't just use me for your own gain?"

He sighed, the sound weary. "Because, Isla, I've watched the footage, seen the wonders of what the IPA has to offer us. But I've also seen how Ky'rn has been treated, how he's been prodded and poked, all for science and ambition. I want to free him, and to do that, I need an insider in the facility. Someone who knows the layout, the security, the staff's patterns…"

"In other words, you need someone like me." I swallowed hard, realizing the weight of what he was proposing. "So, you're saying that by joining forces, we could…"

He glanced around, ensuring no one was eavesdropping, before leaning in closer.

"Free him," Roman finished, determination burning in his eyes. "And maybe, just maybe, give both of you a chance at a life outside these gilded cages. The IPA is willing to give you whatever you want in exchange for setting Commander Ky'rn free."

"Anything?"

He nodded. "My family is collaborating closely with the IPA. We've been offered new technology that would advance our family's business beyond what's currently accessible on Earth. But first, we have to free your Ky'rn.

"I'm the sole owner of my family's business, which makes my offer for your hand that much more tempting to your grandfather—a company merger through marriage. Once you own your family business, you can do whatever you want, but first we must act fast—"

"—or my grandfather may have a change of heart.'

"Exactly, which is why I need you to agree to play your part." A sly, challenging smile danced on Roman's lips, his eyebrow arched teasingly. "You don't have to worry about me falling for you. This is strictly a business transaction. Once Ky'rn is free, we can make our own decisions regarding the future."

"You mean, you aren't interested in a relationship with me?" Some tension in my stomach deflated. "Our marriage will only be for show?"

"Let's just say...you aren't my type." He winked. "I'm not in this to take over your life or business, but to serve as an Earth-side representative for the IPA and help prevent a catastrophe in the making."

Could I trust him? Could we truly be allies in this twisted game our families were playing? Or was he just another player in this elaborate charade?

I leaned in, searching his eyes for a hint of deceit, but found none.

"All right. Let's say I believe you. What's your plan?"

ELEVEN

ISLA

I stormed into my grandfather's opulent office, determination burning in my chest, bypassing his well-dressed secretary and the imposing guards who usually stood sentinel outside. I was on a mission, and nothing was going to deter me. They avoided my gaze, as if they knew why I was here and what I was about to do.

Fuck them.

My grandfather looked up from his desk as I entered, dressed in one of his fancy suits that showed off his influence and wealth. He seemed unsurprised by my unannounced intrusion. He offered a practiced smile, and his eyes twinkled, as if he thought my storming in here was amusing. "Isla," he said in that silky, composed tone of his. "You look lovely today. Would you like a drink?"

I scoffed at his pathetic attempt at pleasantries and confronted him with a stony glare, arms folded across my chest. "I demand the truth, Grandfather," I growled through clenched teeth. "No more hiding behind your lies and half-truths."

He sighed, as though burdened by my question. "The truth about what, my dear?"

With a sigh, I tilted my head back and rolled my eyes. "Seriously? Don't play games with me," I retorted. "I want to know if you've been secretly offering my hand in marriage as part of a business merger deal."

He leaned back in his opulent leather chair, his eyes turning cold and calculating. The once comforting room, filled with bookshelves and warm wooden decor, now felt like a cage, suffocating and intimidating. He was the hunter, and I was the prey, but unbeknownst to him, I wasn't going down without a fight this time.

"Isla, sit," he offered, pointing to the chair in front of his desk.

"I'd rather stand," I retorted, my voice quivering with barely suppressed anger.

He sighed, tapping his fingers against the polished wood of his desk. "Very well. What is it you'd like to know?"

"Is it true?" I spat out, trying to contain the fury in my voice. "Have you been offering me in marriage as part of some business deal?"

He met my gaze with a practiced indifference, carefully neutral, but the flicker of unease in his eyes told me that I was correct. "Isla," he said, his tone softening just a fraction. "You're young, and I want what's best for you. Sometimes, these arrangements are necessary for the future of a family's legacy, especially after what happened a year ago."

I wasn't about to let him sidestep the question, like he always loved to do. "Answer me," I growled. "Have you been trying to marry me off for your own gain?"

He hesitated for a moment, and in that silence, I knew the truth. Roman was correct. My grandfather, a man I had once admired and respected, had been using me as a bargaining chip in his business dealings.

Disappointment and anger welled up inside me, but I refused to let it break my resolve. I was determined to uncover the extent of his manipulation and, more importantly, find a way to free Ky'rn from his captivity, even if it meant allying myself with Roman.

"How could you?" I spat, fists clenched. "How could you trade me off like some...some commodity?"

He rose, his tall frame suddenly towering over me. "I did what I thought was best for the family. For our empire. You have always been sheltered, my dear, protected from the harsh realities of our world."

Tears stung my eyes, but I blinked them away. "Protected? Is this what you call protection? Bargaining me away without my knowledge or consent?"

His face softened a fraction. "It wasn't meant to be like this. I had plans to talk to you, to explain everything."

"But Roman beat you to it," I murmured, my voice choked with betrayal.

A flicker of annoyance crossed his face. "That young man talks too much."

I took a step back, distancing myself from the man I had once looked up to. "This isn't about Roman. This is about you and the choices you've made without considering how I feel."

He sighed, running a hand through his silver hair. "I did it for you, Isla. For your future. Can't you see that?"

"All I see," I whispered, tears streaming down my face, "is a man willing to sacrifice everything, even his own granddaughter's happiness, for power and wealth. I thought you loved me."

He reached out to touch my arm, but I recoiled, the sting

of betrayal too fresh. "I do love you," he murmured, his voice filled with regret. "But sometimes love requires making difficult choices. You will soon learn that."

"I should decide who I want to be with," I told my grandfather, desperation seeping into my tone. "Especially after what happened to me. I haven't even left this place in a year. My friends abandoned me. What makes you believe I'm ready for marriage? You're committing me to a stranger."

His response was like a heavy blow. "This isn't for you to decide, my dear. I just finalized the deal last night." He sat down in his plush office chair, looking disturbingly satisfied. "It's a good thing you had that long conversation with Roman. The wedding is in a month, and he's the lucky groom."

A month.

The news hit me like a tidal wave. I had known that agreeing to this arranged marriage was part of the plan to free Ky'rn, but I hadn't expected it to happen so quickly.

My voice was barely more than a shocked whisper as I repeated, "I'm going to be married in a month?"

"You have nothing to worry about, Isla. Just choose your color scheme, and I'll handle the rest." His calm tone sent shivers down my spine. "The wedding will be in our private rooftop garden, under my watch. There won't be any unwanted guests."

His words hung in the air like a threat, and it hit me. He was using my wedding as bait, a lure to draw out Sam and Rose, who were waiting for their chance at vengeance.

My anger flared, and I couldn't hold back my accusation. "So, you're using my wedding to taunt Sam and Rose into exposing themselves?"

A wicked smile played at the corners of my grandfather's

lips. "Of course," he replied casually. "I know they won't be able to resist showing their faces."

I stared at him, fury and disbelief making me slack jawed. "So I am not just a pawn in your business dealings, but also being used as bait? You would risk my life just to draw them out?"

He leaned back in his chair, studying me with those cold, calculating eyes. "Sam and Rose will not harm you at the wedding. I'll make sure that they won't be able to lay a finger on you."

I felt a numbness spread through me. "And what if they decide to attack during the wedding? What then? You're willing to risk all those lives just to get revenge?"

He waved his hand dismissively. "There will be security. We'll be prepared."

"That's not the point," I snapped. "You're using my wedding day, which is supposed to be one of the happiest days of my life, as a business ploy and a trap. How can you do this to me?"

For a moment, he almost looked sorrowful, but then the professional mask slid back into place, leaving just a stoic blank expression. "Isla, it's for the greater good. You might not see it now, but one day, you'll understand."

I shook my head in disbelief. "You're gambling with my life, my happiness, for the sake of some vendetta, but now I'm not even sure if I'll be able to see that through."

His voice grew stern. "You will play your part and marry Roman. It's for the future of our family, our legacy. Sacrifices have to be made."

Tears blurred my vision, the weight of his betrayal pressing down on my heart. "You have no idea what love or sacrifice means. You're willing to trade everything, even my happiness, for power and control."

There was silence for a long moment.

"I'm doing this to protect you, Isla," he said, his voice gentler. "Because, despite everything, I am still your grandfather, and I do care about you. Just remember that every decision I make is for the betterment of our family."

Defeat weighed heavily on my shoulders as I sat there, absorbing the reality of my situation. Roman had been right about everything. My grandfather had taken my predicament and twisted it, using my life as a bargaining chip for the family's benefit.

While I couldn't say that I fully trusted Roman, at least he had been upfront about everything. He made it clear that he wanted our arranged marriage to be a business transaction, devoid of any romantic notions or illusions.

In some twisted way, that honesty was a relief amidst all the deception.

"Fine, I won't stand in your way," I replied with a resigned sigh. "I'll marry Roman as you wish, but in return, you better promise to let me be. As long as I stay within the facility walls, like I promised." The words left a bitter taste in my mouth, but it was the price I had to pay to free Ky'rn.

My grandfather rolled his hand in my direction, dismissing me as if I were a young child. "And what else do you want in return, my dear?"

I didn't hesitate. "I want you to let me care for my new pet," I replied firmly. "Alone. For whatever reason, he doesn't seem to like Dr. Violet."

He tilted his head and quirked an eyebrow, a sly glint in his eye. "Do you have any new findings to share?"

I nodded. "The frozen food he's being served isn't enough. He requires fresh, live food."

My grandfather's expression darkened as he considered the cost of such a demand. "That'll be expensive."

I locked eyes with him, my chin lifted and shoulders squared. A fire started in my chest, fueling me with a newfound determination. "Too bad," I retorted, my voice firm. "If I'm going to be forced into an arranged marriage, then I'm going to start using my *honorable* position for my own gain."

Without waiting for further argument, I stormed to the door. Just before I closed it, I turned back to face my grandfather one last time. A mischievous grin crossed my face as I glanced back.

"Oh, and Grandfather, just so you know," I remarked, my tone dripping with defiance and amusement. "My wedding colors are purple and blue."

With that, I left him to contemplate the consequences of our new arrangement.

TWELVE

KY'RN

The tank felt like a prison under artificial light, its confines closing in on me, and the water, once so refreshing, now tasted stale compared to the vastness of the ocean. I longed for the freedom to roam open waters, to feel the currents against my scales, and to hunt for my meals.

As I swam lazily through the tank, my gaze kept returning to the large windows that teased me with glimpses of the world beyond, the ocean stretching endlessly. It was a world I couldn't access, a world where I truly belonged, even on this foreign planet. The temptation of freedom danced before my eyes, just out of reach. The tank was nothing more than a cage, and I could only hope that I wouldn't be left here alone for much longer.

The silence was maddening. This was a new form of torture, being cut off from communicating with my people. Every passing moment without contact with my unit felt like an eternity, but I couldn't communicate if I couldn't touch the water beyond those windows.

My thoughts churned like the restless waters of the ocean.

I worried about my unit—the loyal soldiers who had followed me on this mission. Uncertainty gnawed at me. I didn't know what they were doing, whether anyone else had been caught in search of me. I'd been trained to lead, to make decisions, and here I was, confined and powerless.

The humans, so fixated on their own world, likely had no idea of the broader galactic implications of my capture. To them, I was an alien creature to be studied and perhaps exploited. But to my people, I was a leader in command of a vital mission. If I wasn't released soon, my absence could have serious implications. Perhaps it already had.

Humans had always been a complex puzzle to us. They were a peculiar species, so territorial and divided. It was no wonder they were cautious about extraterrestrial visitors. They were a paradox, capable of great kindness and cruelty, often in equal measure.

The IPA had observed their world from the shadows for generations, patiently waiting for the right time to make contact. But now, the *Stardancer* incident and my kidnapping had cast a dark cloud over our efforts.

Loneliness settled over me like a heavy fog. How many hours, days even, had passed since I had last spoken to Isla? There was something about her that had called to me from the moment I first saw her that fateful night. Now that I had touched her mind, experienced her thoughts and emotions, I had to know more about her. Our connection defied reason. It didn't matter that she was a creature of the land, a human, while I hailed from the depths of the sea. Her spirit resonated with mine in a way I couldn't fully understand but desperately wanted to explore.

I had no regrets about saving her from drowning that night. My only mistake, if it could be called that, had been lingering too long to ensure she was safe...

I stretched my arms out and floated in the center of the tank, longing to feel the currents of the sea. I thought of Isla, the way her blue eyes had sparkled with curiosity and compassion. Her energy was unlike any I had encountered before. I yearned to see her again, to hear her voice, to touch her mind.

She was my only beacon of hope—my only source of companionship—

since arriving in this facility.

The laboratory door suddenly slid open with a soft *whoosh*, drawing my attention. Hope flickered within me and my hearts surged as Isla came into view. She was clad in the same sleek black bodysuit that hugged her form so enticingly. Her long colorful hair was tamed into a ponytail that swung with her every step as she pulled a large red container with a white top behind her.

Our gazes locked, and a delicate curl of her lips spread into a radiant smile. The warmth of her expression flowed through me like a gentle ocean breeze, calming my nerves and lifting my spirits. As she approached the glass barrier that separated us, her gloved hand touched it in a wordless greeting. I mirrored her, pressing my webbed hand against the cold, unyielding surface. It was a brief connection, but it was enough to make my hearts skip a beat.

How had I become so obsessed with her so quickly?

She began to speak, her voice muffled by the water but still audible. "Ky'rn," she said, her lips forming my name. I listened intently, struggling to make out her words, as she gestured to the container she had pulled with her.

Confusion washed over me. The thought of her bringing me a gift was a welcome one. I nodded with genuine gratitude, trying to convey all the appreciation I felt through the intensity of my gaze. My eyes sought hers, hoping she could see the depth of emotion behind them, through the dim light that filtered into the tank.

She knelt to pick up the container and carried it up the stairs. It was a struggle for her, the weight of it visible as she strained to bring it to the ledge above the tank.

I followed her up, my eyes locked onto her form. The sight of her determination, her unwavering effort to bring something to me, tugged at my being, filling me with a deep sense of helplessness.

When Isla reached the ledge above the tank, I watched her place the container on the floor with care. She wiped her brow and grinned, her eyes softening with warmth. She opened the container and carefully dropped a large, live fish into the water. I watched it swim, its scales glistening in the artificial light. Visceral hunger clawed at my insides. This was fresh sustenance I had been denied for far too long.

I couldn't resist.

With a surge of power, my powerful tail propelled me forward.

Primal instinct guided me as I captured the fish, the taste of fresh blood an exquisite revelation. It was as if every fiber of my being had been starved, and the simple act of consuming the fish was an awakening. The metallic tang of blood flooded my senses, and I reveled in it, each drop calling to the predator that lay dormant within me.

The succulent flesh of the fish yielded effortlessly to my razor-sharp teeth. Each bite seemed to melt in my mouth. A symphony of flavors that danced on my palate, the fish's life essence fueling me in a way that the frozen, lifeless offerings from my captors never could. I devoured the fish whole, leaving no scraps.

And then, my gaze found Isla.

She stood before me, bathed in the soft, ethereal glow of

the tank's lights. It was as though the universe itself conspired to cast her in an otherworldly radiance. Her sapphire eyes, deep and mesmerizing, held mine, making me want to bathe in their depths.

My instincts, untamed and relentless, roared to life.

She'd offered me a meal—a fish she might have even caught herself—as a sign she thought I'd be a good mate. Did she know what her actions implied?

The predator within me, the ancient force that had guided my kind through the eons, recognized Isla as his mate. It was an undeniable truth, a magnetic pull that drew me toward her, no matter the boundaries that separated us.

My hearts, which had long felt cold, thudded with newfound purpose, and every fiber of my being resonated with the need to be by her side—to accept her offer and claim her as mine.

I traced her body with my eyes, the warm blood pulsed through her veins a tempting invitation. I wondered how she tasted, if she would yield to me, granting me the greatest honor of partaking in her life essence and marking her as mine.

Her blue eyes widened, and her full lips parted as she slowly bent towards the surface, offering me her hand. Despite the shock on her face, there was no hint of fear, only deep interest and intrigue, as her brow furrowed, waiting for me to accept her.

Her bravery honored me. She wanted me as much as I wanted her.

I surged forward, my instincts overriding any hesitation, and grabbed her hand, yanking her into the water. She gasped as the cool depths enveloped her, her eyes wide. She wasn't Makezu, wasn't even an aquatic species. She was a human, a land-dweller, unaccustomed to the depths.

I pushed her against the wall of the tank, making sure to keep her head above water. Her body pressed into mine as if drawn by an irresistible force. Her legs instinctively wrapped around my torso, her fingers finding purchase on my shoulders, and her sapphire eyes locked onto mine, delving deep into my very soul.

Water dripped from her face, her chest heaving as she gasped for air, her breaths coming in ragged bursts. Panic and shock were painted across her features, and I could feel the rapid beating of her heart against my chest. Her fingers dug into my shoulders as if grounding herself.

In that moment, my predatory instincts were drowned by a tidal wave of concern and protectiveness. The need to claim her, to make her mine, was replaced by an even more potent urge to comfort her, to let her know that she had nothing to fear from me.

She should never fear me; I would let the ocean run dry before I hurt her.

Our eyes remained locked as I projected as much reassurance and understanding as I could through our mental connection, trying to soothe the storm of thoughts that raged within her.

"Breathe," I urged her telepathically, my mental voice gentle and soothing. *"You're safe with me, Isla. I accept your offer. Just focus on your breath, let the panic subside. When you're ready, I will take you as mine."*

THIRTEEN

ISLA

I swallowed, my throat dry. "Yours?"

I struggled to grasp the enormity of his statement. What on Earth had I inadvertently offered him, and why did he seem to claim me as his own?

Ky'rn nodded in response, those mesmerizing, glowing amber eyes of his fixating intently on my neck. They bore into me, causing a shiver to run down my spine. Panic surged within me. My swimsuit clung to my body like a second skin, restricting my breath and making me acutely aware of his proximity.

Ky'rn's brows furrowed, sensing my unease, but his gaze remained locked on my neck, taking in the frantic pulse beating there. He probed my thoughts once more, his mental voice dripping with concern. *"What's wrong?"*

"When you say 'yours'..." I touched my throat reflexively, suddenly hyper-aware of my racing heartbeat and the vulnerable expanse of skin exposed by the collar of my suit. *"What does that mean in your world? In your culture?"*

Sensing my unease, his eyes searched mine. *"Isla, I won't...I don't wish to harm or scare you."* Ky'rn shook his head. He seemed to be taking in every nuance of my expression, every shadow that crossed my face.

He moved closer with a predatory grace, like a skilled hunter closing in on its prey. His piercing gaze bored into me with an intensity that made my heart race. He halted abruptly, as though fighting against his own primal desires and scaring me away. The warmth of his breath brushed against my cheek, while his body emanated a chilling aura. But even in his moment of hesitation, there was a palpable chemistry between us, drawing us closer together.

"In my culture, when someone offers another live food the way you did, it means they show interest in that person and consider them fit to be a potential mate. I accepted your offer, but now, I am afraid I've done something wrong."

"I...didn't realize that," I confessed, my cheeks growing warm. *"In our culture, offering food can be a gesture of kindness, hospitality, or affection. But it's not explicitly tied to courtship."*

Ky'rn studied me, the intensity in his glowing amber eyes making me feel like he could see through me—and perhaps he could read me like an open book through telepathic connection. *"Yet, in your world, don't many relationships start over shared meals, over the act of dining together?"*

"They do..." I nodded, drawing parallels to human customs. Animals often displayed their worthiness to potential mates through various courtship rituals, and humans weren't all that different, often exchanging gifts or tokens of affection on a first date. *"So are you saying I unknowingly engaged in a courting ritual with you?"*

"Yes," he confirmed, his gaze unwavering. *"You see, the Makezu are a solitary species. We seldom touch one another due to our natural instincts. This prevents misinterpretation, and it's also a form of defense. So by offering*

food, we're essentially asking if we're worthy enough to touch."

His explanation shed some light on his species' customs, making me realize that despite our differences, there were similarities in the way we sought connection and intimacy.

I bit my lip, considering. *"It's true that human dates often involve meals, and there's something inherently intimate about sharing food. It's a chance to talk, to get to know one another. But,"* I paused, searching for the right words, *"it doesn't have the same...direct implications as in your culture."*

He bowed his head, his shoulders dropping slightly as he took in my words. *"Do you regret offering me food?"*

Ky'rn's question hung in the air, heavy with the weight of what had transpired in the past day. My mind raced through the whirlwind of events—my grandfather's unsettling gift, essentially getting auctioned off in an arranged marriage at dinner, my business conversation with Roman, and the shocking revelations about my grandfather's intentions.

As I pondered his question, I couldn't help but question myself. Did I regret offering him that fish?

Fate had thrust us together, not just once but twice, and I couldn't deny the inexplicable connection that had formed between us. It was strange, almost surreal, to feel so at ease with an alien male who resembled a shark. By all natural human instincts, he should have sent me fleeing in fear.

Yet, I felt safe in his arms, even in this expansive aquarium.

Was it because he'd saved me from the edge of death before?

"Do I regret it? I..." My words trailed off, and I sighed softly, my eyes still locked with his. *"I don't know. But I do*

know that I appreciate you asking me. It's something I haven't had much of lately—control over my own fate.

"But how are we supposed to do this, whatever this is?" I voiced the question that had been gnawing at me. *"You're an aquatic species, and I'm a land-dwelling human. You're trapped in here...and I'm trying to free you. What will happen to the both of us once you're free?"*

The challenges ahead seemed immense, yet the bond we shared was undeniable.

Besides, I was now more or less engaged. I was supposed to marry Roman in a month. Even though we had both agreed it was a business transaction, not a romantic relationship, I still felt guilty.

I shouldn't be here, in this alien male's arms, when it was my obligation to keep him safe until I was able to release him.

There wasn't room for me to become attached to him, to give in to whatever was forming between us, because we were beings from two separate worlds. It would never work.

But why did that make my heart ache?

"The future will always be murky. Why wait for it to clear when tomorrow is never guaranteed?" It was a sentiment that struck a chord in my heart, a reminder that life was unpredictable, and sometimes, you had to grasp opportunities when they presented themselves. *"You feel our bond too, don't you?"*

I couldn't deny the strange, magnetic pull that seemed to tie our souls together. But it was overwhelming, terrifying even. *"This is...a lot to take in."*

His gaze held a depth of understanding, a calm patience that seemed to envelop me. It was as if his eyes were silently communicating a profound empathy, acknowledging and appreciating every unspoken thought and feeling. *"I know it's confusing, Isla. But I promise you, I will never harm you or force you into anything. I hope we—"*

The heavy doors of the chamber suddenly swung open, shattering the fragile tranquility that had enveloped us, revealing a startling sight. Dr. Violet, accompanied by a formidable contingent of guards, stormed into the room, their guns raised and ready.

The sudden intrusion sent a jolt of panic through me. What were they doing here, and why did they have their guns drawn? I instinctively moved closer to Ky'rn, seeking protection and safety in his presence.

"Isla, please, don't panic," she urged, her tone firm but laced with genuine concern. "We will dispatch the threat and safely remove you from the tank. Your safety is our top priority."

My heart pounded in my chest with the instinctive need to protect Ky'rn. I couldn't let them harm him; he was not a threat.

"No! Everything is fine," I said, trying to keep my voice steady. "This is a horrible misunderstanding. Stand down!"

Dr. Violet's expression reflected her concern, but she remained resolute. "Isla, I understand you want to protect him, but I won't jeopardize your life. Your grandfather will have my head if anything happens to you. Please, let us handle this situation."

I clenched my teeth in frustration. "He's not a threat! Stand down, please!"

She hesitated, looking torn. A few agonizing seconds passed, and I could see her giving orders to the guards, signaling them to hold their positions, with their weapons drawn.

Taking a deep breath, she said, "I trust you, Isla. But if anything goes wrong, it's on you."

I nodded, tears blurring my vision. "Thank you."

Ky'rn's amber eyes blazed with frustration as he glared at the guards who had stormed into the room. *"I am insulted,"* he rumbled, his deep mental voice filled with righteous anger. *"I am an honorable commander. I would never harm you or any civilian. Why do they believe that I'm a threat?"*

"Ky'rn, just look at our position," I said, gesturing. My legs were wrapped around his waist and he had me pinned against the unyielding tank wall.

He huffed in frustration. *"I was merely communicating with you, not attacking you."*

I couldn't help but roll my eyes, although the situation was anything but amusing. *"I know you wouldn't harm me,"* I said, my mental voice firm. *"But they don't. In order to defuse this situation, I need to go, before things escalate."*

He looked torn, his gaze shifting between me and the guards who were now forming a perimeter around the tank. *"When will you return?"* he asked, his tone holding a note of longing.

I glanced at the unwelcome visitors, unsure of what awaited me beyond the tank's walls. *"I don't know when,"* I admitted, a sense of uncertainty creeping over me. *"But I promise, I will return as soon as I'm able. I will make them understand."*

My heart thudded loudly in my ears as he nodded, his amber eyes softening with a depth of emotion I hadn't seen before. *"I will wait,"* he murmured, his mental voice brushing against my thoughts like a whisper of a gentle sea breeze, *"until you can grace me with your light once more."*

With a final, tender look, he released his hold on me and gracefully swam away, disappearing into the depths of the tank. The sudden absence of his solid frame caused me to flounder momentarily, my limbs struggling against the buoy-ancy of the water.

I watched, almost mesmerized, as his powerful tail propelled him to the farthest end of the tank. His form, even as it retreated, seemed like a shimmering mirage of strength and grace. His last words to me resonated in the hollow silence of my heart.

Until you can grace me with your light once more.

Those words would haunt me.

Blinking back the sudden surge of emotions, I found myself floating aimlessly in the vast tank. The weight of the bodysuit, mixed with the realization of what had transpired, made every move feel sluggish, every breath a tad heavier.

"Isla!" Dr. Violet's voice echoed from above.

The sound of splashing water and her outstretched hand guided me to the surface. She gripped me firmly, almost desperately, and helped me hoist myself out of the tank. The air outside was a sharp contrast to the water's embrace; every droplet that slid down my bodysuit left me feeling cold and bereft.

"You scared me half to death," Dr. Violet murmured, her fingers brushing wet tendrils of hair away from my face as she inspected me for injuries. There was genuine concern etched into her features, eyes scanning me to ensure I was unharmed.

I tried to muster a smile, though it felt feeble, and my voice was barely above a whisper. "I'm okay, really."

She helped me steady my footing on the slick stairs, the firm grip of her hand a testament to her worry. "I saw him holding you and…I feared the worst."

I squeezed her hand in reassurance. "Ky'rn wouldn't hurt me," I whispered, though the statement was more for me than for her.

We descended the stairs slowly, her arm slung protectively around my waist. The gravity of what had just occurred seemed to hang in the silence between us.

"You need to be careful, Isla," she urged gently. "Regardless of your connection, he's still a wild creature. We don't fully understand him or his intentions."

"I know," I admitted, frowning. "But deep down, he doesn't want to hurt me. He's lonely, Violet. Like me."

She squeezed my shoulder reassuringly. "Come on," she murmured, "Let's get you out of these wet clothes."

With one last lingering look, feeling the power of that silent promise between Ky'rn and me, I finally turned away. Each step took me further from the tank, but I couldn't shake the sensation that those amber eyes of his were still fixed upon me, watching my every move, even as the heavy doors slammed shut behind me.

FOURTEEN

ISLA

Bang! Bang! Bang!

B I stood in the private gun range in my grandfather's sprawling research facility. The question of why he needed such a facility, especially one as high-tech as this, had always gnawed at me. He claimed to be studying the mysterious artifacts he'd collected over the years, restoring them to their former glory.

But something about it had never added up.

The sterile room was dimly lit, the walls lined with cutting-edge equipment and screens displaying its users' data. In the center was a shooting range, far more advanced than any I'd seen outside these walls. The targets were a series of holographic screens that could simulate various scenarios, from simple stationary targets to moving ones. My grandfather had spared no expense in creating this facility, always needing the best, which was more for show of power than necessity.

I adjusted my grip on the handgun, a sleek and deadly piece of technology that felt incongruous in my hand. I had never been particularly comfortable around firearms, but recent events had forced me to become proficient in their use.

With a deep breath, I took aim at the holographic target downrange. My fingers tightened on the trigger, and the gun barked to life, sending a hail of rounds toward the target. The recoil was sharp, but I held my stance, squeezing off controlled shots.

After nearly dying once, I would never be caught helpless again. If I'd been targeted as the heir to my family's business, it would only get worse once I took over.

The holographic target danced with each hit, and I couldn't help but feel a surge of satisfaction as my aim homed in on the bullseye. Each shot was precise, a testament to the training I'd undergone in secret over the last year, against my grandfather's wishes.

He thought it was unladylike of me to carry a weapon, and that I was insulting him and his security by assuming they couldn't defend me.

They had failed once, I refused to let it happen again. Instead of relying on others, I would protect myself if necessary.

I shot my last round, and as the echo of the gunshot reverberated through the range, I felt some of my stress ebb away. My hands were steady, and my aim was true, the bullet hitting dead center.

As I lowered the gun, a sense of satisfaction washed over me. There was something undeniably empowering about handling a weapon with precision. A rush of blood pulsed through me, leaving me feeling strangely alive. I rolled my shoulders back, trying to release the tension that had built up during my target practice.

But the moment of triumph was fleeting. Thoughts of Ky'rn came rushing back, as they often did in unguarded moments like these. It had been days since I'd last seen him, and the guilt stabbed at my heart like a jagged blade.

Despite my heart-wrenching decision to keep Ky'rn at a distance and protect him, I couldn't shake the heavy weight of guilt and longing gnawing at my conscience. It was a crazy notion, but I found myself missing him more than I ever thought possible. Every fiber of my being yearned for him— to see him again, but my mind told me it was for the greater good. Resisting his magnetic pull felt like an impossible task, yet I knew it was necessary for both our sakes.

My grandfather was suspicious of me, and I needed time to sort through my thoughts, to figure out a way to see Ky'rn without the ever-watchful eyes of my grandfather and his security on me.

I knew I had to sort out my thoughts and figure out a way to see him without putting him in danger. I couldn't let my growing feelings for him cloud my judgment, not when there were so many unanswered questions about my grandfather's —and even Roman's—true intentions.

As I stood there, catching my breath, loud claps suddenly pierced the air, snapping me out of my thoughts. Startled, I lowered the weapon and spun around, my eyes widening in surprise. My heart raced as I found Roman standing in the doorway, an unsettling smile playing on his lips. He was flanked by two guards dressed in black, unfamiliar and unsettling.

I swallowed hard. "Roman, what's going on?"

"Who knew the princess of the sea could shoot a gun?" His gaze shifted from me to the holographic target I had riddled with bullets, and he let out a low, appreciative whistle. "Nice shot. I wouldn't want to come up against you…but that's why I have my guards to do my bidding." He gestured casually to the pair of black-clad men who stood stoically beside him.

"Your guards don't look like they've swum with real sharks," I retorted, sliding the safety on my gun and holstering it. I met his gaze head-on, challenging.

Roman smirked. "You'd be surprised, Princess. They've seen their fair share of danger. Besides, they're not here for you. They're here for protection."

"Protection? From what?" My internal alarms were flaring, and I couldn't shake the feeling that this visit was far from casual. "How did you get in here? And more importantly, why are you here?"

He offered a charming smile, the kind that masked his true intentions. "I have a message from the IPA, and they insisted it couldn't wait." His tone was light, as though discussing a trivial matter. He took another step forward, his presence imposing as he closed the distance between us. "Especially now that you've agreed to the mission to free Ky'rn."

I frowned. "A message? What could be so urgent that it required you to interrupt my...practice session?" I glanced around, wondering if this was the right time and place to delve into a potentially sensitive conversation. This environment made me uneasy.

"They have an offer," he continued, reaching into the inner pocket of his jacket and producing a small, ornate box. "I've been instructed to deliver this to you, personally. Consider it a gift."

"A gift?" I echoed, my brows furrowing. My eyes darted upward, searching for the familiar red glow of the security cameras. They were everywhere in the facility, ensuring no corner went unobserved. "Is this really the best time or place to be discussing this?"

Roman handed me the box, his serious eyes revealing the importance of its contents. "My team has ensured we have privacy. The last few minutes have been…lost, so to speak," he explained, a cocky grin forming on his lips. "And by using the device within this box, you can have privacy whenever you need it. As for why I'm here, well, I thought it best to relay the information personally."

The box felt heavier in my hands than it looked. I studied its surface, noting the intricate etchings that swirled like waves, reminiscent of the deep ocean. "And why give it to me now?"

His gaze grew somber. "Because things are about to get much more complicated, Isla," Roman replied, his voice low and intense. "The IPA wants proof that Ky'rn is safe and well, and you are their best bet at a peaceful resolution. You are to meet with him and use the device within the box to contact his leaders. Ky'rn will know how to use it."

The weight of our mission pressed down on me. "Are we really going to do this? Save Ky'rn?"

Roman nodded. "You're the one who can prevent this from becoming a public disaster."

My skin prickled with fear as I imagined the potential fallout. The mere thought of my grandfather finding out about our covert plan and sabotaging it sent a chill down my spine. "I just hope everything goes well," I admitted, my voice shaky. "My grandfather…" I began, struggling to find the right words. "He's more cunning and resourceful than you might think."

Roman chuckled, attempting to reassure me, the sound echoing in the vast emptiness of the room. "You have nothing to worry about. My team will make sure your grandfather remains in the dark. All you have to do is not get cold feet on our wedding day."

His unwavering confidence was both reassuring and unsettling, a reminder of the immense weight of responsibility resting on our shoulders. I had no choice but to trust him. There was too much at stake for me to hesitate now. The future of humanity hung in the balance, and every decision we made would determine our fate.

"I won't get cold feet," I asserted firmly, locking eyes with Roman. "I'll do my part, so you better do yours."

Roman inclined his head in acknowledgment, a glint of respect in his eyes. "I won't fail in my duty," he replied solemnly.

"When can I read the contract for our marriage?"

He gestured to one of his guards, who promptly produced a small storage drive from his jacket pocket and handed it to me. "Take your time, Isla. Read it over, make any changes you see fit, and I'll sign it."

I nodded, clutching the small device in my hand. "I'll make sure to read it thoroughly before I sign it," I assured him, a sense of responsibility settling in.

Roman's next words caught me off guard. "I'm not after your family's company, Isla," he confessed, his expression sincere. His eyes held mine as if willing me to believe him. "But I'm glad you aren't blindly trusting me."

His honesty surprised me, and I couldn't help but smile faintly. "I just want a friendly and respectful business relationship with you," I admitted. "I'm glad we're working toward a common goal. But next time, a warning would be appreciated."

FIFTEEN

ISLA

T he elevator ride down to the lab always filled me with dread.

No matter how many times I'd traveled down this same route, the memory of nearly drowning, of sinking helplessly beneath the stormy waves, still haunted me.

But I had to do this; I needed to do this to help Ky'rn.

It was worth it.

The elevator came to a sudden halt, and with a soft hiss, the metallic doors slid open to a small lobby area. Two guards stood sentinel by the lab's doors, their presence a clear indication of the importance and security of the space beyond.

The metallic doors hissed open, revealing the sprawling research lab. Dr. Violet, who was bent over her station, glanced up with a worried expression as I stepped inside. "I'm glad to see you. I was about to message you."

I approached her, unease growing within me. "What's wrong?" I asked, my heart rate quickening.

Dr. Violet sighed, her gaze shifting to the doors that led to the massive tank that housed Ky'rn. "Ever since your...incident," she began carefully, "the sea creature has refused to eat the frozen fish we've been providing."

I rushed toward the door leading to Ky'rn's tank, my heart pounding in my chest. Slamming my hand onto the scanner, I watched with anxious anticipation as it turned green and the door slid open.

I had to get Ky'rn fresh living fish. He had to be starving by now.

"It's an emergency," I called out urgently. "We need to gather all the living fish we have."

Dr. Violet turned to me, her expression filled with concern. She shook her head slowly. "Isla, I can't do that. Your grandfather has strictly forbidden it."

"Then I'll deal with my grandfather," I replied firmly. "Right now, Ky'rn needs this."

Dr. Violet attempted to follow me, but I turned to her, my tone resolute. "No," I said firmly. "Ky'rn trusts me. After what happened last time, having you here will only create more tension."

She snapped back, "I'm responsible for your safety, Isla."

My hand instinctively went to the gun at my side as I stared her down. "I can defend myself," I retorted sharply. "I don't need a room full of trigger-happy guards who might accidentally harm him."

Desperation flashed in Dr. Violet's eyes as she reached out to try and stop me from going inside. I sidestepped her, slapping her hand away. "He's mine," I declared, my voice shaking with emotion. "No one will keep me from seeing him."

She gasped, clutching her chest, her eyes wide with shock at my outburst. I leaned in, my voice a low and dangerous whisper. "If you breathe a word of this to my grandfather," I threatened, "I'll make sure you never work here again, and I'll ruin your career myself."

For too long, I'd been the obedient, soft-spoken grand-daughter, following every one of my family's whims. But this...Ky'rn was different. My resolve to protect him, to understand him, had brought out strength I hadn't realized I possessed.

I could see the conflicting emotions playing across Dr. Violet's face. She was torn between her loyalty to my grand-father and her duty as a scientist. However, I'd made it clear this was a battle she wouldn't win.

Through the doors, the tank's luminescence reflected on our faces, casting eerie shadows on the walls of the corridor.

"Isla." Dr. Violet's voice was soft, shaky even, a stark contrast to her usual composed demeanor. "I understand your need to protect him. Believe me, I do. But I have to do my duty, too."

"It's my life!" I interrupted, trembling with anger. I took a deep breath, forcing myself to keep calm. "He saved me once, out there in the open ocean. I owe him my life. And now, he's trapped in here, away from his home, with his freedom stripped from him, and it's tearing me apart."

She bit her lower lip, her usually stern expression melting into one of understanding. "I know, my dear. But what you're asking for, feeding him fresh living fish, goes directly against your grandfather's orders. He has his reasons, even if we might not agree with them."

Closing the distance between us, I leaned in and spoke in a firm tone. My eyes narrowed with determination as I made my point clear. "Then let me handle him. You know what's at stake here, and I am willing to risk it all to help Ky'rn. My grandfather gave him to me; he will have to cope with the ramifications."

Dr. Violet's honey-brown eyes searched mine, looking for any hint of uncertainty. Finding none, she sighed, nodding slowly. "All right," she whispered. "But be careful. Please."

I nodded in gratitude and swiftly entered the dimly lit tank room. The cool, moist air wrapped around me like a familiar embrace, carrying with it the unmistakable scent of salt and seaweed.

I turned to face the door, only to see my mentor hovering with concern just outside the threshold. Daring her to change her mind—to report me to my grandfather—I pressed my hand to the scanner, watching as the door closed behind me.

Once the door was securely sealed, I reached into my pocket and retrieved the small black device from the box Roman had given me. Carefully, I placed it onto the scanner and entered the code to engage the master lock. The instructions within the chest had been clear—no one would be able to open this door or use the security equipment within this room unless I disengaged the device with my fingerprints.

Satisfied to see the device glowing green, indicating that the lock was active, I rushed toward the massive tank, my heart racing.

Ky'rn was already there, positioned at the tank's viewing window, awaiting my arrival. His tail swayed gently, keeping him upright in the water, his eyes fixed on me with an antici-patory gaze. He seemed to have been waiting just for me, his magnificent form displaying a serene grace in the aquatic environment.

But today, something was different. His amber eyes, usually so vibrant and full of life, seemed dimmer, lacking their usual brightness.

"Ky'rn," I whispered, pressing my hand against the glass that separated us, the tank cool against my fingertips. His eyes locked onto mine, and I could see longing—and perhaps even relief—reflected in his gaze.

"I'm so sorry," I murmured, tears stinging my eyes. "I promise, Ky'rn, I'm doing everything I can to get you out of here."

Even through the thick barrier, I could feel his intense gaze. Slowly, he raised a webbed hand, mirroring my gesture, until our palms were pressed against the same point on the glass, separated by mere inches yet worlds apart.

Ky'rn's form was captivating. Half shark, half man, he was a mesmerizing blend of strength and grace. His lower half was a dark, almost black, shade of blue, with a contrasting teal underbelly that shimmered in the ambient light of the tank.

The bioluminescent stripes along his back glowed with an otherworldly intensity that shone around his body like an aura of light in the dark water.

His hair, a blend of dark-blue and teal, flowed gracefully, giving him an ethereal quality. His upper body, his human half, was nothing short of magnificent. His chest was chiseled, strong, and statuesque, as if sculpted by the ocean's waves. The way the water caressed his skin was almost hypnotic, accentuating the grace and strength of his aquatic form.

Despite the circumstances, I couldn't deny the attraction that simmered beneath the surface. Ky'rn was a magnificent creature, and being so close to him only heightened his allure. It was impossible not to appreciate his beauty.

However, I couldn't afford to get lost in those thoughts. Ky'rn's coloring had paled, a stark contrast to his usual vibrant hues. Something was seriously wrong, and it was my responsibility to help him.

I pulled my hand away from the glass, tearing my gaze

from his captivating presence, and turned to rush up the stairs.

I could sense Ky'rn following me, his presence like a shadow as I ascended the spiral stairway that curved around the tank. Empty buckets awaited me on the landing, ready to be filled with the fresh fish Ky'rn so desperately needed.

My fingers trembled as I placed my gun in its holster, a silent promise to myself to protect Ky'rn from any threat. Beside it, I set the pouch containing the box Roman had given me.

A loud splash echoed and I spun around to face Ky'rn, his eyes meeting mine as I slowly unzipped my bodysuit and allowed it to drop to the ground. As I stood in only my black one-piece swimsuit, my skin tingling from his intense gaze, I couldn't help but feel like prey in a seductive dance with a predator.

Ky'rn's gaze roamed over my body, tracing the curves and contours as if he were committing every inch to memory. There was a hunger in his eyes, primal and raw, but strangely, it didn't frighten me.

Ky'rn was a predator, but there was something about the way he looked at me that made me feel safe, despite the fear I would feel if I didn't know him—if we didn't have a past.

I felt exposed, vulnerable, and yet, it stirred something deep within me, a forbidden desire that I wanted to explore.

But now wasn't the time to give in to this attraction. I was here for two reasons: to find out why he was refusing to eat, and to help him to contact his people and let them know that he was safe, for now.

My heart thundered in my chest as I sat on the edge of the tank, unable to pull my gaze away from Ky'rn's intense, amber eyes. With trembling hands, I reached for my pouch and swiftly retrieved the small box that Roman had given me.

The box felt heavy in my hand, knowing what was inside would change everything.

I eased myself onto the edge of the tank, the metal cool against my bare skin, sending a shiver racing down my spine.

Before I could even open the box, Ky'rn was before me. His strong hands gently grasped my legs, parting them to make room for him. He pressed himself between my legs, our faces mere inches apart.

My heart raced. I could feel the warmth of his breath against my skin, his powerful presence overwhelming. Heat radiated from his body. It was intimacy unlike anything I had ever experienced.

How could I be this attracted to him?

"Where were you?" he demanded, his amber eyes searching mine.

I swallowed hard. The guilt I'd been carrying pressed down on me even more as I tried to find the words to explain, to make him understand. *"I had to stay away, Ky'rn. For your safety."* I let out an audible sigh. *"I needed time to clear my mind, to figure out a way to help you."*

His expression shifted from one of concern to hurt, and it was like a knife to my heart. *"I was worried,"* he admitted softly. *"I thought…I thought you were banned from seeing me again, and I was starting to think that you may have changed your mind about helping me."*

I shook my head, reaching out to touch his cheek gently. *"No, Ky'rn, never. I could never abandon you, and I would never let my grandfather keep me from you now that I know you're here. But I had to keep you safe, which meant putting some distance between us while I figured things out."*

He sighed and leaned into my hand, seeking comfort from my touch. *"I understand now,"* he said, his voice gentler. *"But how was I supposed to know that? When your mentor came to give me frozen fish, she brought guards, as if she thought I'd attack her."*

I shot a quick, irritated glance at the lab doors, knowing that Dr. Violet was likely just outside, hopefully not tipping off my grandfather. "That woman," I muttered under my breath. Then, I met Ky'rn's gaze again. *"Is that why you refused to eat?"*

"That's part of the reason. My species," he began, choosing his words carefully, *"has incredible endurance. We can survive for an extended period without feeding, particularly during space travel or when in captivity."*

I raised an eyebrow. *"Really? That's an incredible adaptation."*

He nodded slowly. *"Yes, so I can wait to eat until I feel safer. I was hoping your mentor would eventually leave the frozen fish with me and let me eat in peace, without guards watching my every move. Even then, I feared the possibility of her administering some kind of drug or sedative through those meals—"*

"To start experimenting on you again." I took a deep breath, my frustration with the situation bubbling to the surface. I couldn't let things continue like this.

"I'll personally make sure you have a steady supply of fresh fish," I promised him. *"But until then, you shouldn't starve yourself."*

He hesitated for a moment, his amber eyes studying me intently. *"I can endure the hunger for now."*

My anger flared at his stubbornness. *"How am I supposed to get you out of here if you're weak and malnourished?"* I scolded him.

He didn't falter, his gaze steady. *"Then don't leave me alone."*

SIXTEEN

KY'RN

I cursed myself silently for the overwhelming obsession I felt for her.

From the moment I saw Isla, something deep within me had stirred to life, a primal urge that defied all logic and reason.

It was as if the universe had conspired to throw us together, two beings from vastly different worlds, drawn together by an unexplainable force—what others may call Fate, or the Will of the Stars.

Her presence, her scent, her voice, they all haunted my thoughts day and night. I couldn't focus on anything else. It was maddening...

I had to be close to her, to touch her, to claim her, and in turn, be claimed by her kind and compassionate soul.

I wanted to taste her, to know every inch of her body. It was a hunger that couldn't be satiated by food alone.

I had to have her, in every sense of the word.

I knew the dangers of this obsession. It could cloud my judgment, make me act irrationally, put both of us in danger. And yet, I couldn't help myself. Isla had become my everything, and I would do whatever it took to protect her, even from myself.

Her sapphire eyes, as deep as the oceans' depths, held no fear or hatred as one might expect for a creature like me. Instead, they radiated concern and care, warmth that thawed the ice around my heart.

She was a remarkable female, one worth saving and, dare I think it, a worthy mate.

The sounds of her heartbeat and heavy breathing were a sweet symphony in my ears, their rhythm dancing in harmony with mine. The warmth of the blood running through her was a seductive heat where her skin touched my palms.

My gaze was torn between the depths of her eyes that seemed to hold an entire universe and the delicate curve of her neck, which beckoned me. It was there, on the fragile line between her throat and shoulder, that I wished I could taste her, just once…

Drinking from her, consuming her essence, would be a solemn honor. Just the thought filled me with a strange longing. I wondered how she would taste. Would her flavor be as exquisite as the intoxicating scent that surrounded her?

Isla's delicate fingers traced the rough scales on my cheek, a gesture that felt more intimate than anything I'd experienced in my captivity. Her touch was gentle, hesitant, but filled with a warmth that radiated through me.

"If I had it my way," she began, her voice soft with a hint of sadness. *"You wouldn't be trapped in this tank. You'd be free, Ky'rn. Free to roam the depths of your world, and then come back to this one. To me. Without any reservations."* Her eyes, so clear and blue, held mine with a determination I hadn't seen before. *"I believe we can help bridge the gap between Earth and the IPA and end this madness before there's any more suffering, on both sides."*

I swallowed hard, my gills flaring momentarily as I processed her words. *"I wish I could believe that, Isla,"* I said, sounding rougher than I intended. *"But it's not our reality."*

She sighed, her hand dropping away from my face. I immediately felt the void her touch left behind, my skin tingling in its absence.

Her gaze lowered to her lap, where her fingers worked meticulously to open a small, ornately adorned box, its hinges whispering softly in the quiet space. *"You need to eat, Ky'rn,"* she pathed, her eyes meeting mine once more. *"You have to maintain your strength, even if I have to feed you myself."*

"You wish to feed me by hand?" I asked, my voice resonating with a deep, rumbling tone, each word tinged with an undercurrent of desire, hinting at a profound appreciation for the intimate gesture. *"I must admit, I would quite enjoy that. To be fed by you, Isla, would indeed be an honor."*

She looked up at me, and for a moment, her eyes sparkled with mischief. But it was short-lived, quickly replaced by an emotion I couldn't decipher. Her cheeks took on a deeper hue, and her gaze flitted away, a wistful smile playing on her lips. *"Perhaps another time,"* she replied, a touch of regret in her voice. *"We have other matters at hand."*

My interest piqued, I followed her gaze, only to be met with a sight that left me reeling with shock. Sitting inside the ornate chest was a piece of equipment I recognized all too well—a long-range communication device. Its sleek black surface stood in stark contrast to the watery blues and greens of the box's protective cushion.

My eyes darted back to Isla's face, searching for an explanation. *"Where did you get that?"* The words came out in a rush, a mixture of amazement and suspicion.

This was no common device; communicators like this one were highly sought after in the IPA.

She pinched her lips, a simple gesture, but in that moment, it was as if a curtain fell over her mind. A shadow, cold and nebulous, flickered within her consciousness. I felt her push against our telepathic connection, trying to shield herself, to barricade a piece of her mind from me.

With a heavy exhale, her gaze anchored on the open box. *"Ky'rn, after…after everything that's transpired between us, I had to distance myself. My grandfather—he watches my every move, analyzes each interaction. I had to prove my loyalty to him, show him that I was still the dutiful granddaughter he raised."* She hesitated, her eyes hardened. *"I had to fulfill certain duties for him, to ensure he wouldn't get suspicious about us."*

A storm of concern and worry surged through me. The weight of her words, heavy with hidden secrets and fears, hung in the saltwater that cradled my form. They brushed against my scales like a persistent, unsettling whisper, igniting an urgent need to comfort and protect. My hearts pounded against my chest, each beat a resonant echo of my growing apprehension for what she might have endured.

"What are you hiding, Isla? Why are you keeping secrets now? You've always been an open sea to me. Now you pull away like a receding tide. And that device." I gestured to the long-range communicator with a swift flick of my eyes. *"How did you come by it?"*

She hesitated, and for a moment, I thought she would cast aside the shroud and let me in once again. But instead, she shored up her defenses, even as her eyes glistened with her unshed tears.

"I've made promises," she admitted quietly, her gaze fixed on the delicate hands in her lap. *"Certain things—*

certain actions were necessary to secure this device. There were some decisions I had to make, choices that I'm not proud of. To procure that communicator, I had to…compromise."

My stomach coiled in unease. *"Compromise? What did you do?"*

A silent plea shimmered in her eyes, begging me to understand, to not press further, to accept the concealed truths as they were. Her secrets cast a pall on the bond that had grown between us.

"Isla, whatever you've done, whatever shadows lurk behind your eyes, know this: They do not change my perception of you. But don't drown alone in whatever troubles you. Share your burden with me, and I will make it lighter."

She swallowed hard, her fingers trembling slightly. *"I can't say, not yet. But know this, everything I did—and will do—I did with the belief that it was for the greater good. For our future. For your freedom."*

"I wish…" Now wasn't the time to be unreasonable; I needed to keep my emotions in check, or I'd drive her away again. *"That you'd trust me enough to share your burdens. Not because I want to pry, Isla, but because I can't bear the thought of you sacrificing anything for me."* My gaze bore into hers, every scale of my body tingling with the raw emotion of our connection. *"What sense would it make if I saved your life, only for you to throw it away for mine?"*

She met my gaze, her eyes like deep ocean pools, swirling with currents of conflict and determination. *"A life for a life."*

I shook my head vehemently, my fins bristling in agitation. Reaching out, I tightened my grip on her thighs, feeling the warm pulse beneath her soft skin, so different from my cold, scaly touch. *"If that's your reasoning, then you'd do well to forget me, Isla—to stay away. Allow me to perish in this prison. I can't bear the weight of your life being traded for mine."*

Shock registered on her face, a gasp escaping her lips, yet she countered fiercely. *"You're asking for too much. Never, Ky'rn. I could never leave you here..."*

My gaze fixed on the sleek, shimmering device nestled securely in Isla's hands. *"Then you must tell me."* My voice shifted between the authority of a commander and genuine concern for what she'd given up in order to aid me. *"How did you acquire that communicator?"*

Her gaze faltered for a split second, but she gathered herself, meeting my eyes squarely. *"I have an outside connection, Ky'rn,"* she began hesitantly. *"Someone with ties to the IPA. They're willing to help get you out of here, but to proceed, they need proof that you're alive and well."*

As I gazed into her eyes, I attempted to delve deeper into her mind, seeking any trace of stray thoughts or mental fragments that might unveil who had provided her with such a costly device. My abilities, slightly dimmed by a barrier that separated us, brushed against the fortress she'd constructed around her thoughts.

A mental fortress that now seemed to shield something—or someone—deliberately.

How could she know how to protect herself from me? She was a human, and they weren't supposed to know...

"How did your contact know about me? Who are they?" The question, tinged with suspicion and a prickling concern, slipped free as my eyes probed hers for any whisper of deceit.

My instincts wrestled with the reality before me. I was not her superior, she was not a member of my crew, yet my experience and rank in my homeworld told me to prod further, to decipher what she wasn't saying.

Isla hesitated, her fingers fidgeting with the edge of the

device. *"My contact...their family works alongside the IPA, aiding in the rescue of beings like you—IPA citizens trapped on Earth during these precarious times."*

My instincts flared. Having commanded countless missions and interacted with various factions across galaxies, I sensed that there was more to this narrative, perhaps more than she knew. *"And you trust them? This outside connection of yours?"*

Her breath caught, her eyes darkened with determination, and she nodded. *"I trust their intention to free you. But as for everything else, trust is...complicated."*

She was withholding information, and while my instincts screamed for answers, my respect for her autonomy held me back.

"Isla." My mind strained with my conflicting desire for her and loyalty to my work and people. *"I want to believe in you and your plans for my escape, to believe that my dream of freedom might soon come true. But you must understand my apprehension. Secrets can be fatal."*

"I do trust you, Ky'rn." She nodded slowly, her shoulders sagging slightly under the weight of our shared burdens. *"For now, I'm asking you to have faith in me. Can you at least offer me that?"*

"I can accept it for now." My gaze sought hers. *"But I need to know the truth, Isla. Everything. Before my release, I want to know the price you've paid for that device."*

She met my gaze, those sapphire eyes holding a world of emotions—resolve, fear, and defiant courage. *"It's a deal. I give you my word."*

A low growl emanated from the base of my throat, not out of anger but concern. *"You must tread carefully, Isla,"* I cautioned. *"Don't promise me if you cannot, or will not, deliver. When I make a commitment, I hold it sacred, and I expect the same in return.*"

She looked surprised for a split second, a touch of vulnerability flickering across her features. Amid the hushed sounds of the chamber, water lapping gently against the tank walls, I watched as Isla's hand slowly rose, her fingers forming a tight fist, save for her smallest digit extended outwards. The playful yet earnest smile on her face caught me off guard, especially given the gravity of our situation.

Her smile, radiant and genuine, broke through the gloom. "*It's a pinky promise, Ky'rn. In my culture, it's a bond of trust, often made between children. It signifies that the promisor will hold true to their word.*"

A soft chuff of amusement escaped my lips. Here we were, in a web of intergalactic politics and undisclosed agendas, and she offered me the simplest gesture of trust from her world.

"*It sounds…serious.*"

Her laughter was soft, a brief but melodious note. "*Oh, it's* very *serious,*" she replied with a teasing glint in her eye.

"*And if the promise is broken?*"

She nodded, her brow furrowed. "*It's a breach of trust, one that's not easily mended.*"

Matching her gesture, I extended a scaled digit, wrapping it around hers as the coolness of my skin met the warmth of hers. Our pinkies entwined, the gesture surprisingly intimate given its simplicity.

"*Then I'll hold you to your promise,*" I rumbled, my tone gentle yet firm.

"*Great.*" She released our intertwined fingers and handed me the communicator. "*Call your people, Ky'rn. They've been waiting for you.*"

SEVENTEEN

KY'RN

A rush of excitement coursed through my veins to finally be able to communicate with my own people.

As the cool, sleek device nestled into my hand, I swiftly bit into the flesh of my thumb. The sharp tang of my violet blood mingled with the salt water on my scales. Pressing my thumb against the communicator's scanner, I watched as it absorbed my essence, confirming my identity. A soft hum emanated as the device awakened, its lights flickering into life and reflecting in Isla's wide, wonder-filled eyes.

I gently placed the device on the tank's rim beside her, and we watched as it projected a holographic display into the space between us. My fingers moved with practiced grace, each motion ingrained through countless years of training, entering the passcode that linked directly to my leaders in the IPA.

The insignia of the Intergalactic Protections Agency, a planet orbited by a moon and two spacecrafts, spun briefly before transforming, showing the familiar face of Prince Rivu.

The prince, was an imposing figure even in holographic form, floated with the regal bearing of our species: purple skin that shimmered like the vastness of a nebula, golden eyes reflecting strength and leadership from many years of duty, and a waterfall of jet-black hair that cascaded down his broad shoulders. The prince's eyes bored into me with a ferocity I'd almost forgotten after all my time in captivity.

"Commander Ky'rn?" Prince Rivu's voice was deep, resonating in the chamber. He spoke aloud in Galactic Common. Unless we shared the same waters, we couldn't speak telepathically.

I bowed my head respectfully, even as a multitude of emotions churned within me. "Yes, my prince," I replied, my voice betraying my own relief. "It has been a long time."

His eyes, although initially hard and scrutinizing, softened momentarily as they found mine. Recognition flickered through them, followed by a surge of silent questions.

"Commander Ky'rn," he muttered in a soothingly familiar timbre. "We thought we'd lost you…I didn't believe the stories that you were still alive, yet even after a year, here you are."

I exhaled, a shuddering breath. "The thought is mutual, my Prince."

Prince Rivu's gaze briefly shifted, noticing Isla beside me. He arched a slender eyebrow, his curiosity evident. "You are not alone."

I peered down at Isla, her beauty and strength only amplified by the otherworldly light of the communicator. "No, I am not." I said with a hint of pride. "This is Isla. She recently took on the responsibility of looking after me."

"Are you well?" Prince Rivu's voice cut through the hum of the chamber vibrations. "Tell me the truth. Has she treated you well?"

"I'm alive," I responded, pain apparent in my voice, "and for that, I'm thankful. But these walls…they are not meant for beings like us. My health isn't at its peak, and captivity certainly isn't doing me any favors. My stamina has suffered, but with your help, I hope to regain my strength and eventually be free."

Prince Rivu moved closer to his vidcom, his concern evident. "As soon as you're back in IPA territory, I'm granting you leave. You need time to heal, to rest."

"I'd appreciate that, Prince Rivu. Perhaps on X'thyrl…" I paused, allowing my hand to find Isla's, intertwining our fingers. The warmth of her touch was comforting. "I was hoping Isla could join me, in one of those vacation pods."

His eyes slid down to our intertwined hands, narrowing slightly. "The shore-side dome residences? With dual access for both aquatic and terrestrial beings?"

I nodded. "Yes, those. I believe it would be beneficial for me. Once I'm out of this place, I'd like to request my leave there, and have Isla by my side."

"But why?" His golden gaze studied her. "Why would you want to bring one of the people who trapped you for a year?"

I squeezed Isla's hand lightly and kicked my tail, bringing my body higher above the surface. I leaned closer to the communicator, gripping the tank's edge, and spoke with a firm, resolute tone. "My prince, I've been through volcanic waters, but this female, this beautiful, brave human beside me, has been the beacon of hope in my darkest moments. I will not abandon her—not now, not ever—to the wrath of her people. I'm not foolish. I'm sure there will be backlash once word of my rescue gets out. I refuse to let her take the fall. It's not her fault that I'm here."

"Can she understand us?" He flicked his gaze to mine and frowned. "Is she putting you up to this request?"

"No, she doesn't speak Galactic Common. Nor is she forcing me to make this request." I relaxed a little, letting go of the tank as I lowered myself back into the water, still clutching her hand. "I just want the best for her until things settle down between our people."

His fangs flashed in what I interpreted as annoyance or perhaps apprehension. "That might not be as straightforward as you hope. Relations with Earth have become…complex. Taking her off-planet might stir up tensions."

Isla's grip tightened, her mental voice tinged with worry. *"Ky'rn, what are you talking about? Who is this? He doesn't sound like he's too fond of me."*

Her eyes filled with a mix of confusion and concern. She must have sensed the shift in atmosphere of our tense exchange. *"This is Prince Rivu,"* I explained, motioning to the three-dimensional display. *"He's my superior and represents our species in the IPA."*

Isla quickly turned her attention to the holographic image of Prince Rivu with a fierce determination in her eyes. *"Tell him,"* she commanded, her voice firm and unwavering, *"that I will use every resource at my disposal to ensure you get out of here. And I'll do so quietly, without drawing attention."*

Translating her words into Galactic Common, I watched my prince's golden eyes assess Isla's resolve.

"Ask her if three Earth weeks is a workable timeline for your release and rescue."

The question seemed straightforward, but as I relayed it to Isla, her complexion drained of color. Her gaze darted between the holographic projection and me, her mouth opening as her fingers trembled ever so slightly. *"Three weeks?"* she echoed, her voice tinged with shock. *"Are you certain he said three weeks?"*

Confusion clouded my senses. My own tension mirrored Isla's as I relayed her concerns. "Prince Rivu," I began cautiously, "Isla wishes to confirm the three-week timeline. Is that accurate?"

His voice, sharper this time, carried an undertone of warning. "Affirmative. The fleet at *Atlantis* is ready, waiting on my command. We will not delay the mission any longer than necessary."

"It's true. Three weeks until my rescue mission is executed."

Her vibrant blue eyes widened and bore into mine, her lips parting. Her voice was barely a whisper, her fingers trembling in my hand. *"That means…you'll soon be free."*

The enormity of the situation weighed heavily on my heart. Freedom—a notion I had begun to regard as a distant dream—was suddenly tangible, almost within my grasp. *"Yes,"* I replied softly, allowing a flicker of hope to seep into my voice. *"It seems so."*

Turning slightly, I reassured Prince Rivu. "All will be well."

"Commander Ky'rn," Prince Rivu replied, his voice a deep rumble, "I trust you understand the importance of this timeline. Ensure you're prepared. Regain your strength, for your rescue will not be without its challenges."

I nodded, trying to swallow the lump forming in my throat. "I understand. I will be ready."

The Prince's visage softened, the barest hint of a smile playing on his lips. "Once you're safely within our territory, I will arrange a vacation pod for you on X'thyrl. You'll have time to recover and heal. We haven't forgotten our duty to our own."

Gratitude welled up within me. Relaxing in the serene waters of X'thyrl, surrounded by the comforting embrace of my home planet, was a wonderful prospect.

"Thank you, Prince Rivu," I murmured. "Your kindness means more than you know."

As the holographic connection faded, leaving Isla and me in the dim light of the containment unit, she turned to me, her gaze brimming with tears of joy and relief.

"Ky'rn." Her fingers tightened around mine, her voice choked with emotion. *"Soon, you'll be free. And I'll be with you until then. I won't let you go through the next few weeks by yourself."*

EIGHTEEN

ISLA

Withdrawing my hand from Ky'rn's felt like pulling my very soul away from a warmth and connection it craved. My heart fluttered mournfully as I sighed, turning my eyes towards the Makezu commander who, against the odds, had become my unexpected savior.

Three weeks.

The knowledge tasted bitter, tainted with both hope and sorrow. In a mere twenty-one days, Ky'rn would be saved from this terrestrial prison, likely whisked away from Earth and its turmoil forever.

Why would he ever consider returning?

Humans, with our insatiable curiosity, had initiated this chaotic spiral, falsely believing our species to be an unassailable force in the cosmos.

"Curiosity killed the cat…" I whispered to myself, gazing at the small communicator lying dormant on the ground. It was our very curiosity that had led to the *Stardancer*, humanity's first venture into the cosmos, exploding into shimmering debris, lives extinguished or cast adrift in the vast expanse of space. Those brave souls, propelled by dreams of exploration, had been lost due to faulty leadership.

Bending down, I lifted the communicator. It was impossible not to feel the weight of human inferiority. It was such a small, innocuous device, with a complexity and power far beyond our earthly technologies. The gap between human technology and the advancements of the IPA was vast. It was proof of how much humans had to learn…and perhaps, how much we had to fear.

Sighing, I nestled the device back into its box, securing the lid with a soft *click* that seemed to reverberate with finality through the chamber. Roman's promise to marry me, a deal to secure Ky'rn's freedom, lingered like an echo in my mind. His rapid adherence to the arrangement was unsettling, barely giving the metaphorical ink a chance to dry before actioning his end of the deal.

In three weeks, not only would I potentially lose Ky'rn, but I'd face the fiery tempest of my grandfather's wrath once he found out he was being duped. An unsettling dread about the impending confrontation with my grandfather lurked in the shadows of my mind. There would be no way for me to hide from him.

My resolve steadied my trembling hands as I prepared to climb out of the tank, yet before I could fully retreat, Ky'rn's fingers coiled gently yet firmly around my ankle. His touch was both cool and electric, sending a shiver racing up my spine.

I paused, looking down into the depths of his piercing eyes. They searched mine, probing for answers I wasn't sure I could give.

"Why do you wear that clouded expression, Isla?" he asked, his mental voice a soft, rumbling murmur.

My heart clenched. I hesitated for a moment, collecting

my thoughts, teetering on the edge of escape and confrontation.

Ky'rn deserved honesty...

"I..." The swirling whirlwind of emotions threatened to swallow me whole, but Ky'rn's piercing amber gaze sought clarity in mine, grounding me. *"I realized how little time we have left before you're gone forever from my life."*

It was a brutal truth, but it needed to be said. It was foolish to think otherwise—to fantasize about anything else.

"How little time?" His voice rumbled, as if the very thought of it was too foreign, too painful for him to understand. His aquatic features tightened, puzzled and wary. *"What do you mean?"*

My fingers twitched, longing to touch the ridges and contours of his face, but I held back and managed a feeble smile. *"I'm overjoyed at the thought of you being free soon."* I sighed audibly. *"But I'm not blind to reality. Given the political climate and bitterness between Earth and the IPA... you might never come back."*

Silence suspended between us before he finally spoke. *"You're right, I will leave Earth. But if I find a way back, it would be to find you."*

He sounded sincere, yet I scoffed, a defense mechanism to shield my fragile heart. A laugh escaped me, the sound more bitter than I intended. *"Why? Why return for me?"*

The raw honesty in his eyes almost broke me. *"You see me, Isla,"* he whispered, his voice rough with emotion. *"I've become attached to you. Perhaps it's the circumstances of our meeting, or maybe it's because you alone among your species saw me for who I am, not what I am."*

My lips quivered, averting my gaze. *"We could never be together."*

Suddenly, the world spun as I was yanked below the water's surface. Water enveloped me, yet fear was strangely absent, replaced by an electrifying awareness of his body against mine.

He pulled me back to the surface and pushed me against the tank's wall. He captured me in his arms, his eyes—intensely focused—branding mine.

His voice cut through the silence. *"If it could never be, why is your soul echoing with pain, Isla? If we could never be, why does every fiber of your being make me want to forsake it all?"*

I gazed into his eyes, impossibly deep, finding a truth I was hesitant to admit to myself. *"It's Stockholm Syndrome,"* I murmured, defeated.

His brow furrowed. *"I do not know what that means."*

My breath hitched. *"It's when a captive becomes empathetic, even affectionate, towards their captor, aligning with their goals, sometimes falling..."* I hesitated. *"... falling for them."*

A smirk, tender and amused, played on his lips. *"But, Isla, you're not my captor, and certainly not my abuser. At this moment, aren't you the captive?"*

Ky'rn's body surrounded me, large and protective, and as he nestled his nose into the junction of my neck and shoulder, the tension seemed to ebb from my muscles.

Ky'rn's closeness was intoxicating.

His natural aquatic scent, combined with the salty water, created a heady mixture that left my mind in a whirl. Every touch, every word, and the very weight of his presence pushed all rational thought aside. This was the embodiment of an alien, dangerous yet alluring.

The sensation of his rough tongue on the soft skin of my neck was completely unexpected. The lap of cold water over the sensitive spot created a contrast that sent shivers down my spine.

My heart rate, already accelerated by our proximity, seemed to double. Every nerve ending in my body was alert and alive, tingling with anticipation, sending a myriad of emotions coursing through me.

Confusion, fear, excitement…and an overwhelming desire to be close to him, to feel the gentle touch of his scales and the coolness of his embrace. An involuntary gasp escaped my lips.

Ky'rn paused. His glowing amber eyes locked onto mine, seeking consent.

"I'm not trying to frighten you, Isla," he murmured. His deep mental voice sent vibrations that caressed my skin. *"You smell divine. It's a call I can't ignore."*

It was a primal assertion, and though every rational thought warned me to push him away, to create distance between us, I remained frozen, ensnared by his unyielding gaze.

"What are you saying?" My heart pounded in my chest, even as some intrinsic, ancient part of me recognized that he didn't intend to harm me.

A gentle smile curled the corners of his mouth, his teeth gleaming white in the artificial light. *"I wish to sample you. I carve to know how you taste, to mark you as mine in a way that all will recognize."*

"What? Why? Are you saying you want to eat me?" The words were out before I could think them through. *"Why do you want to mark me?"*

"From the moment our paths crossed, I felt a pull towards you, Isla." His eyes, those intense amber orbs, searched mine as if trying to pierce through to my very soul. *"In this place, where I'm confined and stripped of my freedom, you've been*

a beacon. Your fight for freedom against your grandfather, and those who want to control you, mirrors my own. We are the same.

"And I can't go on without knowing how you taste, without feeling your life force joined with mine...I don't want to leave Earth with any regrets."

I swallowed hard, my throat suddenly dry. I wasn't sure if it was fear or the intensity of our conversation that was making it difficult to breathe. *"What does the marking entail?"*

He looked down for a moment, contemplating, before meeting my eyes once again. *"It's a scar, a bite mark visible only to those with heightened vision."* A gentle smile curled at the corners of his mouth, his teeth gleaming white in the filtered light. *"A way of showing others that you're under my protection, and in turn, that I'm in debt to you. It can be... intimate, but it doesn't always have to be."*

A myriad of thoughts raced through my mind. What would people think? Could I keep a mark hidden, especially on my wedding day? And more importantly, what would this mean for our already complicated relationship?

He must have seen the hesitancy in my eyes because he quickly added, *"Only if you wish it, Isla."*

I took a deep breath, weighing my options. I could refuse and potentially alienate Ky'rn, who had already proven I could trust him...

Or I could accept, deepening our bond but also complicating our already uncertain future.

"Will it hurt?" Vulnerability bled into my voice.

His fingertips brushed my cheek, the touch gentle and reassuring. *"At first,"* he admitted as he eased closer, the tip of his nose brushing against mine, an intimate, almost-human gesture that stilled my trembling. *"But then, I prom-*

ise, it will be a sensation unlike any you've ever felt before."

My fingers traced over the rough texture of his shoulder, a contrast to the soft vulnerability in his eyes. This was a decision that would forever change the course of our intertwined destinies.

"All right." With a gentle nod, I gave him my consent, placing my trust in him. *"Mark me."*

His amber eyes never left mine, in their depths a desire and longing that mirrored my own. There was deep hunger there, a primal instinct to claim what he desired, but there was something more too, something tender and profound.

As he leaned closer, our breaths mingled in the small space between us, warm and erratic. I felt the gentle brush of his lips against mine, a feather-light touch that sent a shiver down my spine. It was a silent request, and in that moment, I knew there was no turning back.

As Ky'rn's lips pressed harder against mine, I was consumed by a sensation unlike any other. His mouth was cooler than mine, with an odd textured roughness that was strangely enticing. It was as if the very waters we floated in flowed between us, making the connection electric, alive.

The world around us faded, and all I could feel was him.

His lips trailed from my mouth, down the line of my jaw, to the vulnerable expanse of my neck. A soft growl rumbled in his chest, sending delightful tremors through my body. Before I could react, one of his hands wrapped around my long hair, twisting it gently but firmly, tilting my head to expose more of my throat. His other hand, strong and unyielding, held my opposite wrist against the cool surface of the tank, effectively immobilizing me.

He pressed his lips hard against my skin. *"Don't struggle, Isla..."* His whispered words made my heart race. *"I can't control the hunger I feel for you. It's primal, it's deep...I only want a taste..."*

I steeled myself, holding my breath as his tongue lapped at the juncture of my shoulder and neck, teasing and tasting, preparing me for what was to come.

Ky'rn's sharp teeth grazed my neck, a gasp escaped my lips—and then he bit down.

The sensation was indescribable. It wasn't pain—far from it.

It felt as if a door had been unlocked, a connection so profound that it felt like our souls were intertwining. Warmth spread from the point of contact, a mingling of pleasure and surprise.

The sensation was so erotic that a moan slipped from my lips, unbidden. It was a delicate dance of give and take—him drawing life from me, and in return, flooding me with an incredible feeling. His feeding felt intimate, like he was sharing a piece of himself with me and taking a piece of me in return.

As the world started to blur, Ky'rn pulled away, licking the small wounds to soothe where he'd bitten, a mix of coolness and warmth that sent a jolt through me.

When he finally pulled away, his eyes were filled with a storm of emotions. The weight of what had just occurred settled over us, and for a long moment, we simply floated there, lost in each other. I touched the spot on my neck, still feeling the hum of our shared connection.

"We're..." I started, searching for the right words.

"Connected," he finished for me, his voice husky. *"Bound."*

NINETEEN

KY'RN

With eyes wide, Isla peered at me in shock. *"What do you mean?"*

I was too lost in her—her scent, her touch, her essence. The barriers between us felt thin, almost nonexistent. *"I mean this."* I released her hair and trailed my nose down her throat, sealing my lips over my mark.

She responded with a ferocity that took me by surprise, gripping my hair, her legs wrapping around me, her feet hooked under my dorsal fin. Every motion, every grind against me ignited an inferno that threatened to consume us both.

A hot pulse of desire surged through me as my hearts thundered in my chest. The scents and sounds of Isla so close tempted the very core of my being. The rhythmic cadence of her heartbeat was an intoxicating song that drowned out all other sounds.

Her fingers tightened around my hair, pulling me closer, our faces mere inches apart. The warmth of her skin mingled with the coolness of the water, creating a tantalizing contrast.

She ground against me, lost in the throes of passion, and I couldn't help but respond.

A fierce need took root.

Her response, her closeness, it all made my instincts roar to the forefront. I felt a hunger, a deep-seated need not just for pleasure but for connection. It wasn't just physical—it was emotional, spiritual even.

I was what she yearned for, what she craved—the one she trusted the most, with her life. But the anguish that would follow my departure was a looming shadow that she feared.

When I pulled away, our mingling breaths came out ragged and uneven. My gaze bore into her half-lidded eyes. *"It can't be…"*

She blinked. *"What can't be?"*

The sight of her mark, pulsating gently, had changed something between us. My intimate act had unknowingly created a deeper bond, a tether neither of us had anticipated.

Gritting my teeth, I tried to find the words. *"It's not what I intended. The bite is supposed to be simple. Purely nourishment. But with you…it's different. Everything's different."*

She swallowed hard, her eyes searching mine. *"What's different?"*

"The mark…It was supposed to be a sign of trust, of mutual need. My people will take on the mark during times of war when a comrade is in dire need of healing—something to show others that you've sacrificed your life force to help another. It earns you protection in turn if you ever needed it. But it wasn't meant to be…this."

She seemed to tremble, her voice quivering. *"What's wrong?"*

I pulled her closer, hoping my body could communicate what words could not. *"I did not expect this. Our mark is not just any mark. It has bound us, perhaps more deeply than I ever thought possible, especially with a human."*

Her breath caught, and she shivered against me. *"Bound us? How?"*

I sighed, choosing my words carefully. *"In my species, such a bond is not formed lightly. It links the souls on a level deeper than friendship, beyond mere intimacy. It's a connection that defies all. Usually shared only between mates. I don't know how it happened, Isla, but we are. You and I, we are now irrevocably linked. It means that I will feel you, no matter where you are...and you will feel me, too, if we seal it."*

She looked down at her mark, now understanding its significance. Her hand gently caressed it, and the sudden jolt of emotions bursting from her made me shiver, too. *"But... you said your bite was just for feeding."*

"It was." A growl rumbled from deep within me. *"But somehow, I've anchored you to me. And no matter where I go, no matter the distance between us, I will always carry a part of you with me. Your lifeforce will always be a part of me, connecting me to you."* I searched her face, trying to find the right words. *"Your spirit called to me in ways I've never experienced. Your life force...It's different. Richer. More potent. I can't explain it. I fear if I taste it again so soon, I won't stop."*

Her realization was swift, her body disentangling from mine, pulling away. Fear flashed in her eyes, and I could see the mental walls she was erecting to protect herself.

"I'm sorry," she whispered, a hint of fear in her voice.

Reaching out, I touched her cheek, my thumb brushing against her soft skin. *"I won't harm you,"* I promised, my voice gentle but firm. *"I promise. I can control myself. The* bond between us is stronger than I realized, and I won't risk losing myself—or you. I just need...some space and time. If I weren't trapped in here, things would be different..."

Isla's eyes searched mine, and she nodded slowly, her gaze still wary. *"I understand."*

The silence between us buzzed with intensity as I felt a turmoil of emotions rising within me. Watching her, I wondered what I could do to calm her...to make her understand that I didn't mean to mark her in the way mates did.

As she pulled herself out of the tank, water cascaded from her, each droplet reflecting the ambient light of the room, casting luminous patterns on her pale skin.

She hugged her knees to her chest, radiating vulnerability. Her delicate form glistened as she sat on the edge of the tank, her gaze a blend of uncertainty and defiance.

It was a look I was becoming all too familiar with.

"Isla..." My voice broke, heavy with the weight of regret, reaching up to touch her foot, hoping to bridge the widening chasm between us. *"Why do I feel like I've made a grave mistake?"*

She didn't meet my gaze, the rhythm of the water dripping from her the only sound filling the void between us. Her vulnerability, the way she sat there with her hair plastered to her back, her eyes downcast, was both beautiful and haunting.

She drew a shuddering breath, her eyes avoiding mine. Her mental voice was a mere whisper, silencing the raging thoughts. *"You haven't done anything wrong. It's just...complicated."*

The weight in my chest grew heavier. *"Please,"* I implored, my fingers grazing her ankle in a gentle plea. *"Don't push me away. I didn't mean for this to happen. I don't want to lose what we have."*

She exhaled, her gaze lifting, meeting mine, her blue eyes filled with a storm of emotions. The walls she'd erected around her heart had replaced the warmth from before with guarded caution. *"I don't fault you, Ky'rn. But I need some time, too. To process everything."*

The weight of her words, the shift in our dynamic, bore down on me. I could see her defenses rising, her once open heart now walled off by doubt and fear. *"I will respect your needs. But please don't push me away. Not now. Our time is limited already."*

Her fingers trailed over the fading mark, her touch almost reverent. *"It's not you. I'm not afraid of you, Ky'rn,"* she admitted, her voice thick with emotion. *"But you represent something I can't have: Freedom. I'm afraid of getting too attached to you, only to be left with this mark as a reminder of what might have been."*

My heart thudded painfully. *"Isla, you can have freedom, too. With me. If you truly wanted it. All you have to do is—"*

She shook her head, a pained smile curving her lips. *"It's not that simple. And soon…it won't matter."*

The sinking feeling in my stomach grew more profound, and a rush of emotions washed over me. I could taste her despair, her frustration, her resignation through our new connection. It made my insides coil with dread. I couldn't fathom what she was going through, but I yearned to ease her pain.

"What do you mean, it won't matter?" My voice came out as more of a growl, the urgency palpable, but she was already pulling away.

She faced the door, her gaze distant. *"I've been here too long. I need to go."* The resolve in her voice was absolute, and it shattered me.

My gut twisted, and I watched in mounting panic as she began to distance herself from me.

She was leaving.

Retreating from whatever bond was beginning to form between us. The distance between us grew with every step she took away from the tank. My instincts raged. The predator within me roared in protest, desperate to reach out and pull her back.

Every fiber of my being screamed at me to climb out of the tank, to pull her into an embrace, to reassure her, to make her stay. But I knew I couldn't. Our worlds, our lives, our circumstances were complicated. And perhaps my recent actions had only made things worse.

My gaze followed her, taking in the way her wet hair clung to her shoulders, how she methodically packed her belongings with a kind of finality that gnawed at my insides.

Each step she took was a dagger to my heart. As she descended the steps, my desperation grew. My heart constricted painfully.

Isla, don't go.

Racing along the tank's edge, I placed a palm flat against the glass, willing her to look back, to see my regret and desperation.

Isla!

She paused, and then turned, her gaze meeting mine. Her hand lifted, fingers splayed against the glass, mirroring mine.

It was a fleeting touch, a silent goodbye, and it tore at my soul.

But as quickly as it came, the moment was gone. Isla withdrew, her expression unreadable, and moved towards the door.

Her next steps seemed more determined as she disengaged some device, pausing briefly to stow the box securely in her pouch.

The door slid open, revealing the corridor beyond, and without a backward glance, she stepped across the threshold, disappearing from sight.

The door closed with a soft hiss, leaving me with a haunting void and an ache deep within.

TWENTY

ISLA

The instant I emerged from the chamber, Dr. Violet's piercing eyes locked onto mine. Her features, sharp and intelligent, softened with a wash of concern. She dashed over, her lab coat billowing behind her, abandoning her post without hesitation.

"Isla!" Her fingers wrapped around my wrists, the touch clinical but underscored with genuine concern. "Are you all right?"

The walls I'd built around my emotions threatened to crumble.

My lips quivered as I sucked in a deep breath, my mind a whirl of thoughts concerning the alien behind the sealed door. Now wasn't the time to be swept away by the whirlwind. I swallowed hard, pushing Ky'rn's magnetic presence to the back of my mind.

His well-being had to take priority over our connection.

I forced a nod. "I'm fine, Dr. Violet. But Ky'rn…He's not doing well."

Her brows knitted together. "What do you mean?"

My voice quivered. "His hue has shifted, his energy

seems to be waning. He needs the live fish he requested. We can't risk his health."

Her expression softened, her earlier alarm morphing into determination. "We'll make sure he gets what he needs. We can't afford to have him deteriorate under our watch."

A sigh of relief escaped me. "Can you accompany me to the kitchens? We need the head chef to arrange a constant supply."

She offered a nod and gently let go of my hands. "We can go now, if you want." She motioned. "I bet you're famished. You missed dinner."

I bit my lip, gratitude flooding me. Her offer wasn't just professional between two scientists—it was personal, an unspoken bond between two people who understood the weight of their responsibilities.

I hadn't even noticed my hunger until she mentioned it. A pang of emptiness hit my stomach, and I swayed slightly, light-headedness creeping in.

"Thank you, that means a lot."

Dr. Violet's gaze sharpened, shifting to my still damp hair. "Why is your hair wet?"

The memory of the water, the way Ky'rn's skin had felt against mine, surged to the forefront. I pushed it away with a casual shrug. "Oh, just felt like taking a relaxing swim with him."

She folded her arms across her chest, unimpressed. "And that wouldn't have anything to do with the chamber surveillance mysteriously going offline?"

I shrugged, feigning ignorance. "Couldn't tell you."

Dr. Violet's usually stoic face twisted with a mix of compassion and regret as she took a moment to gather herself, taking a deep breath.

The fluorescent lights of the lab cast a harsh glow, making

the clinical surroundings seem even colder. Dr. Violet's voice trembled with emotion, something I had seldom seen in the composed scientist. "You were right about your grandfather. He wasn't just content with exploiting Ky'rn once he found him. He...he actually orchestrated his capture."

Shock rippled through me, a cold fury surging up in its wake. I had suspected many things of my grandfather, but not this level of cruelty.

"So, you're telling me he put a bounty on Ky'rn? That Grandfather not only knew about him but was the reason he was captured? The reason he's here, in this..." I waved around, the unnatural environment we'd caged him in. "...prison?"

Dr. Violet winced, nodding slowly. "Yes, but it wasn't just Ky'rn," she admitted; her gaze was heavy with regret. "He placed bounties on Sam and Rose that night, too. He was desperate for control, to undo anything that threatened both his position and yours. Your grandfather believes they'll come out of hiding once news of your impending wedding spreads, and the ceremony has been designed to flush them out, if they don't show up beforehand."

I felt bile rise in my throat, the weight of betrayal stinging sharp.

"All this time I thought Ky'rn was just a victim of circumstance. I never imagined my own family was responsible for his capture."

Violet's expression softened, and she reached out, placing a comforting hand on my shoulder. "Isla, I, too, wish things were different, but you can't dwell on the past," she began, her voice filled with the wisdom of her years. "We can't change what's been done. But now that you know, you have the power to change the future. To right the wrongs."

Frustration bubbled up within me, my voice edged with

bitterness. "I'm just one person. I don't even know the first thing about running a conglomerate."

A smile played on her lips, tinged with a hint of mischief. "Well, you have a fiancé, don't you? One who's quite familiar with leadership and power. Perhaps he could be of assistance?"

I scowled. "A fiancé I never asked for," I muttered bitterly.

She tilted her head, her gaze sharp. "I know how you feel, Isla. Your grandfather has cornered me into many decisions I've regretted too. But I believe in change, and I believe in you. With new leadership, things can change. You can shape the future."

The dimmed artificial lighting of the lab created long shadows as the weight of her words sank in. The hushed silence felt almost suffocating.

I took a moment to study Dr. Violet, her face worn from years under my grandfather's oppressive influence. The creases around her eyes, the lines of stress across her forehead, all hinted at the weight of the guilt she carried. Her weary eyes spoke of countless sleepless nights and confrontations with a man neither of us could defy. Her gaze was sincere, pleading almost. It reminded me of Ky'rn's eyes when he looked at me, filled with longing for a life of freedom.

Maybe I couldn't undo my grandfather's sins, but I could ensure they weren't repeated.

"Dr. Violet." My voice was barely above a whisper. "I need to know if you're on my side. Can I truly trust you?"

"When I began working here, I dreamt of discovery, of pushing the boundaries of science, of understanding our world and perhaps worlds beyond. But over the years, those dreams were crushed under the weight of greed, ambition, and a relentless pursuit of power."

I took a hesitant step closer, feeling a kinship with this woman whom, until now, I'd seen as just another part of my grandfather's machine. "I didn't know," I whispered, guilt seeping in for not seeing past the façade earlier.

She took a deep breath. "Not many do. Your grandfather is skilled at keeping secrets and even better at ensuring loyalty—by any means necessary. He has his claws deep in many of us. Some, by choice, seeking power and wealth. But many, like me, are trapped. Fearful of what he might do if we tried to break free."

She hesitated, fortifying herself to continue. "Your grandfather, he rules with an iron fist, using fear as his primary tool. I've seen brilliant minds come and go, crushed under the weight of his ambitions. Leaving isn't an option for me. If I did, he'd ensure I'd never work again, not in any reputable institution."

A faint smile touched her lips. "I've been waiting, Isla. Hoping against hope that someone with integrity would take the reins. That someone could be you."

My heart swelled with a mix of emotions—sympathy for Dr. Violet, anger at my grandfather, and determination to make a change. I reached out, taking Dr. Violet's hand in mine.

"I'll make it right, Dr. Violet. Not just for Ky'rn, but for all those who've suffered under my grandfather's tyranny."

She closed her eyes momentarily, taking a deep breath. "You remind me so much of your mother. She had that same fire, that same drive to change the world for the better." Her voice wavered with a mix of admiration and sadness. "But she was taken from us too soon."

A pang of sorrow hit me at the mention of my mother.

She'd been my guiding star, and her absence was a void that couldn't be filled. "I want to continue her legacy," I whispered, tears threatening to spill. "I want to make her proud. But I can't do it alone."

Dr. Violet's eyes darted around the room, and she let out a shaky breath. "But Isla...your grandfather is a master manipulator. He has connections, resources. He knows exactly how to twist people to his will, and he's done so with many of us here. I've seen him destroy people who've crossed him," she whispered, her fingers playing with the edge of her lab coat. "Your assurances are comforting, but you should know that his reach extends far beyond this facility. What makes you think he won't do the same to you, or me?"

"I'm well aware of his influence and the power he wields." I took a deep breath, drawing upon all my courage. "If you truly want to help me, you need to help me undo the damage that's been done. As I said earlier, I need help caring for Ky'rn, and right now, he needs a fresh supply of live fish. The larger, the better. And whatever you do, don't ever bring security in there. He isn't a danger...not to me or anyone."

She took a step closer, her expression conflicted. "He's an alien," she began slowly, letting the words sink in. "He's sentient, intelligent. While you might trust him, we don't know what he's capable of. He could use you as a hostage."

A soft, melancholic smile crept onto my face as I remembered Ky'rn's gentle caress, the way his eyes lit up when he saw me, and the indescribable moment we had just shared. My fingers instinctively went to the mark on my neck, the one that faintly pulsed with a warmth that seemed to echo Ky'rn's emotions.

It was as if I felt his support through the mark....

I let out a long breath. "All I'm asking is for you to trust me. Trust my instincts on this matter. I know Ky'rn, and he wouldn't harm me or anyone else, not unless provoked."

Dr. Violet's eyes flitted away, uncertainty clouding her features. "I want to believe you, Isla. But it's not just about trust. It's about safety. Yours, mine, everyone's."

I met her gaze head-on. "Dangerous or not, I won't stand by and let my grandfather, or anyone else for that matter, treat him like a mere object."

Her gaze lowered, and she bit her lower lip, contemplating. "But he's a captive, Isla. He's far from his home, from his kind. Desperation can make even the gentlest soul act out. What if he turns on you?"

There was truth to her words, and I couldn't deny the possible danger. But I also couldn't deny what I felt, what I knew deep in my heart.

"Ky'rn has had ample opportunity to hurt me, but he hasn't. Instead, he's saved me, protected me. I trust him, more than my grandfather." I paused, taking a deep breath, trying to find the right words. "I know the risks. But if you want to help me, if you want to stand by my side, you have to believe me."

She sighed, running a hand through her graying hair. "I'm aware of that. But what you're proposing is a huge risk to your safety. And what if your grandfather finds out? He has methods for extracting information. He'd be upset to learn that you've been spending time alone with the 'pet' you've been given rather than completing the research he wants."

I absently caressed the mark that sat just below the base of my neck, and I felt its warmth radiate through my skin. Her eyes darted to where my fingers brushed my skin and then back to my face.

Had she noticed my mark? Had she simply chosen not to mention it?

I sighed, feeling the weight of her concerns. "I understand your fears, but you said you want to make things right. This is our chance. You've seen how he is with me, and you know he's the one who saved me a year ago. I'm not in danger. But Ky'rn is. Every second he spends in that tank, his life is at risk.

"But things will change. I promise you that. In just a few weeks, I'll be in a position to ensure Ky'rn's safety. Yours, too."

"If he means that much to you," she said, pausing as if weighing each word, "then I'll do what I can to help. But you need to promise me something."

"Anything," I replied, eager for her support.

She let out a shaky breath. "I'll help you care for him. We'll get him the fish he needs, and I'll keep security away. But promise me, Isla, if things start to go south, you'll let me know. Promise me you won't let your feelings for him cloud your judgment."

A small, grateful smile tugged at my lips. "Thank you. I promise."

She hesitated, raising her eyebrow as if she didn't believe me. "If your grandfather or Ky'rn becomes a threat to you, promise me you'll do whatever it takes to protect yourself. Promise me you won't sacrifice yourself for the sake of sentiment."

I nodded slowly, my fingers lightly brushing over the mark as a painful knot formed in my chest. It was clear Dr. Violet had witnessed, and perhaps even endured, some of the darkness that shadowed my grandfather's ambitions.

"I promise," I murmured, though deep down, I knew I wouldn't keep that vow if it came down to it. "But my goal is to stay off Grandfather's radar until the wedding, and then I won't have to worry about him."

Her gaze softened, and for the first time, I saw the real Dr. Violet—worn out, but with a core of steel. "Then I'd stand by your side. It might mean I'll never work in this field again, but at least I'd regain some semblance of honor."

A tear formed in the corner of my eye. "Thank you."

TWENTY-ONE

KY'RN

T hings had changed.

The brief encounters we used to have, where I'd see a flicker of emotion or longing in her gaze, were gone.

She was distant, removed.

Every morning and evening, like clockwork, the door would hiss open, and in would come Isla, accompanied by her mentor. She'd push in a cooler, filled with a feast that, under any other circumstances, would have delighted me. But it was hard to enjoy the bounty when all I longed for was a real conversation with her.

Each time she entered with that cooler cart, my hopes would rise, only to be crushed when she began her routine check-up.

Their clinical demeanor was almost robotic. Discussing my health, taking notes, and occasionally extracting samples from me. I appreciated that they treated me with respect, always asking for consent. But the impersonal manner was maddening.

Why was she maintaining this distance?

Every time I tried to address the gulf between us, she'd avoid eye contact, answering in clipped, professional tones. It was as if she'd erected a wall, separating us.

My eyes would always linger on her mark, the one I'd accidentally given her. It made me recall the last intimate moment we'd shared. The warmth of her skin, the urgency in her movements as she clung on to me, the connection I'd felt.

The marking had been instinctual, satisfying a deep yearning from within.

Had that moment scared her? Pushed her away?

I needed to understand. If there was a chance of fixing this, I'd take it, before it was too late. I didn't want to leave Earth with this wall between us. In order to tear it down, I needed her to talk to me, to open up.

As they concluded their methodical examination, I sensed the familiar pattern of departure. An aching weight had settled in my chest, too heavy to ignore as Isla and her mentor turned their backs, heading for the exit.

With a swift motion, my fingers encircled her wrist. *"Isla."*

She jerked in surprise, her blue eyes widening in alarm before settling where my fingers encircled her wrist. Her breath caught, and for a split second, a barrage of emotions danced across her face—fear, confusion, longing.

"Why are you keeping your distance from me?" My voice, though soft, carried the desperation I hadn't intended to show.

She swallowed, her delicate throat bobbing as she seemed to struggle with her thoughts. Casting a quick glance at her mentor, she wordlessly gestured with a fist, the thumb raised —a signal she seemed to understand as she stepped back, giving us a semblance of privacy.

"It's...complicated," she murmured, her voice carrying a heavy weight.

My thoughts immediately drifted to the unintentional bond I had forged. *"Is it because I marked you? Is that why you avoid being alone with me?"*

She shook her head, her colorful locks cascading like a waterfall. *"The mark is...a conversation we need to have, but it's not just that."* Her gaze faltered, a flicker of pain crossing her beautiful face. *"My grandfather has been relentless. Meetings, appointments, obligations...Every minute of my day is accounted for. He's ensured I barely have a moment to myself. I'm trying to maintain appearances, to keep his suspicions at bay. If he senses any deviation, any hint of our... plans, it could become dangerous for both of us."*

While understanding doused the flames of my frustration, another feeling sprouted in its place: longing. *"You're trying to shield me."*

She nodded. *"In a week, you'll be free. But until then, every moment I spend with you is under scrutiny."*

I drew her closer, bridging the gap between us. *"I may be free in a week, Isla, but I don't want that day to come without us clarifying what's between us."*

Her eyes welled with unshed tears. *"I want that too, Ky'rn. Just a little longer. Bear with me."*

"For you, Isla, I'd wait an eternity." I nodded, releasing her wrist.

TWENTY-TWO

ISLA

The lavender hues of the ocean enveloped me, a world that was alien yet strangely comforting. As I swam, the saltless water felt silky against my skin, almost velvety.

I spotted a shadow ahead, a silhouette that bore a striking resemblance to Ky'rn's distinctive form. The familiar curve of his powerful tail, the strength in his streamlined form, beckoned me forward, and I couldn't resist the urge to follow.

My heart raced in exhilaration, a result of the thrill of the chase and the yearning to connect with him again. Every time I felt I was close enough to reach out, to touch him, to confirm it was him, he'd accelerate, his form blurring into the lavender around us, always just out of reach.

The water grew cooler as I dove deeper, chasing the tantalizing shadow. As I descended, the lavender hue darkened, transforming into a deep plum, then almost black.

The harsh buzzing of the vidscreen echoed painfully in the early morning silence, ripping me from the depths of a restless sleep. In a flurry of tangled sheets and disoriented thoughts, I grabbed my robe, clumsily shrugging it on.

Stumbling to the door, I activated the vidscreen. Roman's expectant face greeted me.

Rubbing my temples in an effort to shake off the remnants of sleep, I groaned, "Roman? What are you doing here so early?"

His brows knitted in confusion. "Did you forget? We have marriage preparations with the lawyers before the rehearsal today."

Cursing silently, I let the weight of reality sank in. The wedding was tomorrow. How could I forget? "Do I have time to freshen up, at least?" I mumbled.

Roman's sharp gaze bore into me, one eyebrow raised in challenge. "You do, if you let me in to discuss a few things first."

A sigh escaped my lips as I relented, disengaging the lock.

Once the door slid open, Roman's imposing figure stepped inside, the scent of his expensive cologne filling the room. I watched as he took in my living space, decorated with a blend of professional tools and personal mementos.

His voice, softer than I'd anticipated, broke my reverie. "Were you able to make contact?"

I nodded, steeling myself. "Yes, I did. Ky'rn was able to communicate with his leader. Everything is in order."

He paused, looking thoughtful. "The wedding is tomorrow. Do you really think you're ready for this?" His fingers picked up a frame from the tabletop. An image of my younger self with my parents on a sun-drenched beach stared back at him. Emotion thickened the air. "You're not having second thoughts, are you?"

"Look, I just want this all to be over with." I said, frustration leaking into my voice. "Tomorrow, Ky'rn will be free."

He studied me, his gaze unrelenting. "I wasn't aware you were in such a rush to become my wife."

My eyes rolled involuntarily. "It's not the position I'm after, but the security it brings. After all, our marriage is for business. Purely platonic."

"I want it no other way." Roman stared at me for a moment, the depth of his gaze making me shift uncomfortably, and then he sighed. "Go get dressed. Once you're ready, we can make sure everything is in place before we have to report to our first appointment."

"You might as well make yourself comfortable," I said, gesturing toward the snack bar. "I'll only be a few minutes."

He raised an eyebrow, taking in my half-awake state. "Take your time," he replied with a smirk. "No need to worry about me."

With a huff, I entered my room, leaving him to his own devices. As soon as the door closed behind me, I stepped into the RoBo Changing Room.

For a moment, I was transfixed by my reflection, the mark on my skin catching the light. The discoloration against my skin brought back memories of Ky'rn and what we had shared in that fleeting moment.

I frowned as guilt gnawed at me for not slipping away to speak with him—alone. A part of me was afraid of what would happen. What if I got lost in the moment—once again?

Tomorrow, he would be free to reunite with his people, and I would be left behind on Earth, a newlywed bride.

It would be worth it—a life for a life.

Navi's cheery voice broke through my thoughts. "Good morning, Isla! What would you like to wear for today's engagements?"

My mind quickly sifted through my wardrobe, settling on

a favorite. "The violet flowy gown, please. And the matching stilettos."

I watched in awe, as I always did, as the room transformed. Robotic arms seamlessly appeared, moving with grace and precision. The sensation of the fabric sliding against my skin, the brush of the robotic hands arranging my hair, and the gentle application of makeup was both comforting and surreal.

Once they were finished, the arms receded, and Navi's voice returned, now imbued with a touch of pride. "Is this to your satisfaction, Miss Isla?"

Gazing into the 360-degree mirror, I couldn't help but smile at the stunning image reflected back at me—a confident woman, poised and elegant. The gown hugged my curves perfectly, and the shoes elevated me just right. The violet hue complemented my skin tone, making my eyes and hair color pop. "It's perfect, Navi. Thank you."

As I emerged from the RoBo Changing Room, I felt a surge of confidence I hadn't felt in a while. The cool fabric of the gown whispered against my legs, and my stilettos clicked with purpose on the marble floor.

With each step, I felt more and more grounded, ready to confront the world outside, to face my destiny.

Roman had made himself at home, lounging comfortably in my living area. The large window behind him showcased the dazzling view of the sunrise over the ocean, the perfect backdrop to his silhouette. The deep red of his drink caught the ambient light, shimmering as he took a sip.

As I approached, he turned, and for a moment, the surprise in his eyes was genuine. Then came the whistle. "Well, look at you," he drawled, a smirk playing at the corner of his lips. "You clean up pretty good."

I couldn't help but smile at his compliment, however

backhanded it might have been. "Thank you," I replied, letting my good mood reach my eyes. I twirled a strand of hair around my finger, playing with it absentmindedly. "But if I'm being honest, I'm not the biggest fan of all this glamour. Give me my lab coat any day."

His laughter echoed through the room with a genuine warmth I hadn't expected. "Oh, I'm sure," he teased, taking another sip of his wine. "But let me guess, when you're not donning your white coat, you're lounging around in some old, comfy pajama pants?"

My lips curved into a grin. "You caught me," I said, playfully pointing a finger at him. "They're comfortable, cozy, and the perfect outfit for late-night research or just lounging around after a long day."

He leaned in slightly, his blue eyes twinkling with mischief. "Maybe after all this wedding business, I'll gift you a pair. Perhaps with some little sharks on them?"

I laughed, the tension from before ebbing away. "You do that, and I might just have to reevaluate this arrangement."

Roman's intense gaze met mine as he placed his empty wine glass on the side table. "Ready for the day?"

A heavy sigh escaped my lips as I looked down, tracing the intricate patterns made of crystals on my gown. "Do I have a choice?"

Roman's eyes softened, and he approached me, his steps careful and measured. "Isla, you always have a choice. Remember that." He paused, his eyes searching mine. "After tomorrow, both you and Ky'rn will be free."

"I need details, Roman," I pressed, my fingers tightening around the edge of the ornate table separating us. "You can't expect me to walk into tomorrow blind."

Roman's gaze held a challenge. He seemed to cut right to the core of my intentions. He was a formidable ally, but at times like these, I was reminded that we hailed from our own families, each with our own agendas and loyalties.

How exactly was this going to work if he kept me in the dark on purpose?

He sighed, raking a hand through his dark hair. "As I said, my team will wait until our ceremony is over. And once Ky'rn is out of the tank, he'll be escorted straight to them. The scouts will ensure a smooth extraction."

My frustration bubbled up. "But what's the plan inside the facility? How do we ensure he's not caught, or worse, hurt?"

Roman sighed, his shoulders drooping slightly. "What happens tomorrow will largely hinge on your grandfather's reaction to the revised contract." He pinned me with an analytical gaze. "Speaking of which, I've seen the changes you made. Explain them."

Swallowing hard, I straightened my back, determined to make my stance clear. "If you're going to wield power over my legacy, it's only fair I have a say in yours. A merger ensures that neither of us loses completely, and both of us gain something. Our families remain influential in their areas of expertise, but united, we form a stronger front."

He seemed to mull over my words, but it was his next question that caught me off-guard. "What about a…new operation?"

My brows knitted. "What are you talking about?"

He leaned in, lowering his voice. "An alien sanctuary. Think about it, Isla. A place for beings like Ky'rn, far from prying eyes and threats. Away from the likes of your grandfather."

The idea resonated deep within me. Ever since meeting Ky'rn, I'd realized the dangers and prejudices beings like him faced daily. Such a sanctuary could be a true safe haven, both until things settled with the IPA and after. It might take generations for humankind to accept that we were no longer alone in the universe.

My heart raced as the possibilities unfurled.

My eyes searched his for a hint of duplicity, but all I found was sincerity. "How will we ensure its safety? Ensure that what happened to Ky'rn doesn't happen there?"

"Security would be of utmost importance. We'd employ the latest technology, perhaps even seek assistance from IPA allies."

The notion of joining forces, of bridging gaps not just between our two companies, but between races and worlds, was both awe-inspiring and terrifying. "You've been thinking about this for a while," I realized.

He gave a slight nod. "Ever since I saw what they did to Ky'rn. It made me wonder how many more aliens there are, suffering in silence."

I took a deep breath, mulling over his words. The challenge was daunting, but the possibility of making a tangible difference was enticing. "Can we pull it off?"

Roman's lips quirked in a half-smile. "With our combined resources? I believe we can."

TWENTY-THREE

KY'RN

T he dim lighting from above cast shadows on the floor, and my reflection wavered in the water's surface as I continued my restless circuit around the tank. The rhythmic sound of water sloshing gently was a small comfort, but it did little to ease the weight in my chest.

Every time I closed my eyes, images of Isla danced in front of me.

Her presence had always been a soothing balm to my senses. It grounded me, gave me something tangible to hold onto.

But now, her absence was an open wound.

Every anxious tremor, every suppressed pang of fear I felt from her was like a vise around my heart.

An idea began to form in my mind. If tomorrow was to be the day of my departure, then tonight, I needed to communicate with her one last time. I had to make sure she was all right.

I closed my eyes, focusing my energy, trying to reach out to her, beckoning her toward me. The mark I had left on Isla was never meant to be a leash, but a sign of the bond we'd forged, one that few of my kind ever bestowed upon another.

I felt the distant flutter of her emotions, as if carried by the undercurrents of an ocean, but they were muted and distorted. I could sense her anxiety, her restlessness, but not the reasons behind them.

The uncertainty gnawed at me. I wanted to be there for her, to comfort her, to understand what was causing her distress. I had no means of approaching her, trapped in this place. The knowledge that she might be in some kind of danger, maybe even because of her connection to me, was agonizing.

I needed to see her. To look into her eyes and reassure myself that she was alright. The feelings I had developed for her were intense, overwhelming. This bond wasn't just a superficial connection. It was deep, soul-deep, and I feared that if something happened to her, it would shatter me.

I would not leave this planet without seeing her, without understanding the depth of our connection and why she affected me so. And if there was a threat lurking around her, I was ready to face it and protect her, no matter the cost.

A soft chime echoing in the chamber pulled me from my thoughts. When the doors slid open, I couldn't believe my eyes. Isla stood there, alone, dressed in a long, flowing purple gown that draped around her like a waterfall of amethyst. There was a strain on her face, and guilt lingered in her eyes. It worried me deeply, but she had come, and that was all that mattered.

With swift, determined movements, she went to the wall and retrieved the security device from her pouch. Once it was activated, she rushed over to the tank. Ignoring my hand pressed against the glass, she kicked off her shoes before darting up the stairs to reach me.

I jetted to the surface, eager to greet her at the ledge, and raised my hand toward her. She lifted the folds of her dress and knelt down, offering her hand to me.

"I had to see you." Our eyes met in a silent exchange. *"I called out to you. I needed to speak with you one last time,"* I admitted, my voice low and filled with longing.

Her gaze held mine, reflecting a storm of thoughts and feelings. *"Why does everything come back to you?"* Her mental voice trembled. *"There's so much happening and so much I wish I could tell you...I'd like to learn more about this mark and what's happening between us."*

"Speak to me," I implored, sensing her hesitation. *"Don't leave me in the dark when your emotions are laid bare to me."*

"I came to say goodbye," she murmured, tears filling her eyes. *"And to explain..."*

I felt a sharp pang in my chest. *"Goodbye? Why?"*

Isla hesitated, her gaze shifting away, as if the weight of her truths was too much to bear. She blinked back tears, and her grip on my hand tightened. *"There are politics at play, Ky'rn. Complex, dangerous games. Sometimes freedom comes at a cost. And to ensure the safety of my people, and yours...I have to be a pawn."*

My chest tightened at her words, a growing dread creeping in. *"Whose pawn? What have you done?"*

She hesitated, and the weight of unspoken words hung heavily in the air. *"I have a lot to say,"* Isla began, her voice tinged with uncertainty. *"I don't even know where to start."*

"I have time," I assured her, hoping to ease some of the apprehension that seemed to envelop her.

A small, sad smile played on her lips, although it didn't quite reach her eyes. She leaned closer, her curiosity shining through her somber mood. *"How about we start with this..."*

She sighed. *"Tell me about your family. Are they waiting for you on your home planet?"*

I leaned back slightly, considering her question. *"My parents are royal guards for our king and queen. They never leave their side, always at their Majesties' service."* I paused for a moment, my thoughts drifting. *"Even in times of peace. My sister, she's mated to a Krukken prince, living on another planet with his pod."*

Her eyes widened with interest. *"A Krukken?"* she echoed. *"Are they like the mythical creatures we humans have, the Kraken? Giant sea monsters with tentacles?"*

I nodded. *"The Krukken are similar to my kind—part humanoid, part tentacled sea creature."*

The corner of her lips tugged into a smile. *"That's fascinating. But, Ky'rn, don't you find it...unusual? Two beings from different species being together?"*

I shook my head. *"Love is love,"* I replied earnestly. *"When you spend your life on spy missions and battlefields, whom you choose to love doesn't matter so much."*

Her eyes softened. *"That sounds amazing,"* she replied wistfully.

Nostalgia washed over me as I remembered my home planet, its vast oceans, and the city that lay deep beneath its waves. The talk of family, especially my sister, brought a soft warmth to my chest.

"Isla, why do you ask about inter-species unions?" I probed gently, sensing her hesitation.

"It's...complicated," Isla admitted, her voice soft, her fingers lightly tracing patterns on my hand. *"It's just... humans can be so resistant to change, to things they don't understand. Here, on Earth, it's not always easy for two people of different races—let alone species—to be together. It's easier now than it used to be, but still our older genera-*

tions can be stuck in their ways. The idea of two beings from different worlds coming together will be taboo on Earth. There's so much fear—so much prejudice—that it may take generations to come to terms."

I tilted my head, considering her words. *"Why is that? Is it not the same essence of life, the same heartbeats, the same feelings that drive every living being? If people in a relationship care for each other and want to be together, why stand against it? How would our relationship hinder their lives?"*

She took a deep breath, her fingers playing with the hem of her gown, her eyes looking up at the fabric as if searching for answers. *"I think...it's the fear of the unknown. The fear that something might change us or challenge our beliefs. The cultures, the norms, the expectations. It's all so...limited. Hearing about your world, how accepting you are...it's hard to believe that it can be that easy."*

I moved closer, the water gently shifting with me. *"My world isn't perfect, Isla. We've had our own battles, our own differences to overcome. But change is inevitable, is it not? Planets evolve, species evolve, feelings evolve. Holding on to old prejudices seems...counterproductive."*

She looked down, her fingers now tracing the water's edge, causing gentle ripples. *"You make it sound so simple. But yes, you're right. Change is constant. I guess people fear they'll lose themselves in it."*

I gazed into her eyes, lost in their depths, as a question burned within me. *"What do you fear?"*

Her response was almost immediate, as if she had been holding onto this fear, waiting for someone to ask. *"Drowning,"* she confessed, and her cheeks flushed with embarrassment. *"But,"* she added quickly, *"I don't have to worry about that if I'm around you."*

A tender smile curled on my lips. *"Never,"* I assured her. *"I could breathe for the both of us, if necessary."*

She looked touched but a shadow of sadness crossed her features. *"I hope it never becomes necessary. Tomorrow, you'll be free to go home and reunite with your family and your people."*

I held her gaze, my hearts pounding in my chest. *"Tomorrow doesn't have to be a goodbye,"* I whispered, my voice laced with hope. *"You can come with me."*

For a moment, excitement danced in her eyes, but then she seemed to pull back, her expression conflicted. *"I can't."* She shook her head slowly. *"It can never be, Ky'rn. We could never be."*

My hearts stilled, and I frowned, my brows pinching. *"Why?"* I demanded, unable to hide the urgency in my voice.

"Because I have a duty," she started, her voice carrying the weight of her conviction. *"A duty I can't run from, Ky'rn. I've accepted it. It's the only way to stop my grandfather."*

Desperation welled up inside me, and I pressed her further. *"Isla, what would prevent you from coming with me? I'm a decorated commander. I have the money and power to care for and protect you. You don't have to stay on Earth."*

She shifted, lifting her gown enough to dip her legs into the water. I moved closer, slipping between her legs, my hands gently holding onto her, my gaze locked with hers. *"Please, tell me,"* I begged, desperation seeping into my voice. *"Tell me why you can't be with me."*

She sighed, and in that sigh, I heard the weight of her past, her burdens, and her unspoken pain. *"My mother was a genius,"* she began, her voice soft but laced with sorrow. *"She was the leading scientist responsible for engineering the next generation of plastic-eating algae, helping make our oceans cleaner. She was also working on eliminating other harmful chemicals in waste runoff. My father was well-respected too; he was a politician who fought tirelessly for my mother's cause, securing Earth's future for generations to come. When they died, they left me no instructions, only a legacy to protect."*

My hearts ached for her, understanding the profound loss she had suffered. *"Isla, what does that have to do with our relationship?"* I implored, unable to comprehend how her family's legacy could be a barrier to our being together.

"Everything," she replied, her voice heavy with resignation. *"I'm the heir to my family's highly respected and influential legacy, which includes our business. But, unfortunately, there's no spare."*

I furrowed my brow, puzzled. *"What do you mean?"*

"An heir and a spare," she explained, with a shrug. "Typically, the rules of succession only matter to royals. But families with a legacy and old money tend to follow them to prevent their family line from dying out. Unfortunately, my grandparents only had my mother, and my mother only had me. Both generations too busy with their careers, and they didn't want to add to the overpopulation of our planet when they were working on saving it."

"But how does that stop us from being together?" I sighed, pressing my forehead against hers. *"Why do you believe that we could never be? Am I not good enough? Is it because of our differences? Because I am not human?"*

She shook her head slowly, her eyes shimmering with unshed tears. *"No, Ky'rn. It's not that. It's not our physical differences or where we come from. It's…"* She paused, taking a deep breath, trying to find the right words. *"The expectations, the judgment. My grandfather, my family, my position. There are responsibilities and obligations that I can't just leave behind, no matter how much I wish I could."*

The pain in her voice was palpable, and her words hurt, but I wasn't one to give up easily. *"Then let's make it simple. Just for tonight. Forget the world outside this chamber. Forget the responsibilities, the obligations, the judgments. It's just you and me, Isla. Let's lose ourselves in this moment, in each other."*

She looked into my eyes, her resistance slowly melting away. *"Just for tonight."*

TWENTY-FOUR

ISLA

I couldn't bring myself to tell him, not now.

He was the only thing I wanted but could never truly have.

I couldn't leave my duties behind for him, and I refused to beg him to remain on Earth, not when he had been captured and tortured for a year here already. My grandfather, an unethical old man obsessed with power, was the reason Ky'rn was trapped in this tank.

As I gazed into those amber eyes filled with longing and desire, my resolve solidified. My first action as the new leader of my family would be this sacrifice.

I would do anything to protect this kind and honorable male even if it meant marrying Roman.

The words bore on the tip of my tongue—how I would have to bind myself to Roman, all to protect Ky'rn from further harm. But I didn't want to destroy this moment—my last with him—by telling him how I'd bought his freedom.

Unable to speak the words that ached in my chest, my hand trembled as I reached out to touch his cheek, tracing the strong lines of his jaw. *"Pretend that I am yours, just for tonight."*

He didn't hesitate, his fingers gentle as they brushed a strand of hair away from my face. A slow, gentle smile spread across Ky'rn's face. *"You were mine from the moment we met,"* he replied, voice deep and filled with possessiveness and longing. *"And no one else's."*

The depth of his declaration seeped into my bones, warming me from within. For tonight, I would allow myself to bask in that warmth, to forget the looming decisions and the sacrifices ahead.

Just for tonight, I was his. And he was mine.

Ky'rn's powerful grip on my legs pulled me into his tank, submerging me in the lukewarm water. My gown billowed around me, becoming a heavy, constricting mass. Panic threatened to set in, but then, strong arms encircled my waist, pulling me into the solid wall of Ky'rn's chest. The reassurance in his gaze grounded me.

As he pressed me to the tank's wall, every contour of his powerful form melded with mine. My fingers found the strong, sinewy ridges of his shoulders, pulling myself closer. My legs, almost of their own volition, wrapped around his waist, my heels digging into the small of his back. The sensation of being cocooned in his strength was heady, intoxicating. Every fiber of my being resonated with a singular thought: I was his.

His powerful tail thrummed against the current, keeping us both afloat.

Every ounce of me was electrified by his touch. The unyielding desire, the insatiable need to have and be had, coursed through me. I felt wild and untamed, wanting nothing more than to be consumed by the predator before me.

I needed him. I wanted him. I wished to be devoured by him.

His face nestled into the crook of my neck, lips seeking out the intimate mark he'd bestowed upon me. The sensation of his mouth on my skin was electrifying. I whimpered, fingers tangling in the wild mane of his hair, urging him closer, harder. As he sucked on the mark, a moan escaped me, the sound echoing in the chamber.

Every touch, every caress ignited sparks, threatening to set us both aflame.

"You smell divine," he rumbled, his voice dripping with hunger and need. *"I ache to taste you again, to feel you completely."*

His words sent a flare of desire through me.

My breath came out in ragged pants, the heat between us palpable. *"Then do it,"* I urged breathlessly, grinding against him in a silent plea. *"Take me, claim me, mark me as yours."*

A devilish smirk formed on his lips, revealing his fangs, as his amber eyes darkened with passion and locked on to mine. *"I want to fill your veins with ecstasy,"* he whispered seductively. *"To make your blood burn brighter, hotter… sweeter for me."*

The world spun in dizzying circles, my senses over-whelmed by the heady mix of desire and adrenaline. His strong grip on my thigh was the only thing grounding me, his touch a burning brand against my skin. *"Please,"* I whispered, a desperate plea for him to erase the looming choices, the impending goodbyes, and the responsibilities that would soon become mine to own.

His voice was husky with need, a hint of uncertainty shining through. *"How do I please you, Isla? How do I make you feel amazing?"*

A flush of heat raced up my cheeks, but the urgency of

my need silenced any lingering shyness. *"Use your hands,"* I murmured, the words coming out more like a moan. *"Explore me…you'll know when you've hit the right spot."*

A wicked grin spread across his face, the predatory gleam in his eyes sending shivers down my spine. *"Hold on,"* he commanded, right before he released me and dove beneath the water's surface.

Panic flared briefly as I lost his supporting hold, the weight of my soaked gown threatening to pull me under. I scrambled for the ledge, fingers grasping at the slick edge, trying to lift myself, to breathe.

But then, just as quickly as he had left, Ky'rn was back. His powerful chest pressed flush against my back, his arm snaking around me, holding me secure.

It was a primal gesture, one that spoke of possession and protection.

As I gasped for breath, his other hand snaked around my waist and slipped past the slit in my dress, fingers brushing the delicate lace of my thong.

His fingers were deft, exploring my folds through the lace of my thong and the warmth that lay beneath. I shuddered, arching into his touch, moaning softly as his hand began to move in earnest at a pace that set my pulse racing anew. All the while, his lips roamed over the sensitive column of my neck, each nip and kiss sending delicious tingles down my spine.

"Let go," he whispered huskily. *"Just feel, Isla."*

And I did.

Every sensation was magnified, from the press of his solid chest against my back to the rhythmic motion of his fingers against my core. The world narrowed to just the two of us, the heat of our passion, and the sensations he was drawing out of me. The weight of the day, the fears and anxieties that had plagued me, faded into the background, replaced by overwhelming pleasure.

The sensation of his mouth on my neck, teasing and tasting, combined with the deliberate strokes of his hand, was intoxicating. Every touch sent waves of pleasure radiating through me. I leaned back into him, giving in to the sensations, letting him guide me through the whirlwind of ecstasy. My moans mixed with the gentle lapping of the water, the sounds echoing in the chamber, amplifying the intimacy of the moment.

"Pretend we are on a beach," he murmured. *"White sands stretching as far as the eye can see, and waves of the most beautiful shade of lavender washing over them."*

I closed my eyes, letting the vivid image he painted envelop me. The cold confines of the chamber were replaced with the warmth of an exotic beach, the faint hum of machinery drowned by the rhythmic lull of waves. *"Tell me,"* I begged, my voice shaky with desire. *"Tell me what you're doing to me."*

His fingers, both rough and gentle, slid beneath the delicate fabric of my thong. The electrifying touch sent shockwaves through me as he expertly traced the contours of my most sensitive areas. When he found my clit, a jolt of pleasure surged through me, causing me to arch into his touch, a moan escaping my lips.

"I'm claiming you," he murmured, his tone deep and primal. *"Here, on this beach, with only the stars as our witnesses. I want to make you feel like you've never felt before, to make you mine in every way."*

His thumb began to make slow, deliberate circles on my clit, increasing in pressure with every pass. Every touch was calculated, each movement designed to push me closer and closer to the brink. The sounds of the imagined waves became louder in my ears, mirroring the building crescendo of my pleasure.

"Ky'rn," I gasped, my fingers clutching onto his arm, needing something, anything, to anchor me in the face of the overwhelming sensations. I pressed harder against him, craving more, wanting everything he could offer.

"Yes, my Isla," he responded, his voice filled with a possessive passion. *"Let go. Give in to me."*

I felt on the verge of something powerful, teetering on the brink of sweet release. With a strangled cry, I pushed back against him, seeking more.

My mind whirled with a mix of surprise and burgeoning need when I felt two hard lengths pressing against me. Each movement, each tiny shift sent a new wave of heat to crash over me, pooling deep within. My body reacted of its own accord, arching and grinding against him, desperate for more.

Ky'rn's growl vibrated through me, his warm breath ghosting over the shell of my ear. *"Stop teasing me, Isla,"* he warned, his voice laced with a need that matched my own. *"I refuse to take you here, in this cold tank. When I claim you, it will be somewhere I can fill you with my essence, let you feel all of me until you are lost in waves of ecstasy, seeing nothing but stars."*

His words made my pulse race, setting every part of me on fire.

"Know that you're mine," he whispered fiercely. *"And only mine. I'll make sure you never forget it."*

That possessiveness, the sheer intensity of his need, it made me wild with desire. I couldn't hold back any longer. *"I want you, Ky'rn,"* I moaned, pressing even more deliberately against him, feeling his hard lengths rub deliciously against my ass, only the fabric of my dress between us. *"I want to be free, truly free, with you."*

His growl of approval—deeper and more feral than before—vibrated through me as his fingers moved faster, more insistent against my clit. *"Then I will set you free, Isla. And in doing so, I'll make sure you know, deep down, that you are mine and mine alone."*

His fingers found that pulsing center of my pleasure and rubbed harder, pressing and swirling in a rhythm that had my world tilting on its axis.

The sensations were overpowering; I was on the edge, teetering. The pressure built to an almost unbearable level.

He bit down on my neck, marking me, while the hard lengths at my back pressed even more insistently against me.

Waves of pleasure, more intense than anything I'd ever felt, built up inside of me. My breath came in ragged gasps, and the edges of my vision began to blur. It was as though I was floating, lost in a sea of sensation, with only Ky'rn's touch to anchor me.

The coil of pleasure inside me wound tighter and tighter until I thought I might break from the intensity of it. And then, with one final, expert touch, it snapped.

I cried out, lost in the overwhelming tidal wave of ecstasy that washed over me. The world around me dimmed, and for a moment, everything faded to black as pleasure consumed me entirely.

TWENTY-FIVE

KY'RN

The feel of her body, the taste of her blood, the sound of her soft moans—they had all become imprinted in my mind. Every fiber of my being screamed for her, to claim her, to make her mine in every sense of the word.

The sensations of the night played over in my mind, and I reveled in the satisfaction of knowing I had brought Isla to the heights of pleasure.

Even though I had denied my own desires, the mere thought of her beneath me, of her delectable taste on my tongue, of her sweet sighs in my ears, filled me with a heady intoxication. Each drop of her blood I had tasted left me craving more, making me wonder just how it would taste when she truly became mine.

My mate.

My thoughts drifted toward fantasies of us together, away from prying eyes and the confinement of this tank. In the depths of the vast ocean or in a secluded vacation pod along the coast, I pictured us entwined, exploring one another, letting the hours melt away into days, lost in each other's embrace.

Drawing from my reverie, I carefully laid a sleeping Isla on the edge of the tank. Her dress, heavy with water, I wrung out and placed beside her.

I cradled her face gently, feeling the warmth of her skin against my palm as she leaned into my touch.

"Are you okay?" I asked, my voice a soft rumble filled with concern. The need to reassure her, to make her feel safe and cherished, surged within me.

Her gaze met mine, shimmering with unspoken emotions. *"More than all right,"* she whispered, a sense of wonder lacing her words. *"All of this feels like a dream. I keep thinking I'll wake up, and you'll be gone. This will be gone."*

My hand trailed down from her cheek to her neck, fingers tracing the outline of the mark I had just left there, feeling the heat of her pulse beneath my fingertips. The mark burned against her moonlight skin like a beacon, a symbol of our bond, a symbol of my claim and devotion.

Isla's reaction was immediate; her eyelids fluttered closed, and a soft moan escaped her lips, revealing the depth of her sensitivity to my touch. There was a vulnerability in that sound, a raw honesty that resonated within my soul.

"This is real, Isla," I assured her, my voice firm yet gentle. *"I am real, and so is our connection."* My eyes held hers, willing her to see the truth in them. *"You're not dreaming. Everything that's happened, our connection—it's all real. And it's too late to deny it."*

Slowly, she nodded, a small smile curving her lips.

"I am yours, Isla," I continued, my heart swelling with emotion. *"And you are mine. Forever."*

The words were a vow—a promise to cherish and protect her, to be by her side through whatever the future might hold.

"I wish..." A faint smile spread across Isla's lips as she let out a contented sigh.

Her eyelids fluttered closed, and she drifted off into a peaceful slumber, as her head lolled softly to the side, a serene expression painting her features.

Gently, I removed my hand from her delicate face, careful not to disturb her peaceful rest. As I gazed upon her, I found myself lost in thought, pondering the whirlwind of emotions and events that had brought us to this moment.

My heart swelled with a mix of pride and concern, knowing the challenges we would face together in our deeply intertwined relationship.

Watching her sleep, I pondered over her thoughts, her dreams. Was she finally at peace?

Had I gone too far?

The intensity of our connection, the depth of our bond—it was overwhelming, yet so right. But a part of me questioned if I had gone too far.

Her pleas had resonated deep within me, her desire to escape the weight of her past, to immerse herself fully in the here and now with me. How could I have denied her that solace? Her trust in me was absolute, her surrender complete.

Yet, a part of me questioned whether I had pushed the boundaries of our bond. The intensity of my desire for her, to claim her, to make her irrevocably mine, had been over-whelming. In that brief moment, it felt as though nothing else mattered but the fulfillment of our mutual longing.

But now, in the quiet aftermath, as I watched her sleep so soundly, a sense of responsibility settled over me. I vowed silently to always be there for her, to protect her, to provide her with the love and care she deserved. She had entrusted her heart to me, and I would guard it with my life.

If only we had more time… I cursed the Fates and the Will of the Stars for bringing us together in this manner.

Why couldn't our paths cross in another way? Why hadn't I carried her to the Atlantis, where she might be nursed back to health in the security of the IPA's base?

The rhythm of her breathing, the slight flush on her face, the peace that surrounded her, all held me captivated. My own body, however, was still in turmoil, a whirl of desires and primal urges. The very essence of me wanted to mate, to claim. Every cell in my being cried out for her.

My body responded immediately to those thoughts, my *blavs* twitching from the hunger that raged within.

Climbing up the edge, I sat beside her, letting my fingers brush the soft skin of her cheek. She stirred, her lips curving into a small smile. Even in her unconscious state, she responded to my touch, a soft moan escaping her lips.

With a deep sigh, I leaned down, pressing a soft kiss to her forehead, promising myself that I would find a way.

She was beautiful, not just in form but in spirit. The strength she carried, the burdens she bore, made her even more appealing.

But why did she seem so resigned?

She had spoken about her family's legacy, and the responsibility she carried, but was that the only thing keeping her from me?

Something else was holding her back.

Her eyes, even in their moments of passion, held an underlying sadness, a hesitancy I couldn't explain. I wanted to dive into the depths of her soul, uncover what fears lay hidden, and soothe them away. But no matter how hard I tried, she kept her secrets from me.

Dipping beneath the water's surface, I tried to cool the heat that burned through me. My blavs twitched.

Yet, something was holding her back, making her act as if this would be our last moment together—forever.

Frustration gnawed at me as I circled the tank, battling the insistent arousal that refused to ebb away.

Why did she push me away, when her soul reached out to me?

I surfaced, the cool water dripping from my face.

My gaze once again fixed on Isla. I wanted to shake her awake, to demand answers, to understand the walls she had erected around her heart. But deep down, I feared what those answers might be.

What if she genuinely believed our love was impossible?

Was it fear? Was it duty?

Or was it something deeper, something she hadn't shared with me?

The uncertainty of our future weighed heavily on my hearts.

Determined, I made a silent vow. Once I was free, I would return to Earth. I would seek her out, confront her, and fight for the love I believed we both deserved.

For now, watching her sleep, I clung to the hope I would find a way, that our destinies could be reshaped, and that Isla and I would find our place in each other's lives—together.

TWENTY-SIX

ISLA

I gasped, disoriented.

The remnants of my dreams, with its soothing lavender waves, were replaced by an imposing shade of dark blue, trapped behind transparent glass and cold metal. A rush of memories came back, sending me shooting up in realization.

The chamber. The tank. Ky'rn.

Panic surged within me as I realized where I was. I had fallen asleep after…after our stolen moment together.

I shot up, my heart pounding, my breath coming in ragged gasps. I couldn't believe how foolish I'd been, how I'd let my walls crumble and become vulnerable when it should have been just a goodbye, a single night of pretending.

"No, no, no," I muttered to myself, shaking my head to clear the fog of desire that clung to my thoughts.

Then, a splash sounded beside me, and I turned to find Ky'rn climbing out of the tank. He rested beside me, his majestic tail still in the water, like some high-prized merman statue crafted from marble, longing to whisk me away to a world where we could be together.

His hand found mine, his touch cool and yet reassuring, and then he leaned forward, cupping my cheek. His fingers were gentle against my skin, and I found my gaze being drawn to him, unable to resist. Those mesmerizing eyes mirrored my own internal battle. I swallowed hard, trying to find the words to articulate the whirlwind of emotions swirling within me.

"Isla," he rumbled, a soft vibration that sent shivers down my spine.

My heart hammered in my chest, each beat screaming how much I wanted him, but my mind was a battleground of emotions.

"Isla," he repeated, his voice laced with desperation. *"Talk to me. Tell me what's going on inside that head of yours."*

I swallowed, struggling with the storm of emotions threatening to consume me. *"I shouldn't have let things go so far,"* I whispered, feeling the weight of the words press down on me. *"I can't be here...with you."*

"Why do you pull away now? After what we've shared?" His words seemed to struggle past a barricade of hurt, each one underscored by a raw, aching bewilderment.

My heart ached, and I bit my lip, fighting back the tears. *"It's complicated,"* I whispered, feeling trapped by the emotions that surged within me.

"Talk to me, Isla. Help me understand," he pleaded, moving even closer. The space between us had dwindled to nothing, our breaths mingling, his musky scent surrounding me.

My heart raced, the closeness of him threatening to break down all my defenses once more. *"Ky'rn...I never intended for this to happen. I came to say goodbye. To let go and move on. But..."*

"But?" he prompted gently.

"But you make me feel things I never thought I could feel again. And it terrifies me. Because every time I've let someone in, I've been hurt," I admitted, tears now streaming down my face.

Ky'rn's eyes softened, and he drew me into his embrace, his chest firm against my head. *"I would never hurt you, Isla. I promise."*

Pulling back slightly, I searched his face for any hint of insincerity. But all I saw was raw honesty. *"How can you be so sure?"*

Panic bubbled in my chest. I had always been in control, always focused, but Ky'rn was a variable I hadn't been prepared for. I never thought I would see him ever again—that the phantom with the glowing amber gaze that haunted me whenever I was near water would return, splashing back into my life.

His grip tightened, fingers digging into my skin, the lines of confusion deepening on his face. *"Why, Isla? Why run away from this? From us?"*

The pain and confusion I saw there threatened to undo me. I took a shuddering breath, torn between the pain of pushing him away and the undeniable draw he had on me. *"Because I have to. Being here, with you…it's a mistake,"* I choked out, hating myself for how it sounded, for the hurt I knew I was causing.

"Do you regret it?" His mental voice was low, filled with an emotion I couldn't place. *"Do you regret us?"*

I blinked away the tears, shaking my head slowly. *"No, not us, never us. It's just…the timing, everything. We are in the wrong place at the wrong time."* I hesitated, searching for the right words. "I should've heeded your warning when you told me to forget about you, because I didn't know saying goodbye to you would hurt so much."

His fingers traced my jawline, causing goosebumps to erupt on my skin. *"What changed? Tell me, Isla. What is haunting you? What shadows are you running from?"*

My throat tightened, the weight of today pressed down on me. *"It's not you, Ky'rn,"* I whispered. *"It's the weight of responsibilities—of duties—I can't ignore. And as much as I want to be with you, as much as my heart aches for you. I wish...I wish things could be different."*

"You've already told me this! Let me in, Isla. What are you really afraid of?" He drew closer, his face inches from mine. *"I can afford to take care of you, and by using my position as a commander, I will be able to help grant you citizenship within the IPA, along with a home to reside in, away from here."*

I gazed into Ky'rn's eyes, a swirling pool of emotions churning within me. His face was so close, the warmth of his breath mingling with mine, his concern and determination clear in his intense gaze. His offer was generous, a lifeline for me to grab onto.

"It's not about your ability to take care of me or the life we could have." I swallowed hard, my throat tight. *"I have all the luxury in the world, but it can't buy me happiness... or love. I once made the mistake and thought I understood what love was, but the person I trusted my heart with tore it away... using my life as a bargaining chip to try to acquire a portion of my family's riches."* My gaze fell to his chest, unable to meet his stare. *"And that is when you found me.*

"There's a human saying that says enough money can buy you happiness, but what's the point of money, when people are willing to use and kill you over it?" I let out a shaky breath. *"As much as I want to cast everything aside, I'm*

afraid of trusting anyone, fearing that history will repeat itself once again."

Tears streamed down my face, and I felt the walls I had so carefully constructed begin to crumble once again. Deep down, I knew he was sincere, but my past held me prisoner. The weight of past betrayals, heartbreak, and loss bore down on me.

Ky'rn gave me a glimmer of hope, a possibility of a future where maybe, just maybe, I could forget about all my responsibilities and run away with him, not caring about the legacy forced upon me.

"You can trust me." He brushed away my tears with his thumb. *"Give me a chance, Isla. Give us a chance. We may be from different worlds, but our souls...they're connected. Can't you feel it?"*

I believed him. Perhaps it was the intimate connection of hearing his words, the gentle resonance of his voice, reverberating telepathically through my mind like a soothing lullaby, that convinced me of his sincerity.

I nodded slowly, my resolve wavering. *"I can. And that's what scares me the most."*

"Then why not come with me? Run away with me. Forget your legacy...and those who hurt you," he begged, his mental voice breaking, revealing the depth of his emotions. *"Come start a new life with me."*

"I can't!" The words came out sharper than I intended, and I saw the hurt in his eyes.

"Why?" he demanded, his eyes searching mine for answers.

I took a shaky breath. *"Because your freedom depends on it."*

His eyes, always so intense, darkened further. *"Explain."*

"I'm about to be married...to the man who has orches-

trated your freedom with your leaders. My wedding is today. I need to go."

Shock and hurt crossed his face so intensely that it felt like a physical blow. He backed away from me, his eyes drilling into mine, a depth of betrayal clouding them. *"No. You can't! Why?"*

I swallowed the lump in my throat. *"After today, my life debt will be paid."*

As I pulled away, he reached out, gripping my ankle, preventing me from fleeing. The weight of Ky'rn's gaze felt like a physical tether, trying to hold me in place. The sensation of his fingers brushing against my ankle felt like a desperate plea and made my heart clench in pain. *"I don't want my freedom if it costs you yours,"* he murmured, his voice thick with pain, like I'd shattered him.

I looked down, my vision blurred by tears. *"It's too late."*

His fingers grazed my ankle for a split second before I wrenched away, the ghost of his touch burning into my skin. I felt a part of my heart tear away with it.

"Isla!" He called out, his voice echoing in the chamber as I ran down the stairs.

The cold steel of the stairs bit into my feet as I made my descent, each step resounding. The weight of everything pressed heavily on my chest, making it harder and harder to breathe. Every instinct screamed at me to go back, to stay with Ky'rn, but duty and sacrifice compelled me forward.

"Isla!" he called again with a raw mixture of pain and disbelief.

As I reached the bottom of the stairs, I could feel his gaze on me, begging me to turn around—to return to him.

My discarded shoes were scooped up in haste. My fingers brushed over the security override device, knowing that once I deactivated it, there would be no going back.

Tears blurred my vision, but I forced myself to focus. I knew what I had to do. I deactivated the device, placing it in my pouch, and the heavy doors to the chamber began to open, revealing the empty lab.

"Isla!" His anguished voice reached out to me one last time.

I paused just before the door fully closed, taking one last look at the man—no, the alien male—who had changed my life in ways I could never have imagined. His eyes, once bright with hope and longing, were now shadowed with despair.

"I'm so sorry," I whispered, my voice breaking.

With a resounding thud, the doors shut, cutting off my view of Ky'rn.

TWENTY-SEVEN

ISLA

My white gown cascaded around me, glinting with the gentle sheen of silk strands. It had been meticulously picked out for me…like everything else that had to do with my life. The intricate beadwork shimmered with every movement, reminding me of the sun's reflection on water.

Supposedly, a wedding day was the highlight of one's life. But mine? It felt like an elaborate play, one in which I was the lead but had no say in the script.

The entire affair had been arranged by my grandfather, all in a bid to further our family's legacy. The fact that the only thing I could choose were the wedding colors was testament to how little control I had over my life.

The pale lavender and deep blues were my silent nod to the ocean, to Ky'rn.

I paced the luxurious waiting room, its grandeur mocking me. The thick plush carpets, the ornate furniture—the room's lavish decorations felt like a gilded cage. Perhaps that was exactly what it was.

Every step felt like a countdown. A countdown to a life I didn't choose.

Now I understood the heroines in those fantasy novels I used to lose myself in. That feeling of impending doom, the realization that the climax of the story was nigh.

Only there was no hero to save me from this.

I wandered over to the expansive window, my eyes drawn to the vast ocean spread out before me. Somewhere beyond that horizon, Ky'rn's people awaited his return. A pang of longing pierced my heart.

A knock disrupted my thoughts, and the massive wooden door swung open to reveal my grandfather, dressed impeccably. "It's time," he announced.

I inhaled deeply, willing a facade of calm and happiness over my face. Turning to him, I stretched my lips into the broadest smile I could muster, even though every fiber of my being screamed that I should be anywhere else.

My heart felt as if it was deep in that tank with Ky'rn.

"You look radiant, my dear," he said, his eyes scanning me. "Your parents, and your grandmother, they would be so proud."

The mere mention of my parents brought a sting to my eyes. "I miss them," I whispered, my voice breaking, thinking of the family I'd lost.

He stepped closer, his weathered hand touching my cheek. "I miss them too. Every single day." His face softened, a rare sight. "But know that they are smiling down at you right now."

He then offered his arm, and I took it. Every step felt like a march toward my own personal guillotine.

As we approached the ornate garden doors leading to the venue, he leaned closer. "Once this is over, I can finally retire," he murmured, the weight of his years evident in his voice. "And then, it'll be your turn to make new heirs and continue our legacy."

"Let's just get through today first," I quipped, trying to keep my voice steady, "before thinking about babies."

The mention of children, of heirs, seemed so absurd at the moment.

He chuckled, giving my hand an affectionate pat.

We paused before the garden doors, the sounds of the ceremony beyond faintly reaching us. "I'm proud of you, Isla. Remember to do your part. Bring honor to our family."

The garden doors swung open, revealing the vast assembly awaiting my entrance.

The moment I set foot outside, the live orchestra transitioned seamlessly into the classic wedding march. Every note resonated with years of tradition, echoing with the weight of the ceremony.

The garden itself was breathtaking. A wide expanse of meticulously manicured lawns spread out, with delicate flowers of every hue blooming in carefully designed patterns. The aroma was a gentle blend of roses, jasmine, and lilies. Ethereal fairy lights floated above, illuminating the setting with a soft golden hue. In the middle of the garden, a crystal platform rose slightly off the ground. It was upon this platform that the ceremony would take place.

Beyond the garden, the vast expanse of the ocean stretched, its waves shimmering under the gentle caress of the setting sun. The backdrop of the cerulean waters only added to the enchantment of the setting. Elegant white chairs with sapphire-colored cushions were lined neatly for the guests. Each chair had a small holographic projector, which I knew would display close-ups of the ceremony for each guest.

As I walked, my grandfather's arm providing support, I couldn't help but glance at the many faces that filled those seats. Strangers, diplomats, business moguls—their presence was a testimony to the importance of this union.

Standing on the crystal platform was Roman. With chiseled features, a strong jawline, and bright blue eyes, he was undeniably attractive. His grin was infectious, reaching all the way to his eyes, making him appear genuine and warm.

If my heart hadn't been irrevocably lost to Ky'rn, maybe Roman could've been a possibility.

The marriage officiant, poised and confident, looked striking in her violet pantsuit. The sapphire vest and bowtie added a touch of elegance to her attire. Her blonde hair was slicked back into a pristine bun, and her eyes sparkled with anticipation as she flashed me a welcoming smile.

Ahead on my left stood Dr. Violet, her royal purple gown flowing and shimmering with every movement, the hue complementing her name perfectly. As I approached the platform, she reached out gracefully, taking my bouquet with a reassuring smile.

The officiant cleared her throat, the soft sound magnified through the garden's natural acoustics. "Ladies and gentlemen, we are gathered here today to witness the union of two illustrious families. Two legacies coming together in the hopes of a brighter, united future."

Throughout the ceremony, the officiant emphasized unity and legacy. We recited the generic vows—promises of honor, unity, and commitment. Every word I spoke, every promise I made, felt empty. The future was being decided for me, but the thoughts of Ky'rn and the life I truly desired haunted me.

As the officiant declared, "You may now exchange the rings and seal this union," my gaze involuntarily drifted toward the vast ocean, wondering if Ky'rn was able to escape and where he might be.

Roman's fingers were cool and firm as they clamped

around my wrist, and the proximity of his lips by my ear made the hairs on the back of my neck stand on end.

"Remember how I told you not to blindly trust people, especially me?" My heart raced in tandem with his whispered words, their intent clear as day.

Startled, I jerked back slightly, only to meet his smug expression. He drew out a ring from within the depths of his jacket. As it slid onto my ring finger, his eyes bore into mine —a challenge, a dare.

The moment was suddenly disrupted.

The ground beneath us trembled, a low rumbling escalating into a deafening roar. It felt as though the very heart of the earth was in revolt. The serene garden, moments ago a haven of beauty and sophistication, descended into chaos. The fairy lights swayed violently, and the magnificent blooms were uprooted in the quake. Guests screamed, their terrified cries echoing in the air as they scrambled in panic, their finery forgotten.

Roman's grip on my hand never wavered as he swiftly pulled me away from the chaos, navigating through the mayhem with an unsettling calm.

"What's happening?" I yelled over the cacophony, trying to keep pace with his long strides.

He shot me a sly grin as we entered a concealed workers' passage. "Take a wild guess."

Whirling him around, I pressed him against the cold wall, retrieving the gun from my gown's hidden pocket. "Stop playing games and tell me! What have you done?"

His laughter echoed eerily in the tight corridor. "Consider it my wedding gift to you. I ensured Ky'rn's chamber was demolished, enabling his escape."

Rage bubbled within me. "You used explosives? When I could have released him peacefully after the ceremony?"

His gaze was unwavering. "The ceremony was for theatrics. Once our contracts were signed, they were binding. This facility's cruel experiments on alien life needed to be stopped. That meant destroying all the labs."

"Why the charade? The wedding?"

He raised an eyebrow. "To placate our families, we had to appear as if we were to wed."

"Are we not?"

His laugh was mocking. "No. Our businesses are entwined, but we, dear Isla, are not married."

"Why?" My voice wavered, a mix of confusion and desperation.

"Because," he said, "I knew you didn't desire this union. Ky'rn made it abundantly clear to his leaders that he wished for you to accompany him."

Reality seemed to bend, the weight of his words almost too much to bear. My grip on the gun slackened, and my arm fell to my side in shock.

He leaned in, his voice soft. "Put away your weapon and come with me. There's a boat waiting."

I hesitated for just a moment, then complied. As he grabbed my hand, leading me deeper into the passage, he called over his shoulder, "You deserve your freedom, Isla. Let's claim your happy ending."

TWENTY-EIGHT

KY'RN

Every beat of my dual hearts resonated with pain so profound that it threatened to tear me apart, agonizing over her sacrifice. My thoughts were consumed with an overwhelming mixture of bewilderment and rage.

The human custom of arranged marriage—of mating someone just to further their goals or maintain appearances—was a concept so foreign, so incomprehensible to me. How could her species, one that had journeyed across the stars, still be ensnared in such archaic practices? Did the expanse of the cosmos not teach them the value of freedom?

The recollection of Isla's distant demeanor during our recent encounters now made an aching kind of sense. Had she been steeling herself for this impending union, this unwilling sacrifice, for my sake?

The very thought of her being shackled to another made my blood boil.

I paced restlessly. The cool water currents against my scales did little to soothe the fire of betrayal burning within me, directed not only at the humans but also at my own leaders.

I had naively believed that my leaders would not agree to such a perverse trade. The thought that they had sanctioned this forced union was a betrayal I couldn't fathom. What had they been promised? What twisted agreement had they made?

What was my freedom worth to them, that they'd willingly let Isla be chained to another?

Every fiber of my being roared in outrage.

Isla. My precious Isla, who had become my everything since I'd come across her bound form that fateful night.

She was the one. The one who consumed my thoughts, the one who appeared in my dreams, the one who had awakened a deep yearning in me I hadn't known existed.

From the very first moment I sensed her presence, she had stirred something deep within me, an ancient and primal connection. A bond I could neither explain nor resist. She was not merely an obsession; she had become the very essence that fueled my existence.

Her laughter, her tears, the way her spirit blazed with defiance and strength—everything about her had intertwined with the core of my being. The taste of her blood, shared in a desperate moment, had sealed the unbreakable bond between us.

Her essence, her very lifeblood, flowed through me and gave me strength.

The mere thought of her bound to another male, not of her choosing, tore me asunder. And now, the knowledge that she was willing to give up her freedom for mine was a weight too heavy to bear.

I closed my eyes, memories of our time together flooding back. The way her mental voice danced in my mind, the shimmer in her eyes when she looked at me, the warmth of her skin.

Every moment was etched into my very soul. And with each memory, my resolve solidified.

I would not—could not—let this stand. The universe be damned, I swore upon the Stars themselves that I would come back for her. I'd tear apart galaxies, challenge any foe, and defy our leaders if it meant saving her from a life she didn't choose—to save her from the gilded cage she'd been imprisoned in.

Isla deserved more than a life bound by expectations and politics. She deserved freedom, love, passion—the kind of love I was desperate to give her.

And one day, I vowed, I would return and whisk her away from it all. I would save her—once again—just as she had once saved me.

A life for a life—because a life without her wasn't worth living.

The world erupted around me.

A cacophony of deafening destruction, followed by explosions and the groan of metal being contorted.

Thunderous booms echoed through the base, causing the walls to shake violently. As I surfaced from the water's depths, my eyes were met with a scene of utter chaos.

Dust clouded the air, choking my senses, the sharp scent of smoke and burnt metal biting into my nostrils. The overhead lights flickered, hesitating for a moment in their dim, ghostly glow before plunging the base into complete darkness.

The eerie quiet that followed was broken only by the sound of glass shattering. Then a torrent of water gushed in from every direction, submerging everything in its path.

Instincts kicked in as I navigated through the wreckage,

agile and swift despite the treacherous surroundings. Massive pillars crumbled around me, metallic structures gave way, sending shards of glass and metal flying in every direction. Dodging falling debris and chunks of metal, I made my way through the rapidly flooding base. With every second, the pressure increased, threatening to crush the facility and everyone inside.

In the distance, an alarm wailed its mournful lament, a dirge for the dying facility.

The swirling currents tugged at me, pulling me toward safety, toward freedom.

Confusion clouded my mind. What was causing this destruction? Was this part of a plan or an unfortunate side effect?

And the most distressing question: Would Isla truly sanction something like this?

The woman who had shown me such kindness, such warmth, could she be part of this chaos? My heart refused to believe it.

Despite my instincts telling me she wouldn't willingly partake in such a calamitous scheme, doubt gnawed at me. I struggled to piece everything together.

Voices reached out to me through the murky water. They were familiar, filled with joy and relief. *"Commander Ky'rn!"* they cried. *"You're free! Come, brother, rejoin us!"*

They beckoned me, urging me to join them and return to Atlantis for a flight home. But their words, their jubilation, meant nothing to me. Not when the only voice I yearned to hear was absent. Freedom meant nothing if she wasn't part of it.

My hearts tightened, each thud echoing my growing dread.

Instead of heading toward safety, I ignored their calls, and turned around, facing the imploding structure of the base.

Isla.

Was she safe?

The thought of her trapped within that disintegrating tomb, surrounded by collapsing walls and rising waters, consumed me. The idea that she might be hurt—or worse—clawed at my chest, causing my dual hearts to race in frantic desperation.

"Isla," I called out into the dark waters. *"Where are you?"*

TWENTY-NINE

ISLA

Chaos was everywhere.

The piercing sound of screams intermingled with the sharp echo of collapsing walls. Each footstep reverberated with urgency as Roman and I dashed down the ancient stone cliffside staircase. The air was thick with dust and acrid smoke, but the most haunting sound was that of the screams—distant, echoing cries of terror and despair.

The world around me seemed to be falling apart, but the solid stone under my feet remained defiantly intact, leading me to the sole surviving refuge—the dock.

As we made our way down, my heart raced at the sheer scale of the devastation. The beautiful research center, once carved seamlessly into the cliffside, now lay in ruins. Only the old museum tower stood, its tall silhouette casting a long shadow over the destruction below. Its untouched state was a testament to its enduring strength amidst chaos.

Surveying the dock, I could see the aftermath of the devastation on the once proud fleet of ships. The closer vessels lay broken and battered, their hulls crushed under fallen rubble. But further out, a few ships bobbed, still anchored and intact. Even further out, untouched by the destruction, a small array of vessels floated serenely on the water, including a sleek, modern yacht that stood out from the rest.

"That's mine," Roman said, pointing toward the yacht, his voice breathless. "We'll be safe once we're on board. It's equipped for any situation. The crew is prepared for international waters. They'll get you to Ky'rn."

We quickened our pace, the promise of safety spurring us on. As we approached the yacht, Roman bellowed instructions to the onboard staff. But once we set foot on the ramp, a figure emerged from the shadows, moving with predatory swiftness.

Before I could process what was happening, the figure violently struck Roman with the butt of a pistol. He crumpled to the floor, pain etched across his face.

I reached instinctively for my own gun, ready to defend us, but another shadow blindsided me. A sharp pain flared at the side of my head, and my vision blurred.

The last thing I registered was the cold, hard deck beneath me as the fading cries and the roaring sea became distant, muffled sounds.

A throbbing pain pierced my head, pulling me back from the abyss of unconsciousness.

Soft fabric cradled my body. My eyelids felt heavy as I forced them open, revealing the unfamiliar surroundings of an opulent bedroom.

The room seemed to blend the old and the new, with intricate wooden carvings lining the walls and state-of-the-art tech seamlessly incorporated. But it wasn't the luxurious decor that captured my attention—it was the rippling waves against the evening sky visible through the massive windows. The gentle swaying beneath me was unmistakable. I was on a moving boat.

Despite the room's allure, dread rapidly overtook me.

With great effort, I pushed myself to a seated position, cradling my aching head in my hands. Flashes of memory hit me in rapid succession—the joyless wedding, the deafening explosions, the frantic dash to the dock, and that cold, brutal assault that had left Roman and I defenseless.

A sick feeling of dread twisted my gut, and a cold sweat broke out on my forehead. My breaths became rapid, shallow. Despair bored down, threatening to break me.

Desperate hope made me glance once again at the vast expanse of water outside. The boat's rapid movement, cutting through the waves, left me feeling isolated and vulnerable.

My fingers fumbled along the soft fabric of my gown until they found the familiar weight of my concealed gun. Relief surged, momentarily pushing the fear away. My trusty gun, nestled safely in my gown's hidden pocket, was a glimmer of hope I could cling to.

I took several deep breaths, fighting back the rising tide of panic. I couldn't afford to let fear immobilize me. Not now. The chaos back at the compound meant that no search party would be coming for me anytime soon. Search and rescue would be tied up for days, if not weeks. The likelihood of anyone coming to find me was slim to none.

Guilt gnawed at me. The faceless employees, the innocent souls who may have perished in the explosions—my heart ached thinking of the possible loss of life because of Roman's recklessness.

Drawing strength from the anger simmering within, I slid off the bed and steadied myself. I would have to be cautious, clever, and ready for anything.

I was alone, truly and utterly, with possibly dangerous captors. And the only person I could rely on to navigate through this storm was myself.

The weight of the gown had been both a curse and a blessing. Its layers and layers of silk and tulle had hidden my weapon, but it slowed me down, hindering mobility. It had to go.

Laying my pistol on the bed, I hastily removed the intricately embroidered overskirt and its accompanying underskirts. The layers fell away, each one a weight lifted. When I was finally down to my bridal shapewear, I felt oddly vulnerable yet liberated. Free from the confines of the dress, I was more agile, more capable of defending myself.

I bundled the discarded layers together, shaping and molding them in the dim light until they resembled a figure curled up on the floor—hopefully, at first glance, it would look like me.

Armed with my gun once more, I took a moment to strategize, eyeing the door to the en suite bathroom just across from my makeshift decoy. A plan began to form. The idea was risky, perhaps even foolish, but I couldn't afford to sit here passively, waiting for enemies to come for me.

While the boat was large enough to house several people, I was banking on the assumption that it wasn't too crowded. This wasn't a massive ship; it was more personal, more intimate. And in close quarters, if I had the advantage of surprise on my side, the odds might just tip in my favor.

If I could make it seem like I was vulnerable and attempting to contact the outside world, it might be enough to bait one of them in. From there, I could attempt an ambush.

Creeping over to the bathroom door, I left it slightly ajar, enough for an intruder to see a sliver of my silhouette and hear a fake, trembling conversation, but not enough for them to see my prepared ambush.

My heart hammered in my chest. Fear was a dangerous thing, but it was also a powerful motivator. I steadied my breathing, forcing the rising panic down. If I wanted to get off this boat alive, I had to be brave. I had to be cunning.

With my back pressed against the cold tiled wall and my gun aimed at my gown, I waited.

Whatever happened next, I knew one thing—I wouldn't be a victim. Not again.

I sobbed into the air, echoing around the confines of the room. "Grandpa? Oh, Grandpa, please, you have to help me!" I infused my voice with all the terror and distress I could muster, hoping to sound believable. "I'm so scared…I don't know where I am. They've taken me."

Without warning, the door resounded with a powerful banging. My heart leapt into my throat.

Then a voice, familiar yet dreaded, pierced the air. "Shut up, Isla! Or I swear I'll come in there and make you!" Sam's voice, dripping with venom, froze me momentarily.

I pushed through and called out again, letting the sound of desperation paint the illusion. The more I cried, the more convinced he would be. I could almost see the smug satisfaction in his eyes, thinking he had me cornered, weak and defenseless.

"Please, Grandpa…Please save me," I whimpered, amplifying my feigned crying, making it sound like Sam's threats had broken me even further.

The door crashed open with violent force, and Sam, dressed in a black worker's uniform, lunged toward the bunched-up gown in the corner, assuming I lay underneath.

Hatred emanated from him as he approached, thinking he had the upper hand. He snarled at the pile of fabric.

"I told you to shut up!" he roared, drawing his leg back, preparing to deliver a vicious kick.

But he never got the chance.

Without hesitation, I burst into the room and pulled the trigger twice in quick succession. The deafening sound of gunfire rang out, and the back of Sam's head exploded. Blood and gore splattered onto the white walls, painting the grim picture of his fate. His lifeless body crumpled forward, landing heavily on the bed, burying the gown beneath him.

I took a few shaky breaths, the realization of what I'd done sinking in.

There was no time to dwell on it, though. Others would have heard the gunshots, and I needed to act quickly. Whatever connection Sam had to all of this, it was now clear this wasn't just a random kidnapping. This was personal.

And Rose was most likely on board, too.

The rush of the moment still held me in its grip, sharpening every detail and heightening every sensation. The faint lapping of water against the boat's hull, the muffled cries in the distance, and the metallic tang of blood in the air—all of it was intensified by the adrenaline coursing through my veins.

Then Rose burst into the room, a whirlwind of fury. Her face contorted in confusion and shock as she scanned the room, registering the blood-soaked figure of Sam sprawled on the bed.

"Why, Sam? Why'd you have to ruin my fun?" she cried with petulant anger. Then she saw his mangled head and the horror set in. "Sam!" she screamed, rushing to him, shaking him desperately as if she could wake him from the deepest of slumbers.

As she knelt by Sam's side, trying to shake some life back into his limp form, I stepped forward, my gun still in hand and aimed at her, every line of my body radiating a warning. "Sam won't be waking up, Rose," I declared, icily calm. "And soon, neither will you."

Whipping around to face me, her face paled, her eyes wide with fear that quickly morphed into defiance. "You won't do it, Isla," she spat. "You don't have the guts."

"I can." Drawing upon all the past pain and betrayals, I replied, "By ending you, I can erase every betrayal, every lie you spread about me."

She shook her head desperately, tears brimming. "It wasn't my fault! Sam…he forced me. You know I'd never hurt you. Please, Isla, if there's any part of our past friendship left in you, let me go."

I coldly met her gaze. "Fool me once, shame on you. Fool me twice, shame on me. But a third time? Not in this lifetime."

She dropped to her knees, desperation clear in every line of her face. "Please, Isla," she begged, her voice breaking. "I never meant to take Sam from you. It just happened."

A bitter laugh escaped me. "You think this is about the fiancé you stole from me? Take him." I pointed at Sam's life-less form. "What's left of him, anyway. This is about every time you used me, every lie you told, every wound you inflicted."

"Remember our friendship. All the times we laughed, cried, shared secrets," she stammered. "You were always forgiving, Isla. Always the one to see the good in people."

"No," I corrected her. "I used to be. But after the things you've done to me, there is no forgiveness left."

Her desperate eyes locked onto mine as I kept the gun aimed steadily at her forehead. "Please," she whispered, tears streaming down her face. "I never wanted it to be like this."

But I wasn't swayed. "My biggest regret was ever considering you a friend. For letting you use me for your gain and alienate me from everyone."

"Don't, Isla," Rose sobbed, her voice breaking.

As I stared into her tear-filled eyes, her pleading gaze searching mine, a surge of disgust washed over me. "Cry yourself an ocean, Rose, and drown in it."

Without a moment's hesitation, I pulled the trigger.

Two shots rang out, echoing in the confined space. Blood sprayed, painting red splatters across the opulent room. Rose's body fell lifelessly, landing eerily on top of Sam's feet, her blood mingling with his on the ruined fabric of my wedding gown, now stained with the indelible mark of betrayal and vengeance.

The aftertaste of adrenaline still lingered in my mouth, my breaths heavy. The gun in my hand felt heavier than before, and my heart was still thudding against my chest when the boat lurched.

The sudden movement caught me off guard, and my feet struggled to find purchase on the slick, bloodstained floor. A deafening roar filled the air, and I was violently thrown off balance. The world spun, the walls and ceiling blurring together as a tremendous explosion rocked the vessel.

The force of the impact was like a punch to the gut. As if in slow motion, I watched the rich décor of the yacht splinter and shatter around me. The world outside was a blur, but the horrific screech of metal on metal was unmistakable. There was an ear-splitting explosion, and the very structure of the boat disintegrated.

Suddenly, I was submerged in the biting cold of the ocean. Icy tendrils wrapped around my body, dragging me deeper into its abyss. The world above was a whirlwind of chaos; fiery debris rained down, the fragments of the boat setting the water's surface ablaze. Flashes of searing pain shot through my limbs as the saltwater made contact with my fresh wounds.

Panic took hold as the saltwater stung my eyes and filled my nostrils. Every instinct screamed at me to kick, to push upward, to break the surface and take a breath. But the weight was too much, the dizziness too overpowering.

As I struggled, visions of the burning ship flickered before my eyes—flames dancing on the water's surface, the boat reduced to a flaming skeleton. Desperate gasps for air resulted in sharp stings as saltwater filled my lungs.

Amidst the chaos, a floating wooden door came into view, bobbing in the violent waves. With what little strength I had left, I reached out, trying to grab hold of it. My fingers grazed its rough surface, but I could barely hold on, unable to lift myself out of the icy waters.

Every muscle burned, screaming in protest as I tried to hold on tight and fight against the undertow.

The world darkened around me, my vision narrowing to a mere pinprick. I felt myself drifting, the cold numbing my senses and the sounds of the roaring fire and crashing waves fading into the distance.

The night sky stretched above me, an endless canvas of twinkling stars, their light shining like beacons in the vast darkness.

My vision began to blur, the stars melding together into a hazy river of light. I reached out with my mind, desperate to connect with Ky'rn one last time. *"Ky'rn,"* I thought, my mental voice weak but filled with emotion, *"I'm sorry. Please, survive this. Live... for both of us."*

Tears mingled with the saltwater, blurring my view even

further as I struggled to maintain consciousness. My body felt heavy, my grip on reality slipping as surely as my physical grip on the world around me.

The coldness of the water began to seep into my bones, a stark contrast to the warmth of Ky'rn's embrace that now felt like a distant memory. The darkness beneath the surface beckoned, its icy tendrils wrapping around me, pulling me under.

My hand weakly reached out, as if I could touch the celestial bodies that now seemed so far away. The world above slipped away as I sank beneath the surface, the starry sky replaced by the dark, enveloping waters.

As I drifted into the abyss, my last thought was of Ky'rn. His face, his touch, the way he made me feel whole. I wished for him to know peace, to find happiness in the life that stretched out before him. A life that, heartbreakingly, I could no longer share.

As I sank, I made my last wish, a silent plea to the universe: *"Let him be safe. Let him find happiness."*

And then, the cold darkness enveloped me completely, seeping into my bones, as the ocean claimed me in its silent embrace.

THIRTY

KY'RN

The emotions rippled through our connection with an intensity that left me breathless—panic, fear, anger. It was a cacophony of raw feelings, and though I was used to sensing the emotions of my kin, Isla's were the loudest and clearest of all.

I could feel her.

Her spirit pulsed brightly through our connection, her soul screaming out in the vast expanse of the ocean.

She was alive—but she was also in danger. My entire being responded to that call, urging me to move, to save her.

Closing my eyes, I tried to shut out all distractions and hone in on that tether that linked our souls.

The direction was unclear at first, but something primal within me—my predatory instincts—pulled me away from the flaming wreckage, urging me to move faster, to venture into open waters.

Without hesitation, I accelerated, propelling myself through the water with swift, powerful strokes. I yearned to find her, to wrap her in my arms, to shield her from the horrors she was facing.

It wasn't long before I crossed paths with two familiar figures, both streaking through the water with grace and purpose. Scout Ephi, her deep blue scales adorned with silver markings, met my gaze with worried teal eyes. Beside her, Scout Daixa, her emerald scales contrasting with bronze hair, regarded me with steely determination, her silver eyes evaluating the situation.

"Commander Ky'rn!" Ephi exclaimed, relief evident in her voice. *"We've been searching for you! The destruction... it's everywhere."*

Daixa, ever the stoic, got straight to the point. *"You're finally free. Let us escort you to Atlantis. Our people are waiting for your arrival."*

Their intentions were noble, and under any other circumstances, I would've accepted their aid, but Isla was out there, and she needed me.

"I appreciate your offer," I replied, urgency lacing my voice. *"But I cannot go to Atlantis now. There's someone important I need to find, someone who's in trouble because of me."*

Ephi and Daixa exchanged glances, sensing the urgency in my words.

Ephi's brows furrowed in confusion. *"Who do you need to find?"*

But Daixa's eyes narrowed, reading the desperation in mine. *"You're talking about the female human, aren't you? The one you've bonded with."*

I nodded. *"Yes. Her name is Isla,"* I replied, worry bleeding into my voice. *"I can feel her fear. Her anger. I can't just abandon her, especially not now."*

Ephi hesitated for a moment then nodded resolutely. *"We'll help you find her."*

Daixa's steely gaze met mine. *"Then let us waste no more*

time. Lead the way, Commander."

With newfound determination, the three of us set out into the vast ocean, racing against time to find the one person who meant more to me than anything.

The ocean stretched before us, but as we swam, the pull of the bond between Isla and me grew ever stronger. There was a tethered pull, an undeniable force guiding me toward her, drawing closer with each powerful stroke.

Suddenly, the taste of her blood—a unique flavor I'd never forget—permeated the water, a scent that made my primal hunter instincts flare to life. I could taste every drop of her essence mixed with the saltwater—a taste that made my heart ache and sent a bolt of panic through me.

I sped up, pushing my body to its limits, allowing instinct to guide me. Ephi and Daixa followed closely, their expressions grave. My energy began to wane, but the emotions coursing through me—concern, fear, determination—kept me moving at a relentless pace.

The sight that met me was one I'd never forget.

The shattered remnants of a vessel floated aimlessly, contrasting starkly against a massive ocean buoy. But amid the chaos, my eyes found her.

Isla, my cherished Isla, was there—floating just beneath the water's surface, ethereal and serene. Her hand outstretched toward the sky, she seemed to be reaching for the stars, a silent plea to the Fates to save her.

Cradled by the gentle embrace of the sea, her frail form danced with the rhythm of the waves. She was adorned in a body-tight suit, the white fabric marred with crimson tales of her ordeal, whispering secrets into the water that called to the creatures lurking in the deep. Her body, a canvas of fresh bruises and gashes, spoke of her recent trials. Yet, it was the wound on her forehead, from which life's essence freely flowed, painting a poignant picture of her struggle beneath the moonlit sky.

With a surge of adrenaline, I propelled myself through the churning water, cradling her frail form. My arms ached as I dragged her frail figure to the surface, hugging her tightly. As we broke the surface, her wet locks clung to her face while she coughed up salty seawater. The waves crashed against us, but I held her securely, sheltering her from the relentless ocean waves.

Tenderly, I combed back her hair, finding the mark I had given her and resting my fingers there to feel a weak, yet steady pulse—a frail thread to life.

"Isla," I pathed softly. *"I've got you."*

Though weak, she managed a feeble smile, pressing closer into me. Her mental presence dimmed, but she was still very much alive, and I held onto that knowledge like a lifeline.

Scout Ephi swam closer, her eyes wide with concern. *"Is she...?"*

"She lives," I confirmed, holding Isla tightly against me. *"But she's unconscious."*

Scout Daixa's sharp warrior's gaze studied the wreckage, assessing the situation. *"There are three other bodies,"* she noted with clinical detachment. *"But it appears two died before the explosion."*

"And the third?"

Daixa approached a figure floating in the water, garbed in black and clinging desperately to a floating white ring. As she reached out and touched his shoulder, the male jerked awake, his eyes wide with panic and confusion.

· · ·

Words spilled from him like a torrent, and his native language was a garbled mess to my ears. His gaze locked onto Isla cradled protectively in my arms, and a primal growl rumbled deep within me.

My fangs bared in warning. I instinctively turned Isla away to shield her from him, blocking her body from his reaching hands.

"What's he saying?" I growled, my voice a low rumble of barely contained fury.

Daixa, with a swift and aggressive motion, secured the man, her arms locking under his, pulling him close. *"He claims she is his wife, his mate,"* she spat out, her disgust palpable. *"He declares sanctuary and demands that we take him to Prince Rivu."*

As the harsh words tumbled from their lips, my body recoiled as if struck by an invisible hand. My heart ached with feelings of betrayal and hurt, threatening to overwhelm any rational thoughts. My instincts screamed to abandon him to the sea, to let the waters claim him as they had almost claimed Isla.

But I couldn't—her last words echoed in my mind, a haunting refrain of her sacrifice and duty. She'd stated he was the key to my freedom, the one who orchestrated the sacrifice she'd been obliged to make.

"What should we do about him?" Daixa gestured with a tilt of her head toward the man cradled in her arms. He was slumped forward, his damp hair falling limply over his face, hiding his closed eyes. His skin had taken on an unnaturally pale hue, and his breathing was shallow, barely perceptible.

With a heavy heart, I made the decision. *"We take him with us,"* I ordered, my voice steady despite the turmoil raging within. *"I'll deal with him later."*

As I gazed down at Isla, the pale moonlight revealed the

extent of her injuries: bruises, cuts, and scrapes covered her pale skin. The flickering flames from the wreckage cast shadows on her face, highlighting even more injuries that I had initially missed. My heart ached at the sight of once vibrant skin now looking ashen and fragile in the dim light.

It was a haunting sight, and I felt a pang of guilt for not noticing sooner.

Concern flooded me. I couldn't allow her to be taken away from me, not now, not after everything that happened. *"We need to go."*

"What about the two lifeless bodies?" Ephi twisted toward where they were within the burning wreckage.

A low growl escaped my throat, a primal sound that echoed my fury and pain. *"Leave them,"* I snapped. *"Let the sea creatures feast on their remains. The humans can deal with the aftermath of this disaster."*

The two scouts exchanged a glance, but they didn't question my decision.

With Isla safely in my arms, we began our journey back to Atlantis, knowing that there were still challenges ahead. Her survival depended on my ability to get her to safety as quickly as possible.

The vast expanse of the ocean stretched endlessly around us as we swam, the weight of the situation pressing heavily upon my shoulders. My precious mate lay limp in my arms, her once-fierce grip now just a faint pressure against my chest. Her shallow breaths fanned against my neck, the only indication of her fragile state.

As we moved, the ocean seemed to revolt against us, waves swelling and falling with a rhythm that echoed my own turmoil. Each swell threatened to pull her further from safety, and I tightened my hold, determined to shield her from the relentless sea. Despite the chaos around us, through our bond, I felt an unexpected serenity from her, a calm in the eye of the storm that raged within me, driving me forward, one powerful stroke at a time.

My mind refused to accept the cruel reality of my supposed rescue, my supposed escape. Because this was not what I envisioned when I dreamed of reuniting with my Isla. Not with her teetering on the brink between life and death, a broken and bloody mess.

It was a betrayal of everything I fought for and believed in.

Hadn't she been through enough? Hadn't we both been through enough to not deserve this?

Were we being punished for our connection, our growing love, between a creature of the land and a creature of the sea?

I refused to believe that the Fates willed for this to happen. That our path, our tremulations, were written by the Stars themselves.

Unless this was a test—and if it was, I prayed it was the final one—for us to see if we were willing to fight to be together.

If it was, I was willing to shed all my scales to be with her.

"Ephi, how far to Atlantis?"

Ephi consulted her wristband, her fingers moving with practiced ease as she calculated our distance. She looked up, her eyes meeting mine with a seriousness that mirrored my own. *"A few Earth hours,"* she replied, her voice carrying a note of apology. *"Our journey would be quicker if we weren't burdened with carrying the unconscious humans."*

I nodded, my gaze drifting down to Isla, my hearts aching at the sight of her so vulnerable and frail in my arms. Her pale face was a stark contrast against the dark waters, her usually vibrant blue eyes closed.

I cursed the Stars above for the trials they had thrust upon us, for the endless challenges we faced. The strain on my body was palpable, my stamina waning from the prolonged confinement I had endured.

The ocean around us was silent, stretching out as far as the eye could see. The only sound the gentle whoosh of our strokes through the water. My muscles screamed in protest as I pushed myself forward with each powerful kick of my tail, each stroke through the water fueled by sheer willpower. My hearts pounded in my chest, in sync with the rhythmic sound of my strokes, propelling us closer to our destination.

After a year of captivity, of being confined to tanks too small and environments too restrictive, my body was reaching its limits. Yet, despite the exhaustion that clawed at my muscles, my resolve to protect Isla remained unwavering.

I couldn't—wouldn't—falter. Not with Isla depending on me.

With every kick towards Atlantis, I adjusted my grip on her, making sure she was comfortable and secure in my arms.

But as we made our way through the dark, murky waters, dread settled deep in my stomach. Isla's condition continued to deteriorate at an alarming rate.

Her blue lips and cold, clammy skin against mine were a stark contrast to her once warm and vibrant self. My body was made for the depths of the water, designed to withstand the frigid temperatures, but as I held her in my arms, I cursed my nature for not being able to provide her with the warmth she so desperately needed.

Never had I felt so utterly powerless and devastated by my limitations.

Fear clenched at my hearts as we continued to make our way towards Atlantis, knowing that Isla's life depended on our arrival. But I refused to falter, my determination to save her fueling every thrust forward, knowing that once we arrived, I would have to do everything in my power to save Isla's fading life.

"Ephi!" My voice thundered through our connection across the water, a desperate plea. *"We need immediate assistance, now!"*

Ephi's eyes widened as she took in the dire state of Isla and the human male in Daixa's arms. He wasn't faring any better, his condition just as critical.

Her movements were a blur, her fingers tapping frantically on her wristband, sending a distress signal to Atlantis.

Each shiver that wracked her body sent a spike of fear through my hearts, as a sense of desperation took hold. I was a warrior, used to the chill of the deep, but she was human, fragile and delicate in ways I hadn't fully comprehended until this perilous moment.

"What's wrong with them?" Daixa asked, her voice laced with concern as she adjusted her grip on the shivering male.

"They're humans," I growled, my voice laced with frustration as I tried to rub Isla's arms, to generate even a trace of heat. *"They're not built for these conditions. They need warmth, dryness, and clothing... Things we aren't able to provide them in the midst of the ocean."*

Daixa mirrored my actions and turned the human male in her arms to better shield him from the cold. Her eyes met mine, filled with a question she didn't need to voice.

"Atlantis is sending a stealth rescue craft," Ephi announced, gazing in the direction we were originally traveling. *"They've locked on to our position. Hold on, Commander. Help is on the way."*

I nodded, barely registering her words. All that mattered was Isla in my arms, growing colder by the second.

"Stay with me, Isla," I murmured, my voice a mix of

command and plea. *"Don't leave me now. We've both escaped and are free... We have a future to claim, a life to build. Together."*

I rubbed Isla's arms, trying to stir some heat into her limbs, as I pressed my cheek to hers, whispering reassurances to her, words meant to soothe and comfort, though I knew she couldn't hear me. I poured all my love and determination into our bond, willing her to feel my presence and draw strength from it.

Time seemed to slow down, each second stretching into an eternity as we waited for the craft to arrive. The helplessness I felt was agonizing, knowing I couldn't do anything but hold her close and rub her arms in hopes of creating any substance of heat.

In the oppressive silence of the cold, dark waters, time seemed to stretch into infinity. Then, without warning, the stillness was broken by a disturbance on the water's surface.

The surface tension shattered, water parting in sleek arcs as something advanced with purposeful speed, barely discernible against the night.

As it neared, the craft's cutting-edge design became evident: sleek lines, an almost ghostly silhouette, and a subdued hum of advanced propulsion technology. This vessel was the pinnacle of IPA's engineering, equipped with state-of-the-art tech, making it nearly invisible against the dark backdrop of the ocean.

As the vessel approached us, it gradually slowed down with effortless grace until it came to a complete stop. Its precise movements were a testament to its advanced guidance systems as it halted right in front of us.

The side of the stealth craft rhythmically swung open, revealing a smooth ramp that descended gracefully into the water.

From within, a team of Krukken emerged, their forms a blend of efficiency and urgency. Their tentacles, agile and precise, extended toward us as they surveyed the scene.

The Krukkens' faces registered a moment of horror at the sight of Isla and the unknown human male in our arms. They reached out, their tentacles gently but firmly enveloping them, lifting them from our grasp with practiced care.

I released Isla into their capable tentacles without hesitation. The moment her weight shifted from my hold to theirs, a part of me wanted to growl in protest, to snatch her back and keep her safe within my own embrace, but I knew that it was illogical.

She needed help, help that I couldn't give her.

I was a warrior, not a medic, and they were the only ones capable of giving her the assistance she needed.

Beside me, Daixa followed suit, relinquishing the unknown male into their custody with a silent nod of trust.

As they secured Isla onto a floating hover medbed, my eyes remained locked on her, unable to look away. Her form so pale and fragile against the dark cushion that it only added to my worry.

Our connection was the one thing that gave me the assurance I needed that she was still alive, that there was still hope for her.

The head medic, a figure exuding authority and a calming presence amidst the turmoil, approached me. "Commander, she's in critical condition, but we'll do everything we can." The assurance was there, but it did little to ease the clawing panic inside me.

One of the medics on Isla's bedside, their eyes serious and focused behind their medvisor, turned to me. "There's no need to worry," he reassured. "She's in good hands now."

The medic's words were a balm to my ragged nerves, but it did little to ease the tight knot of fear in my gut.

I hovered close, my gaze never leaving her, watching helplessly as the medics continued to work on her, completing their baseline tests in preparation for departure. The medics worked swiftly, hooking her up to various devices. Their tentacles moved with practiced ease, but it was the concern etched in their eyes that told me the gravity of the situation.

The sight of her, so vulnerable and lifeless, struck a chord deep within me.

Isla, my Isla, was fighting a battle far from my reach.

The unidentified male was given similar treatment, but my focus remained solely on Isla.

The bond we shared pulsed with a quiet intensity, a tether that anchored her to me. I held on tight to it, as if willing her to survive, to pull through, to not drift away from me now that we were both free.

As the medics finished their preparations, one of them approached me. "Commander Ky'rn, we need to get them to Atlantis immediately. Every moment counts. When you're ready, we can be on our way."

I nodded, my throat tight with worry. "Then let's depart," I managed to say, my voice rough with barely contained emotion. "I need her to survive. She's everything to me, and the reason why I'm now free."

"We'll do everything we can, but know that she's in critical—but stable—condition," the lead medic announced, her voice firm and composed, yet I could sense a ripple of concern beneath her professional demeanor. "Hailing us has greatly increased both of their chances of survival."

The assurance was there, but it did little to ease the clawing panic inside me.

My hearts felt like a pile of stones in my chest, heavy and sinking. I nodded, barely registering the other activities around me. The only thing that mattered was Isla, her well-being, and how her life was hanging by a thread because of me.

"Do you need any medical attention?" the head medic inquired, her eyes scanning over me, probably noticing the fatigue etched in my face, the strain in my muscles from the relentless swimming and the emotional turmoil raging within.

I shook my head, my voice a low growl. "No, attend to her." My command was absolute; Isla was my priority, and nothing else held any significance. "I was able to survive a year of captivity, I'll survive the exhaustion and whatever else that I face."

"I advise that you get checked out once we arrive, hopefully before you're debriefed.' The medic nodded solemnly and signaled his team. With efficient movements, they secured Isla more firmly onto the hover medbed, ensuring her safety and comfort.

As they prepared to transport us, I moved closer, my eyes locked onto her pale, serene face. The urge to reach out, to feel her skin, to reassure myself that she was still with me, was overwhelming, but I knew I shouldn't get in the medic team's way.

"She'll have the finest care once we arrive."

I merely nodded, my throat tight with unspoken emotions. I had to trust in their skills, their ability to save her.

The lead medic, her eyes scanning me with a practiced, clinical gaze, stated, "Commander, we have hover carts ready for you and your scouts. Your body isn't in a condition to endure the rest of the journey to Atlantis." Her posture was resolute, embodying her dedication to her ethical and honorable code, as she gestured to the hover carts, sleek and efficient, designed for rapid medical response. "It would be against my oath to let you continue in such a state."

Acknowledging her assessment, I nodded, the weight of my exhaustion evident in my movements. "I have no intention of being stubborn or egotistical enough to ignore my limits," I confessed, a sense of relief mingling with my gratitude. "I'll gladly accept the ride."

Daixa and Ephi moved to secure their places, their faces etched with concern not only for Isla but for me as well. They knew the extent of my suffering, the year-long ordeal that had drained so much of my strength and spirit.

As I settled onto our individual hover carts, the cool surface beneath me a minor relief to my aching muscles, I couldn't help but keep my gaze fixed in Isla's direction.

The medic, sensing my distress, placed a reassuring hand on my shoulder. "We'll reach Atlantis quickly, Commander. Your mate is in the best hands. Our medical facilities are equipped with the most advanced technology. She will receive the care she needs."

I simply nodded, too wrapped up in my thoughts to muster words.

"We'll get you there swiftly. Just rest now."

Rest was a foreign concept at that moment, my mind entirely focused on Isla, her well-being, her fight for life. But her words resonated with a sense of command, reminding me of my own position and the respect I held for those under my charge.

The craft turned, preparing to dart back to Atlantis. My chest felt tight, a mixture of relief and anxiety churning within. Relief that she was getting the help she needed, anxiety because I wouldn't be able to be there right beside her to see it through once we arrived.

Daixa placed a hand on my shoulder, a silent gesture of

support. I barely felt it. My focus remained fixated on Isla's hover medbed, my thoughts and hearts with her.

The brilliance of Atlantis loomed before us as we approached the entry surface level checkpoint.

It was a breathtaking sight, an architectural marvel beneath the ocean, made up of interconnected domes of reinforced glass that allowed sunlight to filter through and illuminate the breathtaking city below. The checkpoint served as a nexus for IPA citizens from land to visit the submerged metropolis, seamlessly fusing alien technology with natural beauty.

Upon nearing the docking area, I noticed something had changed since my last visit. The usual bustling activity of alien spacecrafts was eerily sparse. Only a handful remained, their sleek and otherworldly designs contrasting starkly with the serene surroundings.

It was an undeniable testament to the growing resistance Earth's inhabitants showed toward IPA citizens.

A moss ramp came into view, shimmering with a soft luminescence. Onlookers, both IPA citizens and visiting humans, paused to watch our arrival. Their faces were painted with mixed emotions—some with genuine concern, others with curiosity.

As we approached, the head medic briefed me. "Commander, the emergency crew will meet us at the moss ramp. They're prepared to take her."

I nodded, gratitude evident in my voice. "Thank you."

Two Krukken medics approached us as soon as the vessel's ramp lowered, their tentacles gracefully managing an array of advanced medical equipment. Their eyes, large and expressive, flicked between my scouts and me.

"What happened?" one of them inquired, his gaze sharp and assessing.

"She was in a boating accident," I responded tersely, watching as the vessel's medic team handed Isla's fragile form to them. "She needs urgent care."

The base lead medic let his eyes linger on the mark on Isla's neck. "You've marked her," he noted, more of a statement than a question.

I nodded. "Yes, but our bond isn't sealed. I intend to complete it once she's recovered."

His assistant, a younger Krukken with a more vibrant hue to his skin, spoke up. "We were informed of your arrival by Prince Rivu. She has clearance to be here."

I leaned in. "Then see to it that she's treated immediately," I urged. "And ensure she's provided with AAC. She'll need it to communicate here."

Both medics nodded, understanding the urgency. "We'll do our best, Commander," the lead medic assured me. "You'll be informed the moment she wakes."

With that, they swiftly moved away, taking Isla to the medical wing's elevator and leaving me with two heavy hearts, willing her to recover.

THIRTY-ONE

KY'RN

"Welcome back, Commander." Prince Rivu extended an inviting gesture, his hand sweeping toward his suite's luxurious pool, welcoming me to join him. "Join me in my waters and debrief me on what happened."

Gently, I pressed my palm against the hovercart's control panel, a high-tech interface that responded instantly to my touch. The hovercart obediently glided over to the edge of the pool.

As it came to a gentle stop, I carefully dismounted, feeling the familiar ache in my muscles, a reminder of the recent ordeals.

As I lowered myself into the pool's embracing waters, a deluge of memories flooded my mind. Visions of the sterile experiment tanks and the relentless scientific tests I had endured over the past year seemed to swirl around me, mingling with the pool water that now enveloped my form.

I closed my eyes in an effort to anchor myself in the present, to banish the shadows of the past that clung to me. I focused on the gentle caress of the water against my body, letting its soothing touch ground me in the here and now. I was in Atlantis's main residential dome, a sanctuary within the vast underwater city base, surrounded by fellow IPA citizens.

I was not only free, but safe, and everything would be all right, as long as Isla made a full recovery.

Whispering a mantra to myself, the words drifted from my lips like a caress of soothing current. "I am free, I am safe, all will be well." With each repetition, the heaviness of past traumas began to lift from my shoulders, replaced by a deepening sense of tranquility. My breaths became fuller, my heart rate steadier, as if the very water around me was infusing me with a sudden renewed hope and reassurance.

With a deep breath, I slowly blinked my eyes open and released a long exhale as I sank deeper into the warm pool. The water enveloped me, covering my body until only my head remained above the surface.

Prince Rivu's gaze fixed on me, his eyebrows knitting together in a display of deep concern. His eyes, usually so sharp and commanding, now softened with worry as they roved over my form, seeking signs of distress or discomfort.

He leaned forward slightly, his posture radiating both authority and care. "Should I be concerned?" he inquired, his voice a blend of command and genuine worry. "If you require medical attention, we can postpone our debriefing. It can wait until after we receive positive news about your mate."

His offer hung in the air, a tribute to his willingness to prioritize my health and mental state over protocol and duty. We were more than simply prince and commander; we were lifetime friends, close enough that I would consider him a brother, not just a brother in arms.

While my parents guarded his, we attended the same warrior academy and trained alongside each other until we graduated. I'd asked to be assigned to his fleet and worked my way up to commanding my own squadron under his command.

It meant a lot to me that he stayed on Earth to plan my rescue rather than returning to our capital. He hadn't let anybody else take over his role, managing operations involving humans and Earth, when he had full authority to do so.

"There's nothing to be done at this moment, only time can aid me now," I said, my voice a soft murmur as I sighed and swept my hair back from my face. The scars that marred my soul were invisible but intensely felt; only time could cure them. "Time is the only healer for wounds like mine," I continued, "and news of Isla's recovery, along with our departure from this harrowing planet, will be the beginning of my own path of healing."

"I insist you get examined," he said, his voice firm, reflecting his deep concern for my welfare.

I raised my hand, gently cutting off his protest. "Please, focus all resources on Isla," I urged, my tone soft yet unwavering. "She's the one fighting for her life at this moment. I promise you, once she's safe and stable, I'll submit to whatever checks you deem necessary. But for now, her life hangs in the balance, not mine."

"But you're the one I risked everything for, not her." Prince Rivu's voice deepened, a growl of frustration emanating from him as he struck the surface of the water with his hand, sending a large splash cascading upward. "She's only here at your request. If it were up to me—"

"But it wasn't up to you," I hissed, cutting him off abruptly. "What's done is done, and I won't cast blame on her for the actions of her grandfather or those who imprisoned me. She's the reason I'm here now, safe in your suite's pool, still intact."

His demeanor shifted slightly, the tension in his shoulders easing as he gestured toward the moss-covered ledge beside him. His curiosity was evident as he leaned forward, his gaze piercing yet inquisitive. "So, it's true, then? That you and that human female are mated?"

I gave a solemn nod, my fist pressing gently against my chest, right between where my hearts beat. "She bears my mark," I explained, my voice tinged with a blend of reverence and unresolved longing for wanting more. "But our connection isn't fully established yet."

My muscles stiffened as I glided toward him in the water, resting beside him. As I settled on the ledge, the green moss felt soft and welcoming against my skin.

"Normally, I would say that's unfortunate to hear, but for your situation, it might be a blessing," he muttered, frowning as he gazed at the holographic screens suspended in the air, projected from his elegantly designed stone desk.

"The medics are still attending to the human pair." He gestured toward an image on one of the screens. It displayed Isla and the unidentified male, each on a separate medical bed. Around them, a team of Krukken medics worked tirelessly, assisted by an array of robotic arms. The beds were encircled by a halo of vidscreens, each flashing with vital medical data.

Anxious for any news, I leaned in slightly. "What's their status?"

"Their condition is stable but critical." His expression grew concerned as he waved a hand, bringing up a larger, more detailed view of their medical data. "Isla's body is responding slowly to the treatment. Her injuries and the exposure to the cold took a significant toll on her."

I couldn't tear my eyes away from the projections, watching as each blip of data showed just how fragile she was. It was a brutal reminder of the stark contrast between our species and how vulnerable she was compared to my own kind.

"And what about the male?" I clenched my jaw, trying to control the sharpness in my tone.

Rivu's gaze shifted to the other medbed where the human male lay, surrounded by similar medical equipment. "He's stable, but his condition was not as severe as Isla's. He should fully recover with less difficulty."

My fists clenched involuntarily. It was this male's actions that had led to Isla's current state.

"Who conceived this marriage scheme?" My voice carried a mix of disbelief and possessiveness. "Why was she compelled to pledge herself to him when she was mine first? My mark on her neck proves it."

The idea that she was forced to bind herself to another, despite our prior claim, gnawed at me, a stark reminder of the complex web of politics and personal desires at play.

Rivu raised an eyebrow. "And yet, she didn't call off the plan."

"Because she probably felt she couldn't't!" I pointed at the screens. "It didn't have to be this way. Everything could have been avoided if everyone concerned had communicated with one another."

"I do not know all the details, but it seems Roman improvised beyond the initial agreement," Rivu explained, his voice holding a note of disapproval. "The marriage was supposed to be a facade, a means to ensure her cooperation and safety. It was never meant to be permanent or binding. Roman believed it to be the most effective way to infiltrate

Boze Marine Co. without raising suspicion from Isla's grandfather."

"She's mine. She was mine first." The thought of Isla, swearing herself to another, even under the guise of a plan, sent a ripple of possessive anger through me. "And the destruction..." I pressed on, feeling a surge of anger at the thought of the chaos that had ensued. "Was that his doing or part of the plan all along?"

Rivu's expression softened slightly, understanding the depth of my feelings. "Ky'rn, please... In the grand scheme, their temporary marriage was seen as the most efficient way to free you and dismantle the operations without causing an uproar that could jeopardize everything. Roman's actions, however, were not anticipated. The destruction, the violence... it was reckless and endangered many lives, including Isla's." Rivu shook his head, his expression turning graver. "No, that was not part of the initial plan. It seems Roman took extreme measures beyond what was agreed upon. We're still trying to gather information to understand his motives for deviating so drastically."

My fists clenched under the water, the feeling of betrayal burning within me. How could Roman, who claimed to be aiding us, endanger Isla in such a reckless manner? Seeing her lying in that medical bed, her condition a direct result of this man's actions, ignited a fury in me.

"And now she suffers because of it." I growled lowly. "Was she unaware of the true nature of this plan?"

Rivu nodded solemnly. "It appears so. From what we've gathered so far, she was kept in the dark about the extent of Roman's plans. She believed the marriage to be a mere formality, a way to secure your release and her freedom from her grandfather's control."

The weight of this revelation settled heavily on my shoulders. Isla, my mate, had been manipulated, used as a pawn in yet another game she didn't even know she was playing.

Rivu's hand rested on my shoulder, a silent gesture of support. "Ky'rn, what matters now is Isla's recovery. We must focus on the present and ensure her well-being. As for Roman, we will deal with him accordingly."

An alarm echoed, ringing my ears as Rivu's screens bathed us in a relentless, pulsing red.

As the lead medic's image filled the projection, his tentacles splayed in an unmistakable sign of urgency, I felt a cold dread settle in my gut.

Rivu fixed his gaze on the medic, his voice a command. "Report."

The medic's voice was tight, laced with the strain of the dire situation. "We are losing the female. She's slipping away from us. We require immediate authorization to use our advanced technologies to save her.'

Before Rivu could respond, I interjected, desperation clawing at my voice. "It shouldn't even be a question! Do whatever it takes. I owe her my life; she must be saved."

The medic turned his gaze to me, his eyes somber. "Commander, with all due respect, it's Prince Rivu's call."

Rivu, his brow furrowed, addressed the medic. "What are you proposing?"

"A living suit," the medic replied, his voice even but carrying an undercurrent of urgency. "It's the only way to stabilize her and guarantee her full recovery from her injuries. It's a marvel that she's still alive at this point."

My hearts seized at the words. A living suit. The technology was miraculous, life-saving, but the implications were vast, the commitment absolute. It would bond her to my world, to a life away from Earth, far beyond what she might have ever agreed to.

"No," I muttered, the word a plea, a denial. The thought of her body being altered so fundamentally without her consent tore at me. But at the same time, the desperate need to save her, to keep her alive, warred within me.

Rivu's gaze shifted to me, his eyes reflecting the gravity of the situation. "Ky'rn, I agree that installing a living suit on her is a drastic measure, but it could be her only chance."

I shook my head, my voice barely a whisper as I said, "A living suit... It's a permanent alteration. She won't be the same. I don't want her to hate me for taking away her body autonomy, not after what she's been through."

"She may not have a body capable of keeping her alive if you delay any longer," the medic stated. "It's true, Commander. The suit will bond with her on a cellular level. It will enhance her abilities to survive in various environments, but it will change her, physically, for the better."

Rivu studied the medic's face then turned to me. "Ky'rn, I understand your concerns, but we need to consider Isla's life. This technology would save her... she would be foolish to be mad at you for saving her life."

My thoughts raced, torn between fear of losing her—of her hating me for making this decision—and the desperate need to save her. The living suit was an alien technology, advanced beyond anything on Earth. It could grant her abilities to live in my underwater world, but at what cost?

"I... I don't want to lose her," I managed to say, my voice strained with emotion. "Not when I barely had a chance to be with her.'

Rivu placed a hand on my shoulder, his touch firm yet reassuring. "You won't lose her, Ky'rn. She'll still be Isla, but she'll get to live, to be with you. Isn't that what really matters?"

I closed my eyes, the weight of the decision heavy on my heart. Finally, I nodded slowly. "Do it. Save her."

"Proceed with the living suit implementation," Rivu said firmly. "Save her. Keep me updated on her condition."

Rivu's eyes met mine, a silent understanding passing between us.

Making life and death choices regarding others' lives was part of both of our positions, but this was the most difficult decision I'd ever had to make.

The medic nodded, his image flickering as he turned to carry out the order. The screens returned to their normal glow, but the tension remained, leaving the room in silence.

I remained motionless, my thoughts a whirlwind.

The living suit would save her, bind her to this life alongside me, but at what cost? What would she think when she woke? Would she forgive this decision made in the heat of the moment while she was slipping away?

As I watched the medical team work frantically on the projection, I made a silent vow. I would be there for her, explain everything, support her through every step of this new life.

She had saved me, and now, I would dedicate my existence to being there for her, no matter what the future held... even if she hated me for the choice that I'd made.

THIRTY-TWO

ISLA

I blinked, disoriented for a moment as I tried to process my surroundings. The panoramic view before me was like something out of a dream. I was encased in a clear dome, with a breathtaking view of an underwater city spread out before me. Domes of various sizes and shapes shimmered in the dim light, casting an ethereal glow all around. The brilliant blue and green hues of the water played tricks on my eyes, making me feel as if I'd been transported into some kind of utopian city from the future, only submerged deep beneath the ocean's surface.

The material I lay on was unlike anything I'd ever felt. It was moss-like, moist and cool, spreading over the whole floor —reminiscent of the touch of morning dew. It wasn't unpleasant, just…different, almost as if it were alive.

As my senses fully awakened, I became aware of Ky'rn's presence. He was beside me, his broad, powerful form stretched out in repose. Even in sleep, he looked every bit the fierce warrior, yet there was a softness—a vulnerability in the way his hand splayed out near mine, fingers twitching as though he was reaching for me in his dreams.

How was he even here, out of the water?

As I took in the room, the misty moss beneath us gave me a hint. The environment seemed crafted to cater to both aquatic and land-based species.

Mild discomfort nudged at me. I reached behind my ear, encountering a foreign object. It was metallic and cool, curving smoothly against my skin. Confused, I glanced over at Ky'rn, noticing a similar device behind his ear.

What was it? An implant? A communication device?

Looking down, I received another shock. I was enveloped in a sleek, black material, which clung to every contour of my body. It felt protective, almost like a second skin, leaving only my face, hands and feet exposed. The realization that someone had changed me in my sleep made my breath catch, anxiety threatening to bubble up.

Ky'rn stirred, his eyes snapping open. Those glowing amber orbs searched mine, full of concern. "Isla," he rasped, reaching up to cup my cheek, his thumb brushing my cheek-bone. "Are you all right?"

I gulped, trying to process everything. "Where are we? What happened? And what's this?" I whispered, my voice shaky, pointing to the device behind my ear.

Ky'rn sighed, looking relieved that I was awake and responsive. "You're safe. We're in Atlantis," he began, his voice steady. "After the accident, I brought you here to get medical attention. That," he gestured to the device, "is an AAC—Augmentative and Alternative Communication device. It will help you communicate with everyone here, including me, without needing to touch to speak to me tele-pathically."

I nodded slowly, still trying to absorb everything.

The situation was overwhelming, but Ky'rn's presence, his touch, grounded me. The last thing I remembered was the cold, crushing weight of the water, and now here I was, in an alien underwater city, but with him by my side.

I wrapped my fingers around his, seeking comfort. "Thank you," I whispered. "For saving me."

He gave me a soft smile, his eyes shining with emotion. "Always."

"How are you comfortable here, out of the water?" I asked, concerned for his health. "Shouldn't you be in a pool or something?"

He gently pulled one of his hands from the moss and held it up, showing me the delicate, shimmering scales that covered his skin. "See these?" he said softly. "They're not just for show. They're a part of our respiratory system as well. While we do have gills, we've evolved to have a dual respiratory system. We have a set of lungs to allow us to both communicate vocally and breathe oxygen like land creatures. Our scales absorb oxygen and moisture from the environment, allowing us to breathe even outside of water. But, they need to stay moist for us to stay healthy and comfortable."

I reached out, fingers grazing over his hand, feeling the cool, slick texture of his scales. "That's incredible," I whispered, captivated by his alien biology. My marine biologist instincts kicked in, and I found myself eager to learn more about him, his species, and this underwater world I'd found myself in.

Ky'rn chuckled, a deep, melodic sound that reverberated through the dome. "I thought you might find it intriguing, but yes, it's why places like this," he gestured around the dome with its moss-covered floor, "are essential for us when we venture outside our natural aquatic habitats. This moss isn't just a design choice; it's a necessity. It retains moisture, ensuring our scales remain hydrated in order to keep us healthy while we are out of the water."

I looked around, taking in details I hadn't noticed before. The way the moss seemed to glisten with dew, the slight shimmer of humidity in the air, and the gentle sounds of trickling water from somewhere nearby. Everything was designed to cater to beings like Ky'rn.

"It's all so…thoughtful," I murmured, still trying to wrap my head around everything. "This place, the care that's gone into making it habitable for both of us…"

Ky'rn smiled, his sharp teeth peeking out, but his eyes were warm. "It's a testament to what can be achieved when different species collaborate and learn from each other. And it's also a testament to how much I wanted to ensure your comfort here, with me."

Ky'rn's amber eyes glimmered with emotions—worry, relief, and a vulnerability I hadn't seen before. The ethereal blue glow from the city outside illuminated his face, emphasizing the strong yet gentle lines of his features.

"I felt you," he began, his voice low and thick with emotion. "When you were in danger, the bond screamed at me, echoing with your panic, your fear. Even though you were distant, I could feel the direction you were in, like a compass pointing straight to you."

I swallowed hard, recalling the moments of sheer terror I'd felt in the water, the sensation of drowning, the cold biting at me. "But the shipwreck…"

His hand tightened around mine. "That's where I found you, clinging to life. I couldn't bear the thought of losing you, especially not after everything we had been through. So, I brought you here, to Atlantis, where they have the technology and means to heal you."

A tear slid down my cheek. "Thank you," I whispered, brushing away the tear. "You saved me."

He leaned in, his lips brushing my forehead. "I told you,

Isla, I will always find you. No matter where you are, I will always come for you."

It was a lot to digest.

Tears welled up in my eyes. "I owe you my life, Ky'rn."

He shook his head, adamant. "You owe me nothing."

"This suit…" I trailed off, running my hands over the black material that clung to every inch of my skin.

"The medical staff was able to heal you, but they had to bond a living suit to you," he explained; his voice was calm and reassuring. "It's a bio-engineered living material that bonds to its user, capable of healing them and providing them with protection from the elements, like cold or hot temperatures and high pressure. It also gives you a mask so you can see in the darkness and breathe air through its artificial gills."

While it was concerning that they hadn't asked for my consent before installing such an invasive device, I understood that they had done it to ensure my safety and well-being. I couldn't—I shouldn't—be upset or angry with them, not when they had saved me and were clearly trying to better my life while I was unconscious.

As I considered the gravity of what he'd done and the implications of my new circumstances, I couldn't help but feel overwhelmed.

My life had been altered in ways I couldn't yet fully understand, but as I gazed into his worried, amber eyes, I realized that I wasn't angry at him. Instead, I felt a deep-seated appreciation for his act of desperation to save me.

"Ky'rn," I started, my voice soft yet steady. "I've spent my whole life being controlled by others, being a pawn in their games. You... you chose to save my life, not to control it. That means everything to me.

"You saved me, not just from drowning but from a life where I wasn't really living. Yes, it's terrifying, not knowing what my future holds." His body tenses slightly, as if bracing for rejection, but I continue. "You've shown me a kindness and a love that I've never known. You've given me a choice where I had none. So, no, I'm not angry at you, Ky'rn. I'm grateful. Grateful that in the midst of this chaos, I have someone who truly cares for me. I'm not alone in this, not when I have you."

As I nestled against him, feeling the steady beats of his hearts, there was a flicker of relief in his eyes, and something more, a deepening of the bond that had been growing between us. He pulled me closer, his embrace just enough to make me feel secure but not restrained. His gaze searched mine, his amber eyes filled with apprehension. "But, Isla, this suit, it changes things. You might never be able to go back to Earth, at least not until there's peace between our governments. Can you live with that?"

I sighed a deep, releasing breath, as I considered his words.

The Earth I knew, the life I had here, it was all behind me now. Looking into Ky'rn's eyes, I saw not just my rescuer, but my partner, my equal, regardless of our differences.

"I chose this, Ky'rn. I chose you," I said firmly, a small smile tugging at the corners of my mouth. "I've always been fascinated by the unknown, by the depths of the ocean and the mysteries it holds. Maybe it's time for me to explore a new frontier, with you by my side."

He pulled me closer, wrapping his arms around me in a protective embrace. "I will do everything in my power to make this life, our life, one of happiness and freedom, of love and understanding," he murmured against my hair, a low rumble of contentment vibrating through his chest. "Isla, I vow no matter where we are in the universe, as long as we're together, we're home."

Smiling, I reached out, my fingers brushing against the mark on my neck, a constant reminder of our bond. "I like the sound of that."

"Isla," he whispered, the timbre of his voice sending shivers down my spine. "Do you have any idea what it felt like to think you belonged to another? To him?"

"I'm sorry…" I shook my head, my fingers tracing the hard lines of his jaw. "It was never real, Ky'rn. Just a part of Roman's twisted plot. You should know by now that my heart beats for you, and only you."

A deep growl rumbled in his chest, and his eyes darkened with passion. "Say it again," he commanded, his voice demanding but not harsh.

I leaned in, letting my lips brush against the edge of his ear. "I am yours, and only yours."

Ky'rn's lips crashed onto mine, a fierce and possessive kiss that left me breathless. His hands roamed my back, drawing me even closer, every touch igniting a spark, with a possessiveness that was almost primal.

I clung to him, losing myself in the depths of his embrace.

The weight of his form against mine was both comforting and exhilarating. Every touch, every movement heightened the raw energy that crackled between us.

My fingers threaded through the dark, wet strands of his hair, pulling him closer. The taste of saltwater mingled with our breaths, making the moment even more surreal and intoxicating.

His growls of possession vibrated against my lips, amplifying the throbbing pulse of desire that echoed through our entwined bodies.

Ky'rn's hands slid down to my waist, holding me firmly as he deepened the kiss. I could feel the rhythm of his hearts, wild and untamed, beating in tandem with mine.

The sensation was overwhelming, a heady blend of lust, love, and longing.

After what felt like an eternity, we broke apart, gasping for breath. Ky'rn rested his forehead against mine, our breaths mingling, our hearts racing.

"You have no idea how much I needed to hear that," he murmured, his voice thick.

I smiled, feeling a weight lift off my chest. "And you have no idea how much I needed to tell you."

"I can't lose you," he whispered. "Not again."

I brought my hands up, resting them against his broad chest, feeling the rapid beat of his hearts. "You won't," I promised. "I'm here with you. That's where I want to be."

He leaned in, his lips brushing against my forehead in a gentle kiss. It was a soft, intimate moment—a moment of reassurance and understanding.

"I've seen so much loss in my life," he murmured. "But losing you, even the mere thought of it, terrifies me more than anything. And I almost lost you three times."

"A life for a life," I muttered. "We've exchanged lives. Proof that our fates are forever entwined."

"I told you to forget me—to stay away—yet you defied me." Ky'rn growled. "Thank the Stars for your defiance, because you've become my obsession and my salvation."

"There was no way I'd be able to forget you, even if you hadn't already marked me as yours," I confessed. "From the brink of death, you've saved my life. In your arms, I've found my home. You're my home, Ky'rn. I realize that now."

"I may be a creature of the deep, but it's you who dived deep into my lonely hearts and filled them with hope...and love." He brushed my hair back. "Just as the ocean embraces the shore, let me embrace you tonight."

Every touch, every word, every look from Ky'rn made

my heart race and my skin tingle. It wasn't just the physical sensations, it was the profound emotional connection, the feeling of being truly seen, truly valued, truly loved.

With him, I was whole.

In his arms, the world with all its chaos and uncertainty faded away, replaced by a comforting cocoon of safety and security.

My eyelids grew heavy as the events of the past few hours weighed on me. The adrenaline that had kept me going was now receding, and in its place, a deep, bone-weary exhaustion took hold.

His voice, deep and soothing, penetrated the haze of fatigue. "Isla, rest. Let yourself heal," he murmured, stroking my hair gently.

"I love you, Ky'rn," I whispered, my voice barely audible. It was a promise, a vow, and a declaration all in one. "I want to be with you. Every moment, every day. I want to love you and be loved by you."

A soft smile tugged at the corners of his lips, and he pulled me even closer, our hearts beating in sync. "You have my hearts, Isla," he replied, his voice filled with emotion. "And I have yours."

With that, he repositioned us, ensuring I was comfortable nestled against his chest. The gentle rhythm of his heartbeat lulled me, a comforting backdrop to the warmth and safety of his embrace.

He pressed a soft kiss to my forehead, his warm breath tickling my skin. "Sleep, my love," he whispered back. "I'll be right here when you wake."

And with that promise, I allowed the comforting darkness of sleep to claim me, knowing that I would awaken in the arms of the one who loved me most.

THIRTY-THREE

KY'RN

The weight of Isla's head against my chest was a calming balm, reminding me of the precious treasure I now had.

We'd tasted the fear of death—and now we could taste the sweetness of freedom together.

There would be no more *life for a life*—I forbade it.

A bell sounded, a sharp and irritating twinge that sliced through the quiet serenity I had been luxuriating in. My protective instincts roared to life, instantly ready to shield Isla from harm. The intrusive noise threatened to shatter the fragile bubble of intimacy we'd crafted around ourselves.

My skin crawled, a low rumble escaping me. This was our time. Who would dare to interrupt it?

Isla shifted, her lovely face marred with sleep lines and confusion. "Ky'rn?" she mumbled, rubbing the sleep from her eyes. "What's that sound?"

My gaze was fixed on the dome, where the call was coming from. "Someone thinks it's a good time to vidcall us," I replied tersely, the scales on the back of my neck bristling.

This private pod was supposed to be inaccessible to

outsiders. It made my blood boil that someone would dare disturb our peace, especially when there were multiple channels in place specifically to avoid such invasions.

Letting out a low rumble of displeasure, I reached out and initiated the connection. I was already mentally preparing a scathing rebuke for whoever was audacious enough to reach out directly.

But when the dome around us shimmered and transformed, revealing the familiar features of a human male, I was caught off guard. Even more surprising was Isla's sharp intake of breath and the slight widening of her eyes.

The man's arrogant smirk only fueled my agitation. He looked far too pleased with himself, given the situation. The sleekness of his long brown hair, the piercing blue of his eyes —everything about him screamed overconfidence.

Isla's sharp intake of breath confirmed my suspicion. She sat up, rubbing her eyes. "Why are you calling, Roman?"

"I wouldn't contact you unless it was absolutely necessary. But we have a situation. A big one."

Every instinct in me screamed to cut the connection, but I also knew that if he had gone through the trouble to find us here, it must be urgent. Grudgingly, I sighed. "Speak."

Roman swallowed hard, his gaze shifting between me and Isla. "Wifey, I needed to check for myself that you were still alive, especially since the destruction of the lab and my prized yacht is all over the press."

"*Wifey?*" Isla's anger flared, coursing through our bond like hot flames. "None of that needed to happen—not the fake wedding ceremony, and certainly not the destruction of my family's property. You could have just told me the truth."

Roman raised an eyebrow, crossing his arms defensively. "I was merely fulfilling the IPA's request to get rid of all experimental data and research equipment from Boze Marine

Co. I also rescued your commander. And judging by the remains that have been collected from the boat crash, you were able to seek sweet revenge on those who'd betrayed you in the past."

"But not you," Isla muttered under her breath.

"What was that, my dear?" Roman taunted, his eyes gleaming.

"Wifey?" I spat out the word, incredulous. The sheer audacity of the man to use such an intimate term for Isla after all he had done was infuriating. He wasn't her mate.

Roman, however, seemed amused. He reveled in the control he thought he had over the situation.

I should've had my way with the ungrateful male while he was still here in the medbay, but Rivu insisted he was released as soon as he was able, to be placed on clean up duty for the mess that he'd made.

My fingers flexed, itching to lash out, wishing I could grab Roman by the collar and make him regret every decision he'd made. But the digital barrier between us kept me from doing so.

The only weapons I had were my words.

"I am not 'Wifey' or 'Dear' to you," Isla growled. "Thanks to you, I almost died. Again!"

Roman smirked, seeming to enjoy the distress he caused. "I made sure you were safe, Isla," he said, leaning slightly toward the screen, trying to convey sincerity. "Every move, every decision was calculated."

I could feel the fury radiating off Isla. "Calculated? You played with our lives as if we were mere pawns in your twisted game!"

My heart ached for her, seeing her so torn, so wounded by someone she once might have considered an ally, if not a friend.

Roman's gaze shifted to me, his expression bemused. "Commander, you should be thanking me. If not for my machinations, you might never have found your mate."

My eyes narrowed at him, my voice a low growl. "Don't pretend your actions were altruistic. You acted for your own benefit, and Isla nearly paid the ultimate price."

"Why, Roman?" Isla's voice shook with suppressed rage. "Why pull me into this dangerous game?"

Roman's nonchalant facade finally cracked, a hint of regret shadowing his blue eyes. "Look." He sighed. "The IPA reached out with a deal I couldn't refuse. They wanted those labs gone. Your family's research facility was at the top of their list."

Isla's anger shifted to confusion. "But why? We were researching for the benefit of our planet."

Roman scoffed, running a hand through his long hair. "Benefit? Torturing and experimenting on sentient beings is not for the benefit of anyone. Your grandfather hid a lot from you. And the IPA wanted to stop those atrocities, so they needed someone on Earth to do their dirty work."

I clenched my jaws, trying to keep my anger in check. "So, you used Isla as a pawn? Risked her life to get rid of some tech?"

Roman's gaze met mine, challenging. "Sometimes sacrifices need to be made for the greater good. I knew Isla would oppose the plan, so I kept her in the dark. Yes, it was a risk, but I believed she would survive. And look, she did. She's stronger than you think."

"You manipulated me, Roman!" Isla's voice was ice cold. "You had no right. No right to use me, to lie to me, to destroy everything I cared about. You played with me, and now you expect gratitude? The fact that I'm alive is not due to your benevolence. It's pure luck."

Roman shrugged, his gaze never wavering. "Business is business. And in the end, everyone got what they wanted. The IPA got rid of a threat—the unethical practices of your family have been exposed and terminated, I gained new technology, and you…you're free from the shackles of that legacy. You got your freedom, something you've always desired."

Every word that spilled from his lips deepened the furrows on my forehead, and I had to remind myself to keep my breathing even, lest my agitation show.

Isla's face was a painting of mixed emotions—shock, anger, and a hint of sadness. Her family's legacy, one she'd been so passionate about preserving in her parents' honor, had been sacrificed in this elaborate game. To see her so devastated made my insides churn with fury.

"You never cared for anyone but yourself."

Roman's sharp gaze met mine, and I could sense the calculating nature behind those cold eyes. "It was necessary." His voice was almost soothing. "A necessary sacrifice. You should be thanking me. I was able to free Isla from the chains of her family's expectations and deliver her into your arms."

I growled, my patience wearing thin. "Enough of this. You have done enough damage. Stay away from her."

"We'll see about that. We're still business partners, after all." Roman smirked, his arrogance apparent. "Especially since her grandfather is no more."

"What do you mean, 'no more'?" Isla asked, frowning. "We signed the merger contract. He has no rights to either company anymore."

Roman's cocky demeanor deflated, his face appeared apologetic. "Your grandfather had a heart attack during the evacuation. He's no longer with us."

Isla frowned, but I could sense a great whirlpool of emotions from her through our bond.

"I'm sorry, Isla," I whispered, kissing her forehead as I pressed her harder against my side.

"There's no need to be sorry," Isla replied, glaring at Roman. "While I can't say that I don't feel sad about his passing, the truth is, he was no longer the man I looked up to. Ever since my parents were assassinated, he became someone I didn't recognize anymore. It was always about the legacy, keeping power and wealth, and never about family."

"What do you want us to do with his body?" Roman asked, gently. "You're his next of kin."

"Cremation," she replied swiftly, as if she'd thought about it before. "Use his ash to make a cremation diamond. His body can become the one thing he cared about—wealth and legacy."

Roman raised an eyebrow. "Do you want the diamond to be set into jewelry?"

"Have them make a ring...but I don't know if I would ever wear it."

"Understood." Roman nodded. "I'll see to it. Will you be attending the ceremony before you leave Earth?"

Isla's head snapped toward me. "We're leaving Earth?"

"Yes, tomorrow." I sighed, shooting a glare at the human male. "I was going to tell you. I was granted leave. I'd like to spend my time getting to know you in a vacation pod the IPA has purchased for us on my home planet, X'thyrl."

"Purchased?" Isla tilted her head.

"The IPA has compensated you for the damages done to your property," Roman explained. "And for looking after an IPA commander. You've been awarded IPA citizenship and a credit chip, into which I'll deposit money from our company's profits.

"I was telling the truth when I said my goal was to create a sanctuary for IPA citizens, outside of the Atlantis base." He sighed, running his fingers through his hair. "I know I kept you in the dark about some things, and I understand you may hate me for it, but I will keep our agreement. I will run both companies, and you will be paid through the IPA credit system. I understand what I've done and what you've gone through. I understand if you hate me. But I really hope that one day we can work together to help bring about peace between humans and the rest of the IPA...no matter what planet you're on."

"I don't hate you," Isla replied, laying her head against my chest as she stared at Roman's vidcall. "But I need time to adjust. I do wish to continue our platonic business relationship moving forward."

"I understand." Roman nodded and grinned. "I will take care of everything Earthside, and make sure your grandfather's ceremony and diamond are taken care of."

"I'll have to deal with the estate sometime, too."

"I have just the team of lawyers who can help you," Roman offered. "I can put you in contact with them. You might be able to work something out so you don't have to return to Earth to sign anything."

"Really?" Isla's eyebrows shot up.

"Yes, really," Roman replied. "Everything is either signed by blood drop, e-sign, or an eye/fingerprint combo scan."

"I will make sure she has access to the long-distance communicator to keep in contact with you," I added. "Whatever it takes to make this process easier."

"I can't believe I'm heading to an alien planet," Isla muttered, wistfully.

"Enjoy your freedom!" Roman leaned back, looking satisfied. "You deserve it."

THIRTY-FOUR

ISLA

The vibrant glow of the dome city surrounding us was a marvel of alien technology, a glass bubble showcasing the wonders of the ocean depths. Bioluminescent marine life outside the domes created a surreal ambiance around us.

But for all its beauty, it felt suffocating.

We were so far beneath the surface that I couldn't even see a glimmer of daylight from where we were on the ocean floor. The darkness of the ocean above and the deep silence made me feel so small and vulnerable.

I reached for the bubble dome. My hand touched the glass wall. It was difficult to fathom that I was underwater in a hidden alien metropolis with the aquatic male who had changed my life forever over a year ago.

For a moment, the past few days flashed before my eyes —the fake wedding, the explosion, being kidnapped by Sam and Rose once again, killing them, and the boat crash that had almost led to my drowning.

Why did it always seem like my life circled back to the open waters?

Somehow, I had cheated death not once, but twice—because of Ky'rn.

"What's wrong?"

Ky'rn moved closer, his large frame a comforting presence. His dark blue scales shimmered in the dim light, highlighting his muscular aquatic form. Those glowing amber eyes, always watchful, now bore into mine, searching for answers.

"I just…a lot has happened, and I'm still trying to wrap my mind around it all," I confessed.

Ky'rn's expression softened. "I know you've been through a lot," he said softly, his amber eyes filled with understanding. "I'm here for you, Isla. I'll listen, whatever you need to say."

A suffocating blanket of guilt, relief, and raw fear pressed down on me, making it hard to breathe. "Am I…am I a bad person? For what I did to Rose and Sam?" I looked for judgment in his eyes. "Am I a monster for not regretting what I've done?"

Ky'rn studied me with a softness that took me by surprise. "I've been where you are," he admitted quietly. The gravity of his admission hung in the air, laced with fresh sorrow. "I've taken lives, and each one has left a mark. It never becomes easier. But never forget, what you did was self-defense. You protected your own life against those who sought to harm you. There's no shame in survival. It's only natural instinct."

Despite the comfort of his words, a gnawing dread remained. "But what if the leaders here decide to hand me over to human authorities?" I asked, anxiety evident in my voice. "What if the police come for me? I've taken two lives. My face will be all over the news. They'll charge me with murder."

Ky'rn gave a nonchalant shrug, the casual gesture at odds with the serious tone of our conversation. "You're now an IPA citizen. The circumstances of your actions were justified. And besides," he added with a sly smile. "We'll be leaving tomorrow morning. So, you really don't have much to worry about."

A restless energy stirred within me. "But what am I supposed to do once we leave Earth? I don't want to just... exist," I questioned, my voice tinged with frustration.

His smile widened. "You can do whatever you want. You have credits, resources; you don't even need to work if you choose not to."

I bit my lip, hope blossoming. "I don't want to be idle," I declared. "My research...I don't want to lose that part of me, especially now that I've broken free from the shackles of my grandfather's control and Earth's constraints. Do you think there would be a position within the IPA where I can continue my research?"

Ky'rn cupped my cheek, the cool touch of his skin grounding me. "Of course. The IPA values scientific expertise. With your background, you could greatly contribute to our understanding of marine life across galaxies. The universe is vast, Isla, and its oceans are endless. There's no doubt that the IPA would benefit from having you on board. We'll find a way for you to continue your research, even if I have to use some of my connections."

I nodded, grateful for his support. "I appreciate the offer, it's just...I don't want to have to depend on you for the rest of my life."

"There's nothing wrong with accepting help from others," he reminded me. "It doesn't make you weak. Everyone needs help at some point in their life. If I can use my position to get you what you need to feel fulfilled, to find your purpose, then

I will do so gladly. It's the least I can do because I care about you."

I sighed. "Yeah, but it's hard to wrap my mind around it," I admitted, my heart heavy with uncertainty. "How are we supposed to make this work?

"We are from two different worlds, Ky'rn. You're a Makezu commander with responsibilities. And me? I'm just a human marine biologist, and now, the sole survivor of my family's legacy—or whatever's left of it," I whispered, my voice shaky. "The challenges we've faced already are just the beginning. I'm not foolish enough to believe otherwise. How do we build a life from this chaos?"

"I know it's overwhelming. And I won't lie; there will be challenges." He offered a reassuring smile, his sharp teeth peeking out. "Isla, it does not matter where we come from or what our pasts entail. What matters is now. And right now, all I see is a strong, brave female who has faced insurmountable odds and still stands. We will face our future together, one day at a time."

I looked deep into his eyes, seeking the truth in his soothing words, but the uncertainty remained. Its weight bore heavily on my chest, tightening every breath I took.

The underwater city lights outside our dome's window cast their ethereal glow upon Ky'rn's distinct features, emphasizing the ridges and smooth scales that adorned his face. He held my gaze, unflinching and sincere.

It was then that I realized that amidst the chaos in my life, Ky'rn had always been my anchor.

"Isla," he said gently. "I can sense your unease. Speak your heart to me."

I swallowed hard, fighting back the tears threatening to break free. "Ky'rn..." I hesitated, looking down, "won't you desire someone...more like you? Someone aquatic?"

He closed the distance between us, lifting my chin gently with his cool, webbed fingers. His eyes, filled with sincerity, locked onto mine. "Isla," he whispered, his voice like the gentle lapping of waves on my soul. "Our bond transcends physicality. The moment our souls connected, I knew you were the one. It wasn't about species or where we come from, but who we are inside."

A tear slipped down my cheek, and he reached out to catch it, letting the droplet absorb into his skin. "While our external worlds might be vastly different," he continued, "our hearts beat in tandem. You question our future, and rightfully so. The unknown is daunting. But know this. No matter where we end up or what challenges lie ahead, my commitment to you remains unwavering."

The warmth of his words wrapped around me, and I pressed myself into his chest, letting his strong arms encircle me. The steady rhythm of his heartbeat soothed my fraying nerves.

"I'm scared," I admitted, my voice muffled against his torso.

"And that's okay," he murmured into my hair, pressing a soft kiss on my head. "We'll face the future together, Isla. Whatever comes our way, I'll be right by your side."

"Promise?" I whispered, needing assurance.

"Always," he murmured against my forehead, sealing the promise with a gentle kiss. "Love is universal, Isla. It transcends boundaries, cultures, and species. We have already proven that. As for the rest, we'll figure it out. Together."

As I took a moment, letting his words sink in, the doubts and fears momentarily drifted away.

For the first time in a long while, I felt a surge of hope and the comforting embrace of love. With Ky'rn by my side, the future, though uncertain, didn't seem so daunting after all.

THIRTY-FIVE

KY'RN

The warmth of her body nestled against mine, every breath she took seemed to align with the rhythm of my twin hearts. My relief was palpable as I sensed the turmoil in her mind settle, replaced by a cautious hope.

Every inhale of mine took in the scent of her hair, a mix of ocean salt and fresh blossoms. It was intoxicating and grounding all at once.

The Stars knew how much I cherished this fragile, fierce human.

It stung that she harbored doubts about my future, but given what she'd been through, I couldn't fault her. My mark on her was not just a physical bond but an emotional one; a commitment I had made to her.

"I don't care about the differences in our species." I murmured, my voice husky. "We'll navigate these waters together. As long as you're with me, Isla, I have faith that the Stars will guide us."

The warmth of her breath tickled my chest as she chuckled softly. "You really care about me, don't you?"

I tilted her chin up, ensuring her eyes met mine. "When it comes to you? Always."

Everything we'd gone through had, in some strange way, brought us closer.

We were two souls from vastly different worlds, entwined by fate and united in love. The mark on her neck, a symbol of our unbreakable bond, pulsed gently, reminding me of the promise I'd made. My vow.

She leaned back, looking up at me, her eyes sparkling like the luminescent corals of the deep as she took my hand, lacing our fingers together. "I think you're right. We need a fresh start, away from all the chaos."

I nodded. "Then let's explore Atlantis," I murmured, caressing her face. "We have the entire city to explore. I'm not certain when we'll return to Earth, if ever. And honestly, I want to show you the wonders of my world, and what life will be like on X'thyrl."

She smiled, albeit hesitantly. "Considering the current disagreements between Earth's governments and the IPA, it's best if we distance ourselves. Besides," she sighed. "We can return, perhaps, when things settle down, but for now, I am glad we're leaving in the morning. I want to embrace this new chapter, away from Earth's conflicts, away from the shadows of my past."

Her words, though filled with hope, carried the weight of past burdens. I caressed her cheek, the cool touch of my skin making her shiver.

She looked thoughtful for a moment, biting her lower lip, a gesture I found incredibly endearing. A hint of mischief lit her eyes. "How exactly do we traverse the depths of Atlantis…together?"

A chuckle escaped my lips. "My dear Isla, leave that to

me. The wonders of Atlantis await, and I promise you, I won't leave your side."

Excitement flashed in her eyes, chasing away the shadows of doubt. "Lead the way, *Commander*. Show me your world."

I pulled her close, relishing the laughter that bubbled from her lips. "Then hold on tight, my love. Atlantis awaits us."

"Tell me what I need to do."

I turned to the dome's entrance, excited to show her the life under the water's surface.

"All you need to do is touch the entrance to our dome's wall," I instructed, my voice gentle but firm. "Your living suit will transform, creating boots and gloves over your bare feet and hands, and it will form a mask over your head to allow you to breathe, sealing your body from the elements."

"Are you sure it's safe?" she asked, concern clear in her voice.

I nodded, offering her a smile. "Absolutely. You'll be perfectly safe," I assured her. "It was created by some of the greatest minds in the IPA to allow land-dwelling species to visit our cities and homes. While on land, it will shrink to a circlet around your neck, and will only activate when you enter the water again."

Releasing her, I motioned for her to follow me as I used my powerful arms to propel my body toward the entrance on the mossy sea floor. Without hesitation, I dove through the plasma door and into the cool, inviting oceanic waters outside.

The sensation of water against my scales was exhilarating, and I reveled in the freedom of the open sea. I glanced back at the dome, its tinted privacy layer preventing me from seeing inside. However, through our connection, I could sense Isla's fiery determination burning brightly.

I concentrated on projecting my thoughts to her, hoping

that our connection had grown strong enough so she could pick up on my emotions and intentions. *Come, Isla,* I urged silently, my mental message filled with encouragement and warmth. *You can do this. Join me.*

As she emerged, my doubts faded away, replaced by heightened awareness of her presence. Isla, with her newly formed webbed gloves and sleek finned slippers, looked magnificent. The darkness of the material made her ethereal beauty even more pronounced.

It was as if she belonged here, with me, in the heart of the ocean.

She hesitated, her eyes scanning our vast underwater realm, filled with wonder. I could sense her awe, but also her nervousness. Her fingers, covered in the suit's material, twitched slightly.

She tentatively swam toward me, her movements graceful in the weightless water. Tiny air bubbles streamed behind her. Her eyes were wide, absorbing the world around her.

It felt surreal, having her here, in my world.

As I reached out to take her gloved hand, wanting to comfort her, to share my feelings, I was hit by a stark realization as our hands met.

Our touch wasn't as intimate as before.

I felt a pang of frustration at the barrier that the suit created, cutting off our direct contact. Our bond had always been most potent when our skin met, and now I yearned to hear her thoughts and feel her emotions.

Confusion flooded her expressive eyes. She opened her mouth to speak, but no sound emerged. She pointed at her throat, eyebrows furrowing in frustration.

The living suits, as impressive as they were, limited our unique connection. My hearts sank, but I masked my feelings and gave her a reassuring smile.

This was not the time to let her see my doubts.

I cupped her face, trying to convey that everything would be alright.

My instincts demanded that I deepen our bond, making my thoughts spiral around one burning desire: to claim her, to ensure she was irrevocably mine.

Taking a chance, I pressed my forehead to hers, hoping that the proximity might allow for a faint connection.

I focused my thoughts, sending waves of longing, affection, and desire her way, hoping she could feel even a fraction of my intensity. She blinked and then nodded, her gaze deepening with understanding and mirrored need.

Navigating through the waters of Atlantis, my thoughts centered solely on Isla. Every movement she made in the water, every bubble that escaped her lips, every little glance she threw my way—each action served to inflame my desire for her.

The barrier of her suit standing between us was a reminder of the final step we had yet to take.

The need to claim her consumed my every thought. How wonderful it would be to share my mind with hers. Not just for the bond it would solidify but for what it would enable us to share—a connection so profound that only death could sever it.

Every look, every subtle touch, only stoked the fires of my need. I wanted to feel her, to taste her, to claim her in the most intimate way. The primal urges within me grew stronger with each passing moment, as did the realization that Isla felt the same hunger.

This went beyond infatuation. Every fiber of my being insisted that she was meant for me. I wanted to share every part of me with her—mentally, emotionally, and physically.

Her uncertainty about our future together, her fear of not

being enough for me…that she could ever doubt her worth to me was unfathomable.

She was it for me.

My mate, my other half.

The pull I had felt toward her since she first crossed my path was undeniable, magnetic.

Soon, we would be back in our private pod, hidden away from the world outside. And there, I would vanquish her doubts by giving her my mating mark, completely sealing her to me.

It wasn't just a physical act, but an emotional and spiritual one, too. It would be a declaration to the universe that Isla belonged with me, and I with her, binding us in ways words could never describe.

The thought of our union, the way she would sigh into my touch, the sensation of her skin against mine, how she would wrap her legs around me, pulling me closer—it was enough to drive me wild.

Each night, I'd longed for the intimacy, the unity of our souls, the feeling of her heartbeat against my chest, the taste of her on my lips as I fed from her, her soft moans echoing in the chamber as pleasure coursed through her. Her body would coil around mine, her legs wrapping around my waist, anchoring us to each other as we sought solace in our shared passion.

Hopefully tonight, we would finally be one, in every sense of the word.

THIRTY-SIX

ISLA

Surrounded by vast dark water, the iridescent glow from the Atlantean structures was otherworldly. It was like diving into a dreamscape colored with the vibrant hues of lit domes.

Atlantis was a jewel under the sea, its beauty unparalleled.

While I now understood the incredible tech that allowed me to be here—the living suit, the life support systems of Atlantis—I still felt like I didn't belong. I felt like we had already left Earth.

Ky'rn was a solid presence beside me, watching over me.

As we swam, I could sense Ky'rn's efforts to accommodate my slower pace, but it wasn't long before I began to struggle to keep up with his stamina.

In a swift motion, Ky'rn pulled me to him. My heart raced as I felt the strength of his arms encircle me, lifting me up. Instinctively, I wrapped my legs around him, clinging to his sturdy frame. My laughter rang out as I felt like a starfish seeking sanctuary on a rock in the midst of a raging tide.

His touch, even through my protective living suit, sent

shivers down my spine. His grip was firm but gentle, and the way he held me, so gently yet with such possessiveness, made my heart race.

My face was buried in the curve of his neck, feeling safe in his embrace. I felt every powerful surge of his body as he propelled us forward. His strong muscular body moved through the water with such grace and agility that it took my breath away. Every time he glanced down at me, there was a weight to his gaze, a depth of emotion that words would never convey.

Still, how I wished we could talk, share this experience in more than just silent gestures. I yearned to hear his thoughts, to know what he was thinking, to share in his emotions as we explored this underwater paradise.

As we moved, the majestic scenery of Atlantis unfurled before us—beautiful coral formations, schools of multi-colored fish that seemed to dance in synchronized harmony, and structures that glowed with an ethereal light.

It was all breathtaking.

The inhabitants of Atlantis were just as mesmerizing. The Makezu moved with grace and precision, their elegant forms sliding through the water effortlessly. Every nod Ky'rn received was a testament to his honorable rank. It was evident that he was revered and respected. Their gazes lingered on me with silent questions.

The Krukken were another story altogether. With elongated tentacles and sinuous movements, they looked regal, moving in a manner that was reminiscent of the way jellyfish or octopuses glided through the waters.

But as captivating as the surroundings and its inhabitants were, my thoughts inevitably drifted back to Ky'rn and the silence that weighed on me. The need to communicate, to share my thoughts and feelings with him, gnawed at me.

It was strange how I'd taken the simple act of speaking, of listening, for granted.

As Ky'rn continued to guide me through Atlantis, I realized that despite our inability to converse, our connection had deepened. Every touch, every shared glance spoke volumes. And as I nestled closer to him, I knew that no matter the barriers, we would be fine.

We had survived my grandfather. We could survive our future—together.

The moment I stepped into our private pod, the living suit that clung to me like a second skin began to dissolve, retreating into the choker around my neck. The unexpected transformation left me momentarily disoriented, standing bare in the pod's entrance. The moss floor was surprisingly warm under my feet, its softness a stark contrast to the cold, harsh waters outside.

My eyes scanned our surroundings, and I quickly noticed several additions. Placed on a makeshift loft were items that promised comfort: soft pillows, a thick blanket, and atop them, neatly folded, were garments that appeared tailored for my form—a robe and a set of clothes. Nestled among the pillows was a wristband, its screen glowing faintly.

Adjacent to the loft was an intriguing piece of furniture resembling a shallow bathtub. Instead of water, it was filled with the same moss-like material that cushioned the floor.

Was it a bed, or did it serve some other purpose?

Next to the entrance sat a cubic metallic chest, its surface gleaming with a polished sheen. It looked like a high-tech cooler, and I wondered if it contained our dinner.

Ky'rn's appearance in the entrance drew my attention, and I stepped away to allow him to enter.

His powerful form moved effortlessly across the floor, water droplets sliding off his gleaming scales and creating a trail as he made his way to the moss-filled tub.

He settled on his back, leaning comfortably against one end of the tub, gracefully curling up within. His tail, sinuous and graceful, hung lazily over the ledge, its tip twitching occasionally. His eyes, pools of liquid amber, locked onto mine, carrying a silent invitation.

"Looks like the staff dropped off our bedding and meal for the night," he murmured, his voice a deep rumble.

The slow pulsating glow from the room caught his dripping scales, turning them into a canvas of shimmering hues. His eyes, deep and watchful, never strayed from me.

Suddenly, the warmth of the pod seemed too stifling. My breaths grew shallow. My skin tingled, especially around my neck where the choker rested, reminding me of the mark Ky'rn had given me, and how he'd done it.

My mind was a whirlwind of thoughts, dominated by one overwhelming emotion—desire.

The prospect of being devoured, in both the literal and metaphorical sense, sent a flutter of excitement and trepidation through my core.

Was it wrong for these carnal desires to permeate my mind, to want to be completely claimed by him?

This wasn't just about attraction or a fleeting moment of lust. It was deeper, more profound. It was the culmination of an indescribable bond that had been forming between us since that fateful night.

A faint smile tugged at my lips when I remembered his protective and gentle nature, and how he had come to my rescue. The depth of his affection, paired with an almost feral possessiveness, made me feel like his most treasured possession. It was intoxicating, knowing how much he cared, how he had thrown himself into danger's path to ensure my safety, not once but twice.

The world had thrown so much at me, and in the midst of all the chaos and uncertainty, he had emerged as my rock, my anchor.

Our connection was undeniable, woven from threads of survival, longing, and instinctive trust. Deep-seated longing stirred within me, a desire to be wholly his, to share every facet of life with him, far away from the constraints and perils of my past.

Shaking away the barrage of emotions, I tried to clear my thoughts, if only momentarily, and knelt beside the metallic chest. Its design was alien, without any clear indication of how to access its contents.

"Press both side buttons simultaneously," Ky'rn whispered softly. "Then the center one."

I felt the warmth creep onto my cheeks. "Thank you," I whispered, my fingers fumbling slightly before managing to open the box.

There was an unmistakable hint of regret in his voice as he added, "I'm sorry I didn't help you with that."

"It's okay, Ky'rn." I turned slightly, flashing him a reassuring smile. "I understand that your movement is limited in the pod."

He met my eyes squarely, the intensity in them unwavering. "For you, Isla," he murmured. "Every hardship is worth undertaking, if it means I can make things easier for you."

My heart skipped a beat. The raw honesty of his statement, the raw emotion in his gaze, left me breathless.

The blush that burned my cheeks spread down my neck and further. Ky'rn's gaze was intense, dark with promise and desire, and it was directed solely at me. His words always found a way to curl around my heart and squeeze.

Opening the chest, I found an array of food—some alien and some familiar. There were fresh fruits I recognized, like berries and apples, but also some I had never seen before, with glistening exteriors and tantalizing scents. There were also containers filled with liquids—juices, perhaps?

Ky'rn shifted, rolling to his side and resting his head on one of his arms. "I had them include some Earth fruits. I thought you might like them."

I smiled softly, touched by his consideration. "Thank you."

He shrugged, but the warmth in his eyes was unmistakable. "It's the least I can do for my mate."

My heart thudded heavily. "Mate?"

A sly grin appeared on his face. "Well, that's what I hope you'll be. But only if you wish."

My fingers lightly brushed the choker around my neck, concealing the feeding mark he'd left there. All I wanted was to be with him, to learn about his world and discover every facet of our bond.

Picking up the open chest, I moved closer and sat down beside him. Smiling,

I selected a ripe berry from the box and slowly brought it to his lips. The smooth surface of the fruit met his damp lips, and as he parted them, his warm, rough tongue grazed my fingers, sending shivers down my spine.

His amber eyes, filled with affection and desire, never left mine.

"I choose you," I whispered against his lips, sealing our fate with a kiss.

In a swift movement, he reached over and seized the chest that lay upon my lap, setting it soundly on the floor. His other hand cradled the back of my neck, drawing me close until our lips collided with fiery urgency.

His lips, surprisingly soft, moved against mine with a fierce intensity. The edges of his teeth, sharper than a human's, grazed my bottom lip, sending electrifying tingles down my spine. I reciprocated his passion, our tongues dancing as we explored each other.

A deep growl rumbled from his chest, the vibrations resonating through me. He pulled back slightly, just enough for our eyes to meet. The intensity of his gaze was piercing, dark and stormy like the deepest part of the ocean, and it held me captive.

"I've been aching to claim you fully," he confessed, his voice gravelly. "To mate mark you so that everyone sees that you're mine, and only mine. I've wondered, hoping, craving the moment you'd express the same desperate need I feel for you."

His words sent a thrill down my spine, the weight of his possessiveness both overwhelming and exhilarating.

"Guiding you around Atlantis was bittersweet. To be so close yet separated from your thoughts…It pained me that I couldn't hear your voice or feel your emotions, couldn't communicate the maelstrom of feelings surging within me… it was torture. I want to change that."

His emotions, raw and palpable, struck me. "Ky'rn," I breathed, my voice trembling. "How can we change that?"

He deftly slid his arm around my waist, drawing me onto his lap with a swift, fluid motion, pulling me flush against him. His nose trailed a path down my neck, eliciting a shiver as he leaned in, inhaling deeply. His other hand wrapped around my breast, his thumb stroking over my nipple, causing it to harden instantly under his touch.

"If I drink from you," he murmured into the skin of my

neck, his voice thick with desire. "While pouring my essence into you. If we share our life forces, our souls will be intertwined. We'll be tethered to each other. No obstacle or distance can break that bond, until death takes us."

His words left me trembling. Heat pooled within me, a powerful yearning overtaking all other thoughts. The very core of me throbbed with need, every part of me yearning to be closer to him.

"But," I panted, trying to gather my scattered thoughts as I melted into his embrace, "will it allow us to truly communicate?"

He shifted slightly, pressing his lips to my shoulder, the hint of teeth in his gentle bite sending a jolt of pleasure straight to my core. "No matter where you are, no matter the distance, you'll know where I am and sense what I feel. And I will have the same privilege as you. We'll be able to talk, not with words, but with thoughts…with our very souls, through our bond."

His words echoed in my mind. The notion of being so deeply connected to each other was almost overwhelming. "It sounds…so intimate. Binding. So permanent."

"That it is," he murmured, his other hand sliding to the apex of my thighs, even as he continued to massage my breast, sending spirals of pleasure throughout my body. His gaze, intense and burning, locked onto mine. "Is that what you desire?"

My whole being called out in agreement. "Yes," I whispered, my voice hoarse. "I want it all."

His mouth descended to the tender curve of my neck, each nibble sending electric shocks down my spine. His large, strong hand massaged my breast with a possessive touch, the sensation both gentle and demanding.

I was utterly lost in the sensation of him—his scent, his touch, his presence.

His other hand ventured lower, fingers gracefully slipping between my thighs, cupping my core with a boldness that took my breath away. His fingers traced the sensitive lines of my folds, teasing, tantalizing. Every touch was calculated, designed to stoke the flames of my desire until they threatened to consume me.

My back arched, instinctively pressing against him, seeking more of the contact that sent shivers of pleasure racing through me.

As I ground my backside into him, soft moans, unbidden and uncontrolled, escaped my lips, echoing in the stillness of the room. Each sigh and cry was a testament to the building passion and desire he was invoking within me.

Ky'rn responded with a deep, guttural hiss, and suddenly, I felt the unique sensation of two protrusions pressing insistently between my thighs. I gasped, and peered down to see two large, jagged dark blue members with triangular heads. They both emanated warmth, dripping with a slick essence that made my core throb harder.

"I've dreamt of this moment, Isla. Of filling you completely, merging with you in the most primal way." Ky'rn's voice was thick with desire, his words dripping with anticipation. "Your blood is like an intoxicating drug to me, made all the more potent when you're lost in the throes of pleasure."

I wrapped my fingers around each of his cocks, my grip firm yet gentle, my fingers curving around the unique, jagged shape. They felt much like lightning bolts, but with smoother corner tips. The touch was explorative, an attempt to know and feel the entirety of him. With every movement of my hands, my fingers became familiar with the texture, the pulsing warmth, the very essence of him.

Ky'rn's response was immediate and fierce. He hissed sharply, pressing his mouth to the crook of my neck, his teeth grazing the delicate skin there. The primal growl that rumbled from deep within his chest sent shivers down my spine. "Isla," he growled, my name sounding like both a plea and a warning.

Without thinking, driven by a burning need, I pressed my drenched core against him, rubbing against the base of his cocks. Each glide was a dance of slick friction, a rhythm that mirrored the tantalizing circles his fingers were drawing on my throbbing clit.

The teasing and tormenting, combined with the feel of his lengths pressed against my core, sent me spiraling. I ground harder, the friction between us reaching a fevered pitch.

As if summoned by my own growing desire, a pearlescent liquid began to pour from his cocks. His essence, thick and shimmering like liquid moonlight, poured forth in copious amounts, coating my thighs and pooling between us. The sensation was immediate—an intense sizzling heat that magnified the sensations coursing through me.

Ky'rn's breath came in short, ragged gasps, each one sounding more desperate than the last, and I could feel the restraint in his body as he tried to control the primal urges surging through him.

"Isla…what are you doing?" His voice was a raw whisper, filled with an edge of restrained hunger.

My gaze met his, my own breaths uneven. "I need you, Ky'rn. I want to touch you, to feel you, to share everything with you."

His eyes, dark with need, bore into mine. "If you don't stop, Isla," he murmured, voice trembling with barely contained desire. "I'll lose control. I will snap and claim you…and I might not be able to stop."

My fingers trembled slightly, but not out of fear. "I'm not afraid," I whispered, a challenge in my voice. "I know you won't hurt me."

Guided by instinct and need, my feet planted firmly on the soft moss beneath us, I rose slightly, taking one of his cocks to my entrance. I began to lower myself onto him, feeling the intense stretch and the warmth of his essence easing the way.

Taking a deep breath, I began to descend. The sensation was overwhelming—a mixture of pleasure and stretching that was both delicious and intense.

To maintain some semblance of control, I took his other length into my hands, holding it firmly as if it were an anchor in this whirlwind of sensation.

A deep moan tore from my throat, the sensation over-whelming, pleasure coiling tighter within me.

Ky'rn hissed, his hands gripping my hips, fingers digging into the flesh. "Isla, you feel…so tight," he rasped. An invol-untary thrust, born out of pure need, had him bucking upward, seeking more of the exquisite tightness that enveloped him.

The sudden movement and the surge of pleasure it brought had me moaning, and without thinking, I sank all the way down, sheathing him completely inside me.

The pleasure was sharp and immediate, coursing through me like a lightning bolt.

Ky'rn's eyes widened, a deep growl vibrating through his chest.

"What are you doing?" he rasped, his voice ragged.

A sly smile tugged at my lips. "Stroking you as I ride

you," I teased, beginning to move atop him, setting a rhythm that was both tantalizing and satisfying.

Pushing myself up slightly, I began to move, riding him with a passion and fervor I didn't know I possessed. Each thrust intensified the sensations, the world around us fading as our bodies became one.

There was only the sound of our labored breathing, the slick sounds of our joining.

Every movement, every touch, was electric.

His deep growl resonated through me, sending ripples of arousal through my core. "You've shown me salvation, Isla," he rumbled, his eyes burning into mine with an intensity I'd never seen before. "Now, let me show you ecstasy. Tell me what you want, how I can awaken your deepest desires. Teach me."

Hearing his plea, my heart raced even faster. "Touch me," I whispered breathlessly. "Bite me, drink from me, claim me fully."

He obeyed without hesitation.

His fingers, surprisingly soft for their strength, sought out the sensitive nub between my legs, applying just the right pressure and rhythm, rubbing it in time with the rhythmic movements of my hips, making my body sing.

With every movement, I was carried higher, closer to the edge of bliss.

The sensations were exquisite, taking my breath away. I surrendered to the pleasure, letting it wash over me as I continued to ride him.

Suddenly, his hand wrapped around my hair, tugging it back to expose the curve of my neck. He leaned forward, and I felt the sharp pressure of his teeth biting into my shoulder. I gasped as his teeth sank into my flesh, igniting a mix of pain and pleasure that spiraled through me, making every nerve ending come alive.

The feeling was intoxicating.

As he drank from me, something primal within was awakened, a connection growing tighter and more profound. The thickened member in my hand pulsed in tandem with the one buried deep within me, each thrust stretching me deliciously. His skin heated as I felt his essence pouring over and inside me.

Then, like a dam breaking, heat exploded from Ky'rn. His essence drenched us, seeping between our connected bodies, marking me in the most intimate way.

Bright spots of light danced before my closed eyes, every fiber of my being alight with pleasure.

"Mine...mine...mine," he chanted, his voice echoing the rhythm of our joined bodies with a possessive growl that sent me over the edge.

Releasing his cock, I allowed myself to fall backward, nestling against his hard chest, the remnants of our passion still connecting us. I felt peace and satisfaction like never before. His other length remained deeply sheathed within me, connecting us in the most intimate way possible.

Lying there, surrounded by his warmth and strength, I smiled, my heart full. Unable to utter a word, one thought filled my mind, echoing back to him. *"Yours."*

THIRTY-SEVEN

KY'RN

The intensity of our connection left an indelible mark on my soul.

The rush of her lifeforce still pulsed through me, intertwining with mine—a torrent of emotions, sensations, and connections that was as overwhelming as it was intoxicating. She was now an irrevocable part of me, and every instinct within me roared in satisfaction.

She was mine, truly and completely.

Only the grip of death could ever part us now.

However, with that newfound connection came an even greater sense of responsibility. She had given herself to me in the most intimate way possible, and I had taken, relished, and reveled in our union.

She was exhausted, her human frame more delicate than mine. This was not the time to indulge my desires. She needed rest, and I would ensure she got it.

With a gentle touch, I reached for the blanket draped over the portable cot and pulled it over her, cocooning her in its warmth. My own body, adapted to the aquatic environs of my home planet, naturally ran cooler. It might not offer her the warmth she required, but I would do everything in my power to ensure her comfort.

Drawing her closer, I wrapped my arms around her, holding her close, nestling her against me, protective and possessive. My blavs slowly deflated, sheathing themselves. It was an automatic response, my body understanding the need for rest and recuperation.

Guilt nibbled at the edges of my consciousness. I should have seen to her needs, ensured she was well fed before I tired her out. In the heat of our passion, the basic necessities had been forgotten. I would atone for it. Tomorrow, I vowed to feed her, care for her, cherish her.

The dawn of a new day was fast approaching, and with it, the promise of a fresh start.

Gently, I brushed back the stray strands of her hair, my fingers lingering over the mark on her shoulder. It sat just below the dormant living suit she wore, a testament to our bond—my claim to her. With tender care, I lapped at her skin, sealing my mate mark.

Soon, our shuttle would arrive, whisking us away from this place and toward new horizons. The thought of introducing her to my home planet, of building a life with her, brought warmth to my hearts.

A future where we would build a life together, away from all the pain Earth had brought us.

A soft, nearly imperceptible click jolted me from my slumber, pulling me into full alertness. My senses sharpened instantly, the primal need to protect my mate overriding everything else. An instinctual growl rumbled from deep within my chest, my eyes zeroing in on the entrance.

Isla stirred beside me, her eyes widening in fear. "Ky'rn?" she whispered, her voice quivering.

"Get behind me," I commanded, positioning myself between her and the door. I could feel the tension in the air, thick and palpable. *"I'll protect you."*

"What's happening?" she asked, clutching at the blanket.

"Someone's here," I responded tersely, extending my talons in preparation for a potential threat. My senses were on high alert, every muscle coiled and ready to spring into action.

No one would harm my mate. No one.

The plasma door unsealed with a hiss, revealing two figures. They were Ixik'tryl, their feathers a vibrant crimson adorned with shimmering streaks of orange and gold.

The alarm in my chest abated slightly; these were familiar faces. They were Atlantis staff.

The female, carrying a medpack, stared up at us with exasperation evident in her gaze. "By the deep seas, Commander, you two are going to be late," she trilled, her voice carrying a note of amusement. "Why isn't she dressed? Why aren't you both ready?"

I blinked, momentarily stunned. The rush of adrenaline began to subside, and I sheathed my claws, slightly embarrassed. "It's okay, Isla," I murmured, pulling her closer for a brief moment. "Everything's fine. Please, get dressed."

Her eyes searched mine for a moment, perhaps seeking assurance, a hint of color gracing her cheeks, likely recalling the events from last night, before she nodded and began to dress.

I took a deep breath, letting the tension seep from my muscles.

"We're going home," I affirmed, my voice softer now, filled with a tender promise. The female Ixik'tryl rolled her eyes but smiled knowingly as her partner gathered our belongings.

Isla sat beside me, dressed in her tunic and robe, and kissed me on the cheek. "We're going home."

THIRTY-EIGHT

ISLA

K y'rn glided effortlessly through the clear waters of the tank, his strong physique on full display. Every now and then, his gaze would find mine, and there was a twinkle in his eyes that made my heart race.

The mossy lounge chair beneath me was soft and inviting, but I couldn't tear my gaze away from the massive window wall.

The vast underwater dome surrounded us, but as much as I tried to lose myself in its mesmerizing depths, a nagging question kept resurfacing in my mind.

"Ky'rn," I called out, my voice echoing slightly in the expanse of the suite. "How are we supposed to take off from here? Doesn't the water hinder the engines?"

Pausing his laps, Ky'rn floated toward the water's edge, leaning on the tank's rim as he regarded me with a smile. Water droplets cascaded down his sculpted chest, shimmering under the light. "The dome we're in will rise out of the water," he explained. "Then it'll split in four, opening to the sky above. Only then will we take off."

His explanation only gave rise to more questions. "Why

keep such an elaborate setup underwater? Especially if humans can't access or even find Atlantis?"

His expression turned somber, and he sighed. "Because we can never be too safe. The universe is vast, and there are countless threats and unknown entities, one can never truly be safe. Concealing our launch points underwater adds an extra layer of security."

As I processed his words, a chill ran down my spine.

The waters of the tank shimmered with Ky'rn's every move, his mesmerizing form captivating me. But my thoughts were elsewhere, contemplating the vastness of the universe and the unknown entities that might reside there. "Are there…dangerous aliens out there? Ones that aren't part of the IPA?"

Ky'rn stilled. His eyes locked onto mine. "I won't lie to you. There are always potential threats," he admitted. "Even within the IPA, there are many within the same species with different intentions, some not always pure. Just like how not all humans are bad, nor all members of the same species are either. But you have to understand that on my planet, we're united. We have allies, shared understandings. We aid each other in times of crisis and trade with one another openly."

"Will I encounter other species where we'll live?"

He chuckled softly. "Mostly, you'll see more Ixik'tryl. They occasionally vacation in the jungle regions of our planet. Speaking of which, there's the Calyzis, a plant-like species, who reside deep within the jungles. They're biologically tied to their hometree. And in the desert areas, the Szelsei, a serpentine species, have their underground lairs."

"But what about the open waters?" I inquired, curious about who else shared Ky'rn's home planet.

"Just a few settlements of the Krukken," he said. "But the majority, like me, are Makezu."

Before I could delve further, a sudden tremor interrupted our conversation. The ground beneath us shook, and my heart raced as the dome began its ascent from the watery depths.

As we broke the surface, sunlight flooded the room, blinding in its intensity.

A beautiful spectacle unfolded before my eyes. The dome's thick slabs began to move outward, the mechanism so fluid and silent it seemed almost organic. Like petals of a blossoming flower, the dome divided into four segments. They expanded outward, revealing the enormous spaceport that had been hidden beneath the ocean's surface.

I stared wide-eyed, gripping the edges of my seat. "Ky'rn!"

"We're about to take off," Ky'rn warned, a hint of excitement in his eyes. "This is what we've been waiting for."

I glanced around frantically. "What should I do? I've never done this before!"

His laughter echoed with warmth, a reassuring sound in this unfamiliar environment. "Just buckle up and enjoy the view," he advised, pointing to the harness on the mossy chair.

Taking a deep breath, I followed his instructions and braced myself. As the vessel's engines roared to life, a sense of anticipation filled me.

The ground beneath us trembled and then, with an exhilarating rush of speed, we lifted off. I watched in awe as the scenery below began to shrink.

Buildings, trees, and landmarks became smaller and smaller, transforming into mere specks on the vast canvas of Earth. The ground, the seas, the familiar continents, all shrank to minuscule proportions.

As we soared higher, I could make out the entire continent, its intricate details merging into a blue-green mosaic.

And then, the familiar sight of the moon appeared,

looming large and radiant against the backdrop of space. As we flew past, I saw the craters and scars marring its surface.

Then, nothing but the vast expanse of space stretched out in every direction.

Stars twinkled like countless diamonds against the inky blackness, and far-off galaxies swirled in hues of blue, purple, and red. Nebulas painted the cosmos in brilliant strokes of color. It was an infinite, boundless expanse that made me feel insignificant, reminding me of how small we truly were in the grand scheme of things.

How could humans believe they were alone in this universe?

A lump lodged itself in my throat, and tears welled up in my eyes, spilling over as an indescribable weight lifted from my chest. But it wasn't a sorrowful release; it was the profound realization of freedom enveloping me. I felt liberated, as though a colossal burden I hadn't even been aware of had been gently lifted from my shoulders.

The melodic sound of water droplets echoed throughout the room as Ky'rn made his way from the water to join me on the moss lounge sofa.

As he settled next to me, droplets cascaded off his body, creating gentle ripples on the water below. The room's muted lighting bathed him in a soft luminescence, highlighting the dark-blue scales that covered his chiseled physique, making the edges gleam like polished sapphires. Wet strands of his almost-violet hair clung to his neck and broad shoulders, glistening and emphasizing the sharp contours of his chest and arms.

Every droplet seemed to play upon the muscles that were carved with such precision, reminding me of ancient marble statues I had seen in museums on Earth. I couldn't help but marvel at my good fortune—how had I become so lucky to have such a magnificent male by my side?

His amber eyes burned with an intensity that made my heart race. A hint of worry flickered in his eyes as he studied me. His strong, scaled hand reached out, gently cupping my cheek. "Isla," he murmured, his voice deep and rich. "What troubles you?"

I took a deep breath, the weight of emotions threatening to spill. "It's just…" I began, my voice quivering slightly. "The weight of everything we've been through, the sense of newfound freedom and wonder of the unknown in the sheer enormity of the universe we're in…it's just hit me. But in this moment, with you, I finally feel free. As if no one can try to control me and I can finally do whatever I want.

"I love you so much, and I'm so eager to face whatever comes next, as long as it's with you."

He brought his face close to mine, his eyes searching mine for a long moment. "We were brought together by fate, Isla. Despite the odds, the universe conspired to make our paths cross. Every challenge, every hardship…it was all worth it, just to be here with you."

His strong hands cradled my face, the cool contrast of his scales against my heated skin sending shivers down my spine. The world around us seemed to dissolve as the intensity of his amber eyes drew me in, their golden depths swirling with a tempest of emotions.

Then, in a slow, deliberate motion, his lips found mine.

The contact was soft at first, an exploration. His lips were cooler than mine but astonishingly soft, moving with a tenderness that belied the power contained in his form.

The kiss deepened as Ky'rn tilted his head, capturing my bottom lip between his. A soft moan escaped my throat, and the gentle touch became more urgent, more consuming.

His tongue teased the seam of my lips, seeking entrance. Granting him access, our tongues danced together, tasting and savoring each other. I clung to him, my fingers threading through his damp, violet hair, pulling him closer.

The world spun. My senses were flooded with him—the taste of the sea on his lips, the musky scent of his skin, and the powerful thrum of his hearts beneath my touch.

It was a kiss of passion, warmth, and the promise of eternity. The kind of kiss that melted away every ounce of doubt and fear, leaving behind only the raw, undeniable truth of our love.

Pulling back slightly, our foreheads touched. He gazed into my eyes with such tenderness and raw emotion. "I am completely, irrevocably in love with you, Isla," he confessed, his voice barely a whisper. "And I eagerly await to spend the rest of my life with you as my mate."

A warm smile tugged at the corners of my lips. "You're my anchor, Ky'rn. You've become everything I've ever wanted in a partner and more. And just like you, I can't wait to start this new chapter of our life together."

EPILOGUE

ISLA

Three Months Later…

G liding through the lavender-tinted shallows, I immersed myself in the vibrant underwater world that had become our home. Every hue of the coral, every dance of the marine creatures, had a story to tell, captivating me anew each day.

A soft smile tugged at the corners of my lips as I carefully collected samples, securing them in vials with practiced ease. My work as an marine biologist had merged beautifully with this new life off the jungle shore.

Ky'rn had taken on an assignment planetside, overseeing units tasked with defending our precious waters. It was a role that allowed him to stay close to me, and it was clear that his prince had recognized the importance of keeping us together, especially after all he had endured during his captivity.

While the idea of galactic voyages was thrilling, we both agreed that, for now, to prioritize Ky'rn's complete recovery —spiritually, mentally, and physically—was paramount. There would be time for us to explore other worlds in the future. I longed to study new alien marine life on distant planets, but for the present, this underwater sanctuary was our haven.

And honestly, I wasn't comfortable traveling off planet until Earth had settled its differences with the IPA. Even though I was an IPA citizen and officially mated to Ky'rn, I didn't want to take any more chances than I already had.

Being mated to an aquatic alien had its challenges, but Ky'rn was worth it. This life was worth it, and I wouldn't have it any other way.

As I was lost in my thoughts, a familiar thrill coursed through our bond, signaling Ky'rn's return from duty. He was on the hunt—for me.

His resonating presence was palpable, a rhythmic pull tugging at the corners of my consciousness—a pulse that called to me across the watery expanse.

Swiftly, I stashed my vials in a waterproof container and turned my attention to the sleek aquatic cruise-cycle beside me. Mounting it with practiced ease, I smacked the scanner, allowing my wristband to activate the vehicle before taking hold of the handlebars.

He was homing in on my location, and I could feel the intensity of his pursuit.

With a twist of the handle, I surged forward, casting a brief look back at the breathtaking underwater panorama painted in gentle hues of lavender and violet.

Across the calm surface, a dark, agile form cut through the water, drawing ever closer. Sunbeams pierced the water's surface, casting a dazzling dance upon Ky'rn's shimmering scales. I might have been captivated had I not been so intent on eluding him. Surrendering was the last thing on my mind.

"Think you can outswim me, my mate?"

"By all means, chase me," I countered playfully, masking

the truth that lay beneath. This chase was exhilarating, and the idea of being caught thrilled me.

Our playful predator-prey game never failed to excite me —the perfect welcome home treat.

The familiar silhouette of our beachside pod's underwater dome loomed ahead. Would I make it this time without being caught?

But Ky'rn was built for this world. With an astonishing display of speed, he lunged toward me, the strength of his tail granting him unmatched agility.

Laughter, light and bubbly, spilled from my lips into my mask as I expertly navigated the waters, slipping between coral formations and darting through natural archways, all in an attempt to elude him.

A soft, teasing graze against my ankle sent a tingle up my spine, and I couldn't stifle the joyous sound that escaped me.

As the shadow of our dome grew larger, I revved the cruise-cycle to its limits, heart pounding.

But just as the entrance to our home came into view, the world shifted. Powerful arms enveloped me, drawing me back against a solid, scaly chest. The sensation of his scales, cool and silken, pressed against my skin, made my heart race even faster. Within his embrace, I found both thrill and safety.

"Thought you could win, my little fish?" he teased. His mental voice sent tingles down my spine.

I smirked, trailing my fingers along the chiseled lines of his jaw. *"Always worth a try."*

He effortlessly hoisted my aquatic cruise-cycle onto its designated slot on our overwater dock. The contrast of his powerful physique against the cycle's delicate frame was a sight that never ceased to captivate me.

He turned, cradling me in his arms with a tenderness that contradicted his strength. His movements were fluid as he treaded toward the pristine white sands of our secluded beach.

As the waves lapped gently around us, I felt the water receding from my neck, triggering the transition of my living suit. Sensing the change in our environment, it swiftly receded into its dormant state, nestling comfortably around my neck as a delicate choker, leaving me in just my bikini and swimming skirt.

As Ky'rn gently set me down, the cool sand cradled my back while he positioned himself above me, nestling between my legs. His powerful arms created a protective barrier on either side of my head, and his dark-blue scales seemed to gleam even brighter in the sunlight. His intense amber eyes, full of raw desire, bore into mine.

"You might be swift, Isla, with all your clever maneuvers," he murmured, his voice a deep rumble. "But remember this: you can never truly evade me. I'll always be there, hunting you, reminding you where you truly belong."

Feeling the heat rise in my cheeks, I smirked and playfully nipped at his nose. "Maybe I need that reminder," I whispered, challenging him.

His response was a growl, primal and rough, sending shivers down my spine. "If it's a reminder you seek," he said, his voice husky, "I'll gladly provide it...by consuming every part of you."

My heart raced, my desire matching his. I entwined my legs around his strong waist, pulling him even closer. "Then come, my great hunter. Remind this prey where she belongs. I need you, crave you, yearn for you to claim me in every way."

The sensation of Ky'rn's weight atop me was intoxicating, but he held himself up with a strength that seemed both effortless and controlled. I felt the sand below me mold to fit the contours of our bodies, and the salty ocean breeze teased and caressed our heated skin.

His arm moved with a predator's precision, his fingers tracing a sultry path to the juncture of my thighs. Through the soft material of my bikini, he discovered my growing desire, rubbing and igniting a fire deep within me. As his expert fingers danced over my sensitive flesh, he lowered his face to my neck, nibbling and teasing the skin there, sending shivers of anticipation through me.

Every gentle caress, every calculated move was a testament to his mastery, and it sent waves of pleasure coursing through me.

"I've thought of you every moment today," he murmured huskily. "I've yearned to be back here, with you, to show you just how much I've missed you, how much I want you. How incredibly fortunate I am to call you mine."

His words, dripping with raw emotion, stoked the fire within me. My hands found their way into his thick, silky hair, pulling him closer, wanting to meld into him, to erase any distance between us.

With my eyes shut, I tuned into the deep, erotic connection we shared, feeling his desires amplify my own, pushing me to the brink of pleasure. Our bond vibrated with shared desire, the intensity of which threatened to overwhelm.

"Ky'rn," I gasped, my voice urgent. "I need...I need more."

A chuckle, rich and deep, vibrated against my skin. With a swift move, he shifted my bikini bottoms to the side. One finger, then two, plunged into me, exploring and stoking the fire he'd kindled.

As his fingers danced within me, his lips continued their trail of fire across my body, leaving no inch untouched, nipping and teasing.

The sensations coursing through me were almost too much to bear. The weight of Ky'rn's presence, the heat of his touch, and the tantalizing sensation of his dual hardness pressing insistently against my inner thighs—it was maddening. Each drag against my sensitive skin sent shockwaves of pleasure throughout my body, leaving trails of his warmth, marking me as his.

Desperation clawed at me, and my fingers dug into the rippling muscles of his back, scraping and urging him closer, the need to feel him inside me becoming unbearable. "Ky'rn," I gasped out, consumed by fervor. "I need you. Now."

He growled, predatory and protective all at once. "Impatient, are we?" His voice was a dark promise, full of barely contained desire.

In my desperation, I arched upward, trying to ensnare his twin blavs between my thighs, eager to feel them where I wanted them most.

He hissed—a sound of both pleasure and frustration. "I wanted to savor this," he murmured, his fingers drawing torturous circles around my clit, before thrusting three inside, scissoring and stretching in a maddening rhythm, sending me closer to the edge.

My eyes, previously squeezed shut, flew open, locking onto his. The intensity of his gaze held me captive. In one swift movement, I bucked against him, desperately trying to capture one of his blavs. I trembled, and once more, I tried to guide him to where I needed him. "Please, Ky'rn," I begged, my voice quivering, "I need you inside me."

His eyes, always so intense, darkened even more. The depths of his desire mirrored my own. His resolve crumbled, his growl filled with pure, unbridled lust. "I can't resist you, Isla," he admitted huskily. "Your pleas, your demands—they undo me. I want nothing more than to lose myself with you."

"Then do it," I challenged, not afraid of him or his feral predatory instincts.

As Ky'rn pulled his face away. A rush of cool air hit my flushed skin where his lips had been. His weight shifted off me momentarily, making sure not to hurt me. My senses heightened, feeling the soft sands beneath, the distant sounds of waves crashing, and the intoxicating scent of Ky'rn's musk mixed with ocean brine.

His fingers, which had been igniting a sweet torment, withdrew suddenly, leaving a void that sent a shiver of longing up my spine. A whimper escaped my lips, my body missing his touch. But it was a fleeting moment. Almost immediately, the unmistakable feeling of him lining up at my entrance sent another jolt of anticipation through me.

The initial press of his blav into me made my heart race, and as he sheathed himself completely, a moan tore from my throat. The sensation of him, so thick and warm, filled me in a way that made my entire body sing. It felt as though every nerve ending was on fire, the pleasure almost too much to bear.

His broad shoulders flexed above me, muscles taut from the effort of holding himself in check. I could see the struggle in his eyes, the hunger and need, warring with the deep-seated desire to treasure the moment, to savor every second with me. But I didn't want gentle right now; I wanted him, all of him.

I gripped his back, nails digging into his thick skin, leaving faint marks that would heal almost instantly, given his unique physiology. I shifted, trying to draw him even closer, to feel more of him. His low growl vibrated through me, adding to the electric charge between us.

The sensation of Ky'rn inside of me was nothing short of euphoric, a consuming fire that swept away any remaining barriers between us. The stretch and fullness brought forth a pleasure I hadn't known I craved until this very moment. Every push and pull of him inside of me sent ripples of ecstasy cascading through my body.

His sharp predator eyes never left mine. There was a ferocity to his gaze, one of ownership and possessiveness, but also deep, unrelenting love. His lips, slightly parted, were but a breath away from mine, his exhales syncing with my ragged ones.

"You're mine, Isla. Mine," he growled, his voice rich with raw emotion. Each word was punctuated with a deep thrust, grounding his claim within me.

I arched my back, pressing my breasts into his broad chest, my fingers digging into the sinewy muscles of his back, the delicate sting of his scales brushing against my skin. "Yours," I whispered back, the word more of a sigh, a confession, a pledge.

Surrendering to Ky'rn's touch, I allowed the waves of pleasure to wash over me. Each of his movements was deliberate, a testament to his desire to make me feel cherished and desired. The intensity of the connection between us was palpable, as if our souls were dancing in a harmonious rhythm. I felt myself teetering on the edge, the pleasure intensifying almost to the point of overwhelm.

With every push, every glide, he drove me closer to the precipice, my body coiling tighter and tighter.

His thoughts, intense and passionate, reverberated through our bond. He yearned to push our boundaries, to explore the depths of our connection in every way possible. His intentions flooded me with his great need—to worship me, to drink deeply from me, and the tantalizing promise of feeling both his blavs simultaneously.

"Do it," I urged him, needing to feel all of him.

He hesitated, eyes clouded with concern. "Isla," he murmured uncertainly. "I don't want to hurt you more than I already have."

His bites, the way he drank from me, always hovered on the edge of pleasure and pain.

I cupped his face, pulling him closer. "It's a pleasant kind of pain, Ky'rn," I reassured him, trying to convey just how much I craved it. "I want all of you. Both of your blavs."

He seemed taken aback, a frown marring his handsome features. "How could you even…?"

"There are ways," I said, a hint of mischief in my tone. "But I want to feel both of them, right where you are now."

Ky'rn's eyes darkened, the conflict evident in their depths. The sensation of him pulling out was a sharp contrast to the fullness I had felt moments before. The chill of the loss was immediate, and I found myself yearning for him, craving that intimate connection.

"What are you suggesting, Isla?" he rasped, staring down at where both his blavs were now positioned at my entrance.

A coy smile tugged at the corner of my lips. "I think you know exactly what I'm suggesting," I replied, wiggling my hips for emphasis.

He swallowed hard. "You've never taken both before," he said hesitantly.

"That's because we've never tried," I whispered, my fingers trailing down to where he was poised to enter. "But I want this, Ky'rn. And I know you want this too."

His dual shafts twitched in his grip, and I could see the struggle playing out on his face. The desire to fulfill my request weighed against the fear of causing me pain. "Isla," he began, but I silenced him with a finger to his lips.

"I trust you," I murmured, my gaze never leaving his. I bit my lip as the anticipation built within me. "Just go slow. Let me adjust."

The emotions that flashed across his face were myriad—desire, awe, excitement. "I will be gentle," he promised, his voice thick with emotion.

He took a shaky breath, showing just how much he valued my trust. Nodding slowly, he began to push forward. The sensation of being stretched by him, by all of him, was overwhelming. It was a heady mix of pain and pleasure, just as I'd anticipated.

I gasped, my fingers digging into his broad shoulders as I adjusted to his size.

He stilled, his brow furrowing with concern. "Are you okay?" he asked, his voice soft.

"Yes," I panted, willing my body to adjust. "Just…give me a moment."

After what felt like an eternity, the sharpness of the stretch began to subside, replaced by a fullness that left me breathless. I nodded at him, signaling that he could move.

He began to thrust, the sensation unlike anything I'd ever experienced. With every movement, the pleasure intensified, and our shared connection amplified everything. His thoughts, raw and unfiltered, echoed in my mind.

The love, the need, the desire—it was all there, laid bare for me to see.

"You're incredible," he growled, his thrusts becoming more insistent.

"And you," I gasped out, feeling the coil of pleasure tightening within me.

Ky'rn's powerful thrusts gained momentum, each more

intense than the last. The raw, primal need emanating from him was intoxicating. With a gracefulness belying his size, he descended onto his forearms, positioning himself closer to me. The warmth of his breath cascaded over my neck, his moist lips pressing gentle kisses on the sensitive skin there.

Feeling the sturdy planes of his chest against my soft breasts, the sensation sent waves of electricity through me, heightening my awareness of every touch, every movement.

Desperate to be even closer, I wrapped my arms around him, fingers digging into the sinewy muscles of his back. My legs instinctively encircled his waist, pulling him deeper into me, as if we could somehow become one entity.

In that euphoric haze, our minds melded together, our emotions and thoughts intertwining effortlessly, blurring the line between where he ended and I began. His most intimate thoughts, dreams, and desires flowed into me, all became a part of me, and in return, I gave him all of mine.

"Ky'rn, is this the beach?" I whispered, my voice shaky with emotion, gasping between shaky breaths. "The one you had me envision when we shared that intimate moment?"

A momentary pause in his rhythm signaled his surprise. He lifted his head, those dark, intense eyes locking onto mine, a mixture of wonder and disbelief. "You remember?" he rumbled, his voice thick with emotion. "Yes, Isla, this is the very place I dreamed of. The home where I longed to lose myself in you—dreamt of claiming you again and again."

A flood of emotions washed over me, and tears threatened to spill from my eyes. The weight of the love and trust between us was overwhelming. "Bite me," I breathed, tilting my neck to expose the sensitive juncture. "Drink from me, and let's live that dream together."

Ky'rn hesitated for just a fraction of a second before his instincts took over. His teeth, sharper than any human's, pierced the skin of my shoulder. The initial sting was quickly overshadowed by the overwhelming pleasure that followed. A primal sound escaped me as I reached up, fingers tangling in the thick, wet locks of his hair, yanking him closer, needing to feel the pressure of his bite even more.

Every tug and pull from his mouth sent shockwaves of pleasure through me, like electric jolts igniting every nerve ending. I anchored him to me, willing him to drink deeper, to take what he needed. I felt him drawing from me, a sensation that was equally about giving and receiving.

With my eyes closed, it was as if the world faded away, leaving only Ky'rn and me, and the connection we shared in that intimate moment. Every ebb and flow of pleasure mirrored in him, as if our souls were intertwined.

Heat began to build deep within me, spreading outward with every rhythmic beat of our hearts, every drop of blood he took. It felt as though we were on the edge of a precipice, teetering, waiting for that final push.

And then, with a sudden intensity that left me breathless, we plunged together into the depths of ecstasy. The heat inside me ignited, burning away all thought as waves of pleasure consumed us. Ky'rn's essence filled me, his warmth mingling with mine, igniting every cell in my body, binding us closer than ever before.

Our souls danced together in that moment, spiraling upward in a burst of orgasmic bliss.

Slowly, as the waves of pleasure began to recede, Ky'rn released his bite, leaving behind a mark that I'd wear with pride.

Gently, he licked my new bite mark, soothing the raw skin, the rough texture of his tongue sending tiny shivers down my spine. I felt his reverence, his gratitude, in every gentle swipe of his tongue. The rhythmic motion, combined with the afterglow of our shared climax, left me in a state of serene contentment.

Opening my eyes, I was met with the breathtaking sight of Ky'rn silhouetted against the backdrop of a fiery sunset. Vibrant hues of orange, pink, and purple painted the sky, casting a warm glow on his chiseled features. I reached up, brushing the curtain of hair from his face, my fingers lingering on his cheek.

A soft, heartfelt smile blossomed on my lips.

"Welcome home, Ky'rn."

AUTHORS NOTE

This book is a little darker than my usual stuff, but it isn't something I would consider "dark" by today's standards.

I had fun exploring the constraints that a wholly aquatic alien hero imposed, and I have a few more planned in the far future, including Roman's chance at love. 😊

ABOUT THE AUTHOR

USA Today Bestselling author, Jade Waltz lives in Illinois with her husband, two sons, and her three crazy cats.

She writes character driven romances within detailed universes, where happily-ever-afters happen for those who dare love the abnormal and the unknown. Their love may not be easy—but it is well worth it in the end.

Jade enjoys knitting, playing video games, watching Esports, green tea and writing all the stories that live in her imagination.

Website: www.jadewaltz.com

Newsletter link: https://landing.mailerlite.com/webforms/landing/c5y8l5

Email: authorjadewaltz@gmail.com

ALSO BY JADE WALTZ

MF Alien Dragonrider Romance Trilogy:

Across the Stars

Cosmic Threads of Fate #1

Alien dragon riders. Fated mates. She would do anything to protect his world.

Mae's mission was to find a potential location for the next human colony, however, she finds something more...

After landing on a newly discovered moon, she finds what she figured existed only as myths and legends... Alien dragon riders who live in enormous trees.

When one of the warriors, Watai, attempts to teach her about his world, he declares that she's his cosmicmate, and that they share the same cosmicthread—a fated cord, which has destined them to be together.

The more she learns about his home, the more she wants to protect him and his world from the very government that she works for.

Now she is faced with a difficult choice: To stay and embrace her connection with Watai, or to resist its pull, sever their thread of fate, and flee to protect everything she has grown to love.

Across the Stars is the first book of the *Cosmic Threads of Fate* trilogy, featuring the love story between Mae, a human starpilot and Watai, an alien dragon rider.

https://books2read.com/AcrossTheStars

RH Space Opera Alien Romance Series:

Found

Project: Adapt # 1

A failed human prototype. That's all she is…

Born and raised as an experiment, Selena's life has been filled with torture, betrayal, and distrust... but one night changes everything.

Sold, attacked, and on the run, Selena is picked up by a colony ship. Struggling to find her place on this ship and trying to understand the draw she feels toward two alien males, her already uncertain life becomes downright unimaginable when she learns new life is growing inside her.

Terrified her captors will find her and take her and her children back to a life of horror and captivity, she must learn to trust her saviors, and herself.

With the help of her two mates, Selena will fight for her freedom— or die trying.

books2read.com/PAFound

Polycule Space Opera Alien Romance w/MM Series:

Cosmic Valor

Cosmic Honor # 1

She wanted to bring honor back to her family's name and to save her people...

Falling in love wasn't part of the plan...

When Jaiya takes her twin brother's place on a diplomatic mission to end a war that's been raging since her childhood, she discovers how it all really began.

Disguised as a young male diplomat, Jaiya meets Prince Idris—her greatest rival in their space battles—his royal assistant, Erlyn—who never leaves his side—and is assigned to be guarded by Raizxl—who blames humans for losing his mate.

If she cannot convince her people and the enemy to put aside their differences and choose peace instead of war, she risks returning as a traitor to her race instead of as a hero.

The longer she's in their presence, the more she feels at home amongst those in their space station.

Determined to save their people at any cost, something about them calls to her—and she does not know why.

When they discover the truth, will they be able to get past her betrayal to work toward peace? Or will it only add fuel to the fires of war?

Books2read.com/Cosmic1

Made in the USA
Monee, IL
11 July 2024

61573081R10185